The Rise of the Phoenix

Vol. 3 of the Daimones Trilogy

Massimo Marino

ISBN-13 978-1-4993054-5-6
Cover design by The Cover Collection, UK
Editor: Susan Uttendorfsky — Adirondack Editing

First Printing: May 2014

The Rise of the Phoenix is Vol. 3 of the Daimones Trilogy.
Vol. 1, *Daimones*
Vol. 2, *Once Humans*

For those who are no longer with us.

About the Author

Massimo Marino comes from a scientist background: He spent years at CERN, in Switzerland, and at the Lawrence Berkeley Lab, in California, followed by lead positions with Apple, Inc., and the World Economic Forum.

Massimo currently lives in France and crosses the border with Switzerland multiple times daily.

The first volume of the trilogy, "Daimones", is the recipient of the 2012 PRG Award Reviewers' Choice in Science Fiction, and the Seal of Excellence in Quality Writing from both the Awesome Indies (awesomeindies.net) and the indiePENdents.org association.

In September 2013 "Daimones" won the Hall of Fame - Best in Science Fiction Award, Quality Reads UK Book Club.

With the release of volume 2, “Once Humans”, the books received the 2013 PRG Reviewer's Choice Award Best in Science Fiction Series.

The second volume, "Once Humans", starts seven years after the events narrated in "Daimones". The Communities led by the Selected are about to thrive and peace and security reigns on Eridu...not for long.

He also writes short chilling, twisted, horror stories, oftentimes while having breakfast. Go figure why.

If interested in more details about Massimo Marino, please see his full profile on Linkedin:
http://ch.linkedin.com/in/massimomarino

Connect with Massimo Marino:
Twitter:
https://twitter.com/Massim0Marin0

Facebook:
http://www.facebook.com/massimo.marino.750546
http://www.facebook.com/MassimoMarinoAuthor

Author's website:
http://massimomarinoauthor.com

TABLE OF CONTENTS

Chapter 1 – Memories

From Dan Amenta's Journal

Those were days when I doubted what we were doing. The peace we enjoyed in Eridu—the planet once called Earth—vacillated due to the increase in incidents of sabotage. Someone methodically destroyed our plants and livestock—other survivors for sure—and we seemed unable to make the sabotage stop, find the perpetrators, or understand their motives.

The aliens who changed our destiny forever, the Moîrai, and their Selection process to rebuild a new race of man, had offered their assistance at all levels, but I and the other Selected had decided that humans should deal with human problems. Eridu was scarcely populated, so who else—other than discontented wanderers—would perform such barbaric acts? But there was that unmistakable sign they left at each time...the imprint of a mutilated hand. We discovered they were led by another race of aliens, the Kritas, who for eons had been challenging the Moîrai for the supremacy in the galaxy.

The fate of humans hung in the air those days. Only a few years had passed since the Selection, what we Selected called instead the Third Loss, the genocide perpetrated by the Moîrai with the ultimate goal to prevent humans from self-destructing. They played with our destiny, "to save us" from oblivion, they said, preserving only a few of us. They revealed ancient history of the two previous losses we humans had inflicted onto ourselves, plunging our race into millennia of darkness and the loss of our collective memory, of our past. Were we worth saving, or were the latest events—that we could be led to fight each other—the proof that the son of man was once again corrupted?

No matter how hard we tried to rein things in, humans will find a way to cause trouble when jealousy rules. As a Selected, I was getting stronger every day; I discovered new capabilities—previously unknown to me—the existence of which I kept a closely guarded secret. Every year, though, brought bitterness rather than contentment. I'm not aging or, at least, I can't see any sign of it yet. But my wife Mary is, and so are my daughters, Annah and Hope, and Hope's mother, Laura, too. My family: they all will die before me and I'm in constant pain because of this. I'm not alone in this fate, as other Selected face the same cruel destiny, but sharing the pain does not diminish it. It didn't work like that; not for me, anyway.

We thwarted Kritas' plans on our planet; we tracked them down and found the base they'd build underground using the large mines around Pittsburgh. In the last battle, many lost their lives, and we humans had no control on our destiny. I lost Marina, the Selected who shared with me the responsibility for our community, and I felt my life was always marked by losing someone dear to me every time I conceded myself to hope for the future. We discovered treason even within the Moîrai ranks, and received promises of full disclosure, promises that have not been honored.

Our communities are thriving, and a future of prosperity and plenty awaits us. At least, that's what we all think, but the future is uncertain again and the Moîrai hide the truth from me.

I became one of the Keepers, a Moîrai ancient brotherhood organization. The Keepers enjoy a secrecy never violated in the millennia since their birth; feared and respected, their existence is never acknowledged in the open, a shadow force that permeates, guides, and controls the Moîrai Confederation in the galaxy.

A special drug that we call the Fusion makes interstellar travel possible; cells from the nervous systems of billions of dead humans allowed the Moîrai to produce an even more potent formula than the original available before the Third Loss.

Through the Palladium, a wearable device like a crown, the Moîrai made us Selected more similar to them genetically than to the other humans the aliens didn't cull, the ones we call the 'spared ones.' Are the Moîrai using us to keep them in line while they're still alive?

With time, the production of the Fusion went under our control and has brought us riches and good fortune. Eridu is now famous in the galaxy, and for reasons not related to its most ancient history. We are no more a feared race, an uncontrollable monster that could turn against anyone at any moment; others have taken our place in those rankings.

Fortunately, I believe I do have some friends among the Moîrai, but I feel I'm alone in my quest to find the traitors and those ultimately responsible for the apocalypse, for the Third Loss. Who can I fully trust? I question everyone's motives, even the Keepers'.

I feel like we are threatened again by an advanced alien civilization. This time, they're not planning for our physical demise, but they attempt to undermine our morals, to embrace our fate and forget our past. If that's the case, what chance do we have to rise strong again?

Dan of Eridu, I'm called, the watchful eye of the new humans. I represent our interests in the Moîrai's Supreme Council, but I perceive a barrier—an invisible threshold—and I can't yet cross it.

Chapter 2 – Hope

"One more time, please."

I glanced at the memnosphere, the biological computer that contained Marina's memories and thought processes. They were collected from her retrieved body after she died in the disaster of Vatus, the Moîrai base on the floor of the Pacific Ocean, destroyed by saboteurs with the help of traitors among the Moîrai.

The sphere twinkled in the twilight of my office and a three-dimensional scene from the first years of our community in Civita filled the space in front of me once more.

I let my mind drift back to another time, a time when I believed I had reasons to be happy. Yet, ninety years had passed from that fatal day when the Moîrai changed the Selected after they had culled mankind and altered irreparably the history of our race.

Behind me, the wall—set to be transparent at that time of day—allowed me to enjoy the magnificent view of the Tiber Valley, and I could glimpse the last reflections of the sunset off the cusps of Nova Roma and its first lights in the evening sky.

From my terrace at the top of the main tower of Eridu's Council, the dome around the medieval little town of Civita preserved my past and looked small in the distance, like a souvenir snow globe installed to protect the ancient buildings that gave shelter to our first community. My daughter, Hope, and my son, Samuel, were born in Civita, and those old stones had been our home for many years—when my family was still alive.

At times, I expected to see a giant hand descend from above and shake the globe to make its snow fall.

"Why are you torturing yourself, Dan?" Marina's voice echoed in the room.

"I'm not, Marina. I assure you." I followed the images the memnosphere created for me; my wife Mary waved at me. She smiled and turned to play with little Joshua Alaston under the amused watch of our daughter, Annah, his mother.

"It just strengthens my resolve." I glanced back at the memnosphere. "We won't stop until everything is accomplished."

⁂

Millions of kilometres away from Eridu, the transporter was reaching our destination. I felt Samuel getting closer to my quarters. Soon the wall announced his presence, too. I let the wall dilate and Samuel entered.

"Father." Samuel lowered his head. "We're on the final approach to Bridge Station One."

"Very well, Samuel." I looked into my son's eyes and—in a mental fastbackward—the last decades flashed in front of mine. For a moment, Civita and the ghosts of my past haunted me once more. For a moment, I held my breath.

"From now on," I said, "wear your Palladium. You'll be my eyes and ears. There's no need to announce my presence here yet."

"As you desire, Father." Samuel took the ring-shaped alien artifact and donned it before leaving. His Palladium molded as a crown on his head and established contact with mine. Our minds became as one.

He knew well the importance of his mission. After the Academy, Samuel climbed the ranks in Eridu's Space Fleet to become an accomplished top-ranked officer, and was now an Admiral, the Fleet Commander. He had the qualities to make it into the Keepers if destiny and I didn't have different plans.

Everything was in place. Our underground, covert preparation had taken years, but now we only had to finalize the last details before making all possible. Before forcing destiny's hands.

The Bridge Stations controlled the inner space of the solar system, just within the Kuiper Belt but beyond the orbit of Neptune; they monitored the interstellar travels in and out of our star system through the wormhole bridges. We had acquired and mastered the latest Moîrai technology and leaped into the future in a matter of a few decades.

By Eridu's regulation, the authorization for wormholes' creation was granted only at space coordinates beyond the Belt, at an approximate distance of a hundred million kilometres from the sun. And our Fleet protected us from any intrusion. No one could have reached Eridu without our consent, or, at least, not without paying a tremendous price.

Our transporter docked with the station.

⁂

"Commander!" On the main bridge, a young officer walked up to the tall man intent at observing the solar system model floating in the middle of a large ring of duty posts crowded with personnel, all intent on their tasks. "Fleet Admiral Amenta is here." He snapped to attention.

From the entrance, with only a glimpse at the model, Samuel distinguished the six Bridge Stations controlling the approach routes to and from the wormholes' creation points. Two of his personal guards accompanied him.

The controllers monitored in detail all space flight plans of the traffic crossing the Belt and directed all vessels to their next waypoint. They identified the vessels bound for Eridu and assigned them to the inner Traffic Control Stations when they reached forty million kilometres from the Sun.

Samuel suppressed a smile, thinking about the many hours spent on the simulators at the Space Academy many years before.

"Is that so?" The tall man replied without interrupting his activity, nor turning to acknowledge his guests. He nodded. "Thank you, Captain. At ease."

After a few more checks on the model, he finally turned to welcome the visitors. The Bridge Station Commander looked young, as all new humans did, whatever their age.

"Admiral." He raised his chin. "I knew I would have had the pleasure of your official visit one day, but now I can't figure out whether that's a good thing or not." He stared at him.

Samuel bent his head to the right, as his mother used to do when she faced unexpected situations. With his eyes, he examined the station commander from head to toe and back, but didn't reply.

The station's commander didn't seem to notice. "We'll be better off in my private quarters." He gave a stern look to the officer who still stood rigid by his side. "Captain, would you escort the Admiral?"

"Aye, aye, sir." He gestured with his hand. "Admiral, this way..."

"Admiral..." The commander stepped forward and the two men exchanged an intent look. "I believe I'm supposed to initiate the process?"

They both knew it was a rhetorical question. A smile rose to Samuel's lips.

"Please do, Commander." Samuel refrained from adding more, then he followed the captain out of the main deck bridge.

The wall dilated. In front of the station commander quarters, the captain stepped to one side to let Samuel in. "Commander Sage will be with you shortly, Admiral."

Samuel nodded and signaled to his guards to wait in the corridor. The wall coalesced behind his back.

The private quarters reflected the peculiar character of Anton Sage. No amenities, everything had a purpose, a simple and austere taste. He remembered Anton from the years they spent as cadets when the first space squadron delivered by the Moîrai had set base in Eridu.

They both commanded their first ships right after graduating, following the exhausting training years with the Moîrai instructors. Samuel continued his career within the Fleet to reach higher ranks, while Sage opted for more sedentary—and possibly less surprising—kinds of assignments.

He smiled when his eyes fell onto the only luxury Sage allowed himself. Aligned on a few shelves, books of the most rare and old editions must have absorbed most of Anton's time and salary, he thought. Samuel noticed the collection had grown substantially since those years at the Academy.

The wall became translucent and announced "Commander Sage." It dilated and Anton Sage stepped in.

The two men looked at each other in silence for a moment, waiting for the wall to coalesce.

"Your visit, Admiral, wasn't announced." Sage's cold voice broke the silence. He turned to seal the room.

"You son of a bitch!" Samuel couldn't contain himself any longer.

"Come here, bastard!" Sage laughed but stopped when two strong arms squeezed him and made him go "ouff" under the assault. He coughed and gasped for air. "Easy, easy. Good Lord, Samuel. So many years; look at you now... Fleet Admiral."

"I'm glad to see you, too." He smiled. "My mother would be proud to see us both, now," Samuel held the man by his shoulders.

Shorter and thinner than his old friend, Sage looked up at Samuel's face with a veil of sadness. "I remember Mary well. Your mother was the bravest woman I've ever met in all my life."

"Thank you." Samuel sighed. "She would have loved to hear you say 'woman' and not 'spared one'."

"Of course." With a twist, he freed himself from Samuel's grip. "You know, many of us feel the same. Besides, we wouldn't be here if it wasn't for the general sentiment."

Samuel nodded in agreement.

"By the way, how's your sister?"

"She's tired, Anton. It won't be long before she goes, too. We can see in her eyes that it's what her heart desires."

Sage led Samuel to a cozy part of the apartment with two large armchairs. "Come, have a seat."

"It must be tough for you and your father." Sage looked into his eyes without a blink.

"Indeed." Samuel stared back. "She's still young in my memories; I see this old lady on her death bed...I just can't believe that's really Hope."

Sage nodded and stared at the floor. "That's how it's been for everyone."

"Hope had the hardest times, and her termination will mark a new beginning. Father told her and she's ready."

"Oh, I didn't know she was told about the plans...is it safe?" Sage asked and stiffened on the armchair.

"With Hope? You're kidding, right? Don't worry, she's my sister, and my father knows her better than she knows herself."

"You're right. Sorry, it was silly of me to doubt."

Samuel waved one hand as if he was rubbing out the last words that still lingered in the air. "Is everything in place?"

"It is." Sage relaxed again. "I suppose you'll pay a visit to the other Bridge Stations as well?" He saw Samuel nod. "You may confirm with your father that all Bridge Stations have now received the coded message. Preparations must be taking place as we speak."

"Excellent. The operation is ready to be launched at all levels. Eridu's ready, too."

Both men stood. Samuel held out his right hand. "I wish I could stay longer, Anton."

"Don't say anything." He took his friend's hand with both of his. "We are all one, Sam."

Samuel smiled. "The Council of the Twelve is unanimous. We're only waiting for Hope now."

Sage saw a sparkle in his friend's eyes and shivered like he did the first time he met Samuel's father, Dan of Eridu.

"Farewell, Anton." Samuel had the wall dilate and left.

Sage took a deep breath; he had many tasks now to accomplish and new procedures to put in place.

⁂

I waited for my son in my rooms back in the ship. The wall announced that Samuel was outside waiting. I let my son in.

"Well done." I greeted him. "Now everything will happen as we have established."

I felt Samuel's eagerness to fulfill his tasks and go to the next Bridge Stations.

"Have you anything to suggest for my next visits, Father?"

"You did well." I smiled. "The few who still hesitate will join the cause without second thoughts once everything has started." I paused. "Besides, all Stations have received their orders by now; use your skills to rally the troops."

Samuel stood silent in the middle of the room. He nodded.

"I need to go back to Eridu now." I stepped closer and rested my hands on his shoulders, opening my mind to him. "I need to attend to the final preparations."

I let him feel my pride, the love I bore in my heart for him and for all those who had left us.

Chapter 3 – Eridu

The transporter entered into a geosynchronous orbit. On the floating screen, hovering over my desk, the face of the ship commander announced our arrival.

"We are at thirty-five thousand kilometres above the North Pole, sir."

"Thank you." I activated the 3D display to enjoy the view of our planet floating in space. A glowing bluish sphere the size of a soccer ball lit up the room; the default rendering also showed the real-time space traffic. With a gesture, I removed all layers of additional information. The old North America and Russia were visible, and all of Europe down to the larger part of Africa.

Our ship received the landing authorization and left the high orbit; the planet grew and the image shifted as we achieved lower orbits. The continents drifted in front of my eyes, as did my memory and pulled back in—with force—the images of those who were once waiting for me on Eridu.

⁂

Our house in the little town of Civita provided a spectacular view of the valley. Over the years, the spaceport on the plain had doubled in size to accommodate the increased traffic. The flamboyant Phoenix bird that marked the original landing area hadn't changed much since its inauguration twenty years before but for the once-vibrant colors that Mary described now as 'pastel'.

Human and Moîrai ships crowded the docking areas, along with a smaller number from other races from all over the Confederation, which had only recently been accepted in our inner space. The plans for Nova Roma required infrastructure, equipment, and personnel well beyond what we could provide ourselves, so the Moîrai had delegated some of those efforts to their closest allies.

"Dad! Daaad?!" My daughter's voice reached me, charged with anxiety. I knew why Annah was calling, impatient, and I raised my eyes toward the invisible orbiting Space Academy. My grandson, Joshua Alaston, would be living there in the years required for his training to receive his wings, and then pilot his own fighter.

"I'm here, on the terrace." But I realized that wasn't what was being asked. "I'm coming, I'm coming!" I yelled.

Mary and Annah appeared at the French door, both smiling and dressed for the occasion. I looked at them next to each other and shivered. Annah was the image of my Mary in her thirties and my wife... Years made her pay the price; she was perfect in her role as Joshua's grandma.

"Grandpa?" A young man's voice preceded the arrival of a strong and proud Cadet in his brand new uniform. He towered over the two women. Newly admitted to the academy like his Uncle Samuel before him, Joshua was eager to reach the spaceport.

"Look at you." I opened my arms and smiled.

"It's time, Grandpa." Joshua smiled back and invited me inside with a waving hand.

"Yes, it *is* time," I repeated, and followed his steps.

On the terrace reserved for families—overlooking the landing sectors reserved to the space fleet—everyone waved goodbye to the XXI° Space Cadets boarding the transporters aligned on the tarmac, eager to enter a new life.

I sensed exactly where to look for Joshua and had to point him out to his mother and grandmother; they claimed tears prevented them from finding the boy among the others.

The transporters' docking bays coalesced behind the last cadets. The ships left the ground silently, hovering gently above the spaceport for a moment before soaring up in formation to reach their destination.

I sighed and the vision of the past years faded. My eyes focused again on the 3D rendering and I watched the final approach to Nova Roma spaceport. Joshua was a captain now, a fighters' squad leader, and would be among the first involved if things were to turn sour. I knew I would have to suffer more losses of people I loved. With an acute pain, the memory of my wife, Mary, and her last moments tore my heart apart once more.

⁂

Mary never wanted a ceremony nor had any desire to be buried. She died peacefully in my arms. Her blue eyes shone with a bright interior light and held mine until her last breath. "I'm sorry, my love," she murmured.

"Oh Mary. Why do you say that?" I managed to whisper in her ear through the knot that clutched my throat, but I knew what she meant.

The rest of our family stood in a semicircle around her bed. The flood of their emotions crushed against me like waves of a raging ocean. Samuel and Joshua tried as much as they could to ease my pain, but I didn't allow anyone to shield me from my Mary and her last moments; I wanted to drink from that cup until the last drop.

My wife had a smile for everyone, then she looked at me one final time.

"I'm leaving, hon. Think of me." And she closed her eyes.

"No, no, NO!" My voice burst out, but Mary couldn't hear me anymore.

The Moîrai took Mary's body for a special kind of cremation; they turned her into the purest diamond, never to be corrupted.

A few days later, the family gathered in front of the memorial in Civita, as Mary wanted. It was a marble boulder with a niche for every one of us, for all our diamonds to be set into the stone one day, imperishable and united forever. That day, her diamond shone bright for us.

The boulder stood in the main square, at the place of the pedestal where once my Palladium sent a bright beam to the sky signaling everyone the new beginning. It bore the inscription Mary and I had written together only a year before:

WOULD I WERE WITH THEE[1]
Would I were with thee, every day and hour
Which now passes so sadly, far from thee.
Would that my form posses'd the magic power
To follow where my heavy heart would be!
Whatever thy lot, o'er land or sea —
Would I were with thee eternally!

Would I were with thee, when, the world forgetting,
Thy weary limbs upon the turf are thrown —
While bright and red, our evening sun is setting
And all thy thoughts belong to heaven alone:
While happy dreams thy thoughts employ —
Would I were with thee in thy joy!

Would I were with thee, when no longer failing
The hurried laugh that stifles back a sigh!
When thy young lips put forth its sweet complaining
And tears have quench'd the light within thine eye:
When all seems dark and sad below —
Would I were with thee in thy woe!

Would I were with thee when the day is breaking,
And when the moon has lit the lovely sea —

Or when in crowds some careless note awaking,
Speaks to thy heart in memory of me.
In joy or pain, by sea or shore —
Would I were with thee evermore.

Even if much younger, Laura's diamond joined Mary's only a few months later, while I still grieved, as if they had decided together to end our relationships at the same time. Laura had joined our family when we thought we were the only ones left alive on the planet, when we believed it was our duty to start again, all together. Then, Laura stayed with us more for the bond that had grown between the two mothers and their daughters than for me. The battles for survival wounded her with cruelty and she never recovered from the physical and emotional scars.

Thirty years later, my daughter, Annah, and her husband, Federico, joined them as well. Four diamonds now ornated the boulder in Civita, and four more slots awaited theirs. I knew with pain that mine would probably be the last.

Within a few more years, Eridu lost all but one of the remaining true humans, the frail remnants of the doomed race of man, leaving the entire planet in sorrow. We felt the lifetimes of the last humans as brief as a breeze at the end of a warm day. A sudden gust of wind that left you with only a shiver to remember its passage.

Now Hope was ready to go, too. Born from Laura and me soon after the Selection took place, she was the last child who was born with only human genes, the only human the Moîrai never had to spare. She was the youngest of the last humans. Then the Moîrai transformed us Selected and a new human race was born.

The Palladium created in my mind the image of Manfred, interrupting the flow of my reveries.

Among the Selected, and as one of the twelve members of the human's Council, Manfred knew everyone in my family, including the ones who now had left us; he was the closest to a friend I had.

"Manfred!" I greeted him as the Palladiums connected and his figure appeared in my room.

"Dan, welcome back. I'm already at the spaceport. A shuttle's waiting; we'll reach the Council together." Always frugal with words, his image took its place on the seat that blossomed from the floor.

The Twelve, men and women, constituted the highest decisional power in Eridu. Nothing happened on the planet that wasn't blessed by the Council. As its thirteenth member—a planned oddity—I was the Primum Inter Pares, known elsewhere as 'Dan of Eridu.'

Moîrai's Keepers had inducted me into their secret Brotherhood as "Eridu's Keeper." Unbeknownst to them, I had shared the acquired knowledge with my own Selected, which led to the creation of the Council of the Twelve in Eridu.

"How's Hope?" I asked.

"Well, I'd say. Nothing's really changed in her life since we moved her to the facility in Nova Roma." Manfred bent forward. "From her point of view, she's still in her house in Civita."

I nodded. "Are we ready?"

He replied with the two most welcomed words he could ever pronounce: "We are."

The transporter landed, I left the ship, and reached Manfred waiting in front of our shuttle.

The shuttle rose in silence over the city, Nova Roma, one of the new metropolises whose buildings had soared toward Eridu's sky in the past decades. I looked at the skyline and at the Council complex in the distance. Manfred respected my silence and my privacy.

During the last eighty years, as the population expanded, the new generations moved to the growing urbanizations that resembled Moîrai's capital, Protusa, for the architecture and for the technology solutions made available to the citizens.

The spared ones became old and frail, and they tended instead to search for each other and stay together. They secluded themselves from the rapid changes the planet went through. They clung to the past and became revered ghosts, always present but living in another dimension and in another time.

Their numbers dwindled, and their loss hurt the Selected and the newest generations. The pain stung deep inside; we were indeed experiencing the fabled Third Loss of the human race, a loss the Moîrai pretended to have avoided with their intervention, cutting by force all branches of humankind's history and leaving only a few to a new start.

But the spared ones' fate, with their presence and their demise, had created a resolve and a sense of unity the race of man had never experienced in all its troubled history.

The shuttle touched ground with a sigh, its side bulkhead dilated, lowering to the ground. Together with Manfred, I stepped outside on the landing platform perched atop the Council Tower.

"Welcome back, Dan of Eridu." The greeting sounded in my head and I smiled at the fellow Moîrai Keeper.

"Thank you, Ohtlinell." I replied in the same way.

Two members from the Council waited for us, too. They and Manfred heard my mental exchange with Ohtlinell but pretended they didn't, as no one but the Eridu's Council—in the whole galaxy—knew that the race of man could already walk the path of the Keepers without their direct training and intervention.

"Welcome, Dan and Manfred. The Council is reunited, as you have requested." They bowed.

"Then let's not make them wait any longer." I led the party on the first step of the new course.

Chapter 4 – Farewell

The facilities built especially for the ceremony had impressed even the aliens. A lottery would be held in all cities, and five hundred thousand people would be granted the privilege to be present in Nova Roma; plus, there was no place on Eridu where whoever wanted to witness Hope's last moments couldn't.

The event would lay a crucial milestone for our race and be the watershed moment for history itself; it will be marked as the day where everything ended and all began anew. I had personal reasons to be involved; I was the father of the one the Moîrai never had to spare.

Late in the morning, the doctors finally told me Hope could receive me now, but warned me to avoid any stress and emotion because she had become much weaker in the last hours.

I had arrived earlier in the morning at the medical center that had only one patient—my daughter. The nurses greeted me with soft and reverential voices and told me she had a fair night. One might believe the special care was due to my position, but—in truth—it was Hope who was venerated on Eridu. It would have been the same even if she weren't my daughter.

The media shared detailed reports of her health, with bulletins every hour and special reports. Everyone knew all details of Hope's life, from the moment Laura—her mother—gave birth. She was more than just 'Dan of Eridu's Daughter.' Hope became the most important human being on the planet, the most precious and the frailest of all. She was known as 'The one who wasn't spared,' the last child born by a man and a woman without the enhanced Moîrai transgenetic modifications.

Army soldiers protected Hope's rooms and held their blasters horizontally—in the Moîrai way—when I approached. I returned the salute and the wall dilated.

That day, Manfred accompanied me, and when I turned, expecting him to follow, he shook his head. "No, be alone with you daughter. You both deserve it."

I nodded and thanked him with a forced smile. Manfred lowered his head and closed his eyes. *"No one will ever forget her, or the others."* His thoughts reached me wrapped in multiple layers of...hope.

The entrance gave visitors the impression of stepping into another place and time; the engineers had reproduced Hope's last home in Civita in every detail. The parquet cracked at the usual spot when I stepped in. The same nurses and doctors frequented the 'house', but acted as if they were just visiting from the Civita's hospital instead.

From the re-created windows, one could see the little medieval town as if it were there, beyond the walls. Hope could still glimpse her beloved town and hear the birds chirping while chasing each other above the roofs. She couldn't leave the med-unit anymore; she was no longer able to sustain the burden of living by her own strength.

The nurse on duty lowered her head when she saw me and left the room. Hope kept her eyes closed, but a smile appeared on a face marked with the lines time had inflicted.

My daughter, the wrinkled and dying woman lying in front of me, was the oldest-looking human on the entire planet. Yet, to the rest of the world, she was leaving us the youngest, as the new humans her age looked like they'd just passed puberty.

The med-unit hummed solemnly. Hope felt my presence and opened her eyes, a tired look but the same as her mother's, Laura.

She didn't have much hair anymore, and it had long since lost its ebony beauty. My heart shrunk in pain. How many times had I watched the people I loved the most leave me? It hurt more each time; there's no drill and no training to teach one's heart how to bear the loss of another. My heart grew colder and harder with each death.

"Dad." Hope greeted me with a broken voice.

I thought I would have been strong, that the Palladium made me stronger. How wrong I was. I'd already lost my wife Mary, and Laura, then my first daughter, Annah, and now Hope's life was vanishing before me and I couldn't do anything about it. With all my resilience, strength, and inhuman capabilities, there I was...a broken father watching his little girl dying. What a cruel destiny the Moîrai had imposed on us Selected.

"How are you?"

"I'm tired." She sighed. "But I'm ready."

I took a deep breath and walked up to her. Unable to say anything, I stepped to her bedside and took that bony hand.

She smiled. "Your hand is warm, and I'm so cold..."

My eyes looked for the nurse. "I'll tell the doctors to raise the temperature."

Hope shook her head. "Inside..."

At those words, my eyes filled with tears. "Darling..."

"Dad..." she whispered. "I want my bed."

I managed to collect some air and sound calm. "You won't last an hour in your bed, sweetie."

"I know." Hope let go a long sigh. "Would you do something for me?"

"Anything." I looked at her, eager to do whatever she needed. My heart hung to her lips and I bent forward.

Her eyes mocked me. "I know where I am."

Befuddled, I probed her mind. "How?" I started.

"Am I not your daughter?"

I blushed. "Hope, I didn't want you to—" I glanced down as she squeezed my hand to interrupt me.

With an effort, she raised her head. "Shhhh. It's okay, Dad. Let everyone watch if they need to, but let me watch everyone, too."

My voice cracked. "You'll never be forgotten." My eyes held hers. "I love you so much."

"I know, Dad." Her hand squeezed mine again. "Please, let me see, let me start the new beginning."

I didn't know then, but those words put the seed of revenge in my heart and found fertile ground.

⁂

The news spread through Eridu like an electroshock; the last-born human was ready to leave. The huge apparatus for the global ceremony had been ready for months and only needed this trigger to be activated.

Other, more secret preparations completed their final details for everything to work perfectly on Eridu, and in space. Confirmations—from all levels—reached the Council, and we crossed the point of no return, resolute as one entity.

On the chosen day, Eridu held its breath. The whole population watched the event, live or remotely, and feelings were shared among all of us.

The Twelve joined me at the medical facility where Hope was getting ready. They bore a grave expression on their faces. We didn't need words and it wasn't just because of the Ultimate Farewell, as people called the day.

Together, we crossed the threshold into Hope's rendered house. The doctors and nurses had freed her from all life support units and Hope seemed relieved. She had smiled when they disabled the last connection, they told me.

"Hope?" I stepped forward. Large pillows kept her raised, half-seated on the bed—'her bed', as promised.

"Dad, I'm so happy." I could feel she was telling the truth. Her soul felt lighter and more vibrant than in, the days before.

"Everyone's here." I bent my head toward the door. "Manfred, and all the others in the Council." I smiled. "Plus, half a million people surround us under a dome and the rest of the planet's population will share in your farewell."

Manfred came in closer. "Hope, your decision saddens me, but I understand. It has been an honor and a privilege to have known you and your family, and everyone who left us before you."

Hope closed her eyes and nodded. Tears wet her cheeks. Through her mind, I saw images of Laura, me and Mary, together with Annah; images of her play-days with Joshua Alaston, her wonders when she saw him staying young while she grew older. And when she could no longer join him in the same games, when age affected her mind and body, I saw how left out and alone she felt.

My tears joined hers. "You've never been alone."

Hope took a deep breath, opened her eyes, and smiled at me. She then greeted all those present in the room. One by one, the Council members lowered their heads in humility and respect.

"We'll leave you, now." Manfred smiled a last time at Hope. "Farewell." Then his thoughts echoed within my mind. *"Everything is ready, Dan of Eridu."*

A bit surprised that he called me by my Keepers' title, I turned to look at him, straight into his eyes. A flow of pride, gratitude, and sorrow accompanied Manfred's next thoughts. *"For how painful this day is for you, and for all of us, this is the final connection; the glue that binds and unites our race. Hope."*

I understood what he meant; I nodded slowly as Manfred left with the others.

I sat on Hope's bed.

"I'll be your next diamond, Dad." She looked at me with anticipation. "I'll always be there, with Mom and the rest of our family."

The knot in my throat intercepted my words, though I managed to smile.

"I don't have much time, Daddy. I feel I'm leaving." We held hands. "Let me see everyone now."

I sighed, turned my head, and signaled to invisible eyes to make the rendering of her house disappear.

"Oh." Hope gasped as everything—the walls, the ceiling, the floor, the windows, and Civita beyond them—faded; the Ultimate Farewell dome, and its crowd, appeared.

Then, the sound of five hundred thousand individuals rising from their seats, humans and other races alike, rolled toward us. Hope's eyes dilated, full of marvel.

"Oh Dad, it's wonderful." A murmur rose from the dome; it spread and shifted in waves and mounted as a flood. Hope's eyes widened as she felt the emotional impact that engulfed everyone there. Her hands trembled.

She looked at me, radiant. "Can they hear me?" she asked with a chuckle.

I stared at my daughter. Her old and tired faced merged with the images that lingered in my mind, vivid as ever. Hope as a toddler, as a teenager, and then as a young woman in her thirties. My heartbeat quickened.

"Yes, darling; they all can hear you." I raised my eyes and looked around. "The entire planet is with you now."

With a slight effort, Hope turned her head to the multitude watching in silence and raised her gaze—as much as she could—toward the highest rows and the screens that reproduced our images in life-like detail. Then she became serious, stared at me; then, in the distance, at the rows of people in front of her bed. The screens zoomed to her face. She filled her lungs. "My time has come," she exclaimed. "Don't be torn in pieces as we once were. I'm the last of the old race, don't commit our past mistakes; be whole, and be forever."

She gripped my hand with a strength I didn't know she still had. "Dad..." Her voice broke, she sighed, and she was gone. I turned to deny myself the excruciating sight of her eyes, now hazy.

A tremor arose from billions of minds, as if everyone on Eridu shivered the moment Hope exhaled her last breath.

I stood up and kept holding her hand within both of mine. My own voice sounded stentorian, as if coming from someone much stronger and detached than I. The seed of revenge grew roots in my heart. "Hope is no more." I paused. *"Let there be no more hope,"* I thought.

For a moment, I hid my shattered tears. Then I rested her hands to her chest and bent to close my daughter's eyes. I faced the multitude. "We honored our oath to the past. We fulfilled our pledge. Now the time has come for us to shape our future."

Chapter 5 – Behind Closed Doors

From my office atop the Council Tower, Nova Roma presented the same fervid aspect of all mornings. The roads buzzed with vehicles and pedestrians. The flight levels between the skyscrapers had reached their traffic peak since the first hours of the morning. On the surface, nothing had changed, apart maybe the spaceport with its now empty sectors—once crowded—reserved to the space Fleet. We raised the Fleet's alert condition to the maximum, and the same happened in all spaceports in the planet. The Fleet had left Eridu and deployed in accordance with the orders.

The day was bright, and with Hope gone, it was day one of a new era.

The Aliens Interim Detention Areas—or the AIDAs as they were known—became operative the moment my daughter left us. We built AIDAs all over Eridu, and the secrecy had doubled the efforts required to make them operational. Secluded areas, unreachable by any known detection devices; our scientists were confident they made them invisible to any probing attempt, internal or external.

In all documentation and during all discussions, the facilities were referred to as 'Assisted IDentification Apparatuses' to prevent diplomatic damages from accidental leaks of their true purpose. 'Paranoids survive' was a lesson I'd learned well in my previous life.

In only a few hours after Hope's death, the tens of thousands of aliens in Eridu, permanently stationed or not, had been tracked down, apprehended, and transported to the nearest detention area; a huge effort, but everything worked as planned. We had minor incidents, of course, and protestations, but we had a cover story prepared for the detainees.

When all reports confirmed the success of the operation, and after my daily meeting with the Council, I sent the guards to bring me Ohtlinell, the Moîrai Keeper I ordered to keep confined in his quarters, instead.

The day before, Manfred asked me to be present for the meeting. As usual, when we discussed his request, he could not remain seated when things heated up; I refused, and Manfred stood up at once and paced the room. "I've been waiting for this day eighty-six years!"

"I know." I remained seated. "But I have to deny you this pleasure."

Manfred stopped, frowned, and tightened his lips. Before he could make any additional remarks, I warned him. "If you make even the most subtle attempt to probe his mind, Ohtlinell will detect you. I remind you, he is a Keeper. It's not yet the time to show them how much the members of the Council have evolved."

Manfred snorted. "Ah, the Keepers. How come with all their capabilities they found no evidence of who really is involved in the conspiracy? I believe they don't want *us* to find out."

"That's exactly why we've reached this point." My voice was calm and my mind went back to old events.

The battle in the city of Corvel, in the old United States, saw our victory in the final confrontation against the Kritas and the humans they subjugated, and brought promises to unveil the treason and bring to justice all those responsible for what happened to us as a race. Moîrai's promises, though, to our disappointment, never materialized.

Alaston—and all the Moîrai I met—denied the process of culling the humans had anything to do with the control of the neurotrophic drug used to form interstellar pilots in all races. In years, though, not one ever showed us, to our Council, any substantial proof that the Moîrai conclusions were founded, or that they'd done everything in their capacity to discover the truth.

But humans grew stronger, we became the major—and then the only—producer of the Fusion drug; we perfected the process of extracting the components from neurological tissue grown from stem cells, and that led us to an even more powerful formula than the one the Moîrai obtained from the brains and hypothalamuses of billions of humans. We prepared, we lurked, we spied, and—unbeknownst to everyone—were now in the position to demand and ask about the truth.

The only one Moîrai blamed as the main orchestrator of the conspiracy, Ekahau the traitor, the one who colluded with the Kritas, had disappeared with no clues, nor explanations had ever been given. Not to us, at least.

Even with my role in the Keepers, the Moîrai's most ancient Brotherhood, a pillar in their governing organization, I had been unable to go beyond certain points, beyond certain individuals. My moves and investigations always hit a glass ceiling that was opaque from my side, but I knew someone watched me and maneuvered from the other side so that all my attempts faced an impenetrable wall.

Alaston, the Moîrai who'd been always by my side, the leader of the Keepers and my mentor, tried each time to make me reconsider, to take into account the Moîrai's efforts to grant humans their rebirth. He made it clear to me many times that he was in no position to help in my endeavors.

Granted, the Moîrai changed us and helped a lot, but I don't think they'd been able to remove stubbornness from our traits, from what we'd become.

The wall warned me the party I was expecting had arrived. It dilated and Ohtlinell entered, escorted by four of our guards. From behind my desk, I opened my right palm and showed him where to sit; a stool emerged from the floor. The Moîrai watched the stool rising but didn't move and stood there, in silence.

I nodded the guards to leave us. I sensed they took their place right beyond the wall that coalesced after them.

After the wall sealed again, *"What's the meaning of all this, Dan of Eridu?"* burst in my mind. The black eyes of the Moîrai searched for mine.

I smiled. "You may talk freely here. My quarters are sealed; no one can track, hear, or record anything said within these walls." I indicated once more the stool.

"As you like." He walked to the stool and sat. "But first, it would please me to know why the guards confiscated my Palladium."

"Ah, yes...the Palladium." I rubbed my chin. "All communications from and to Eridu are now regulated." I looked straight at him, but he didn't reveal any emotion, as he had shielded his mind.

"It's normal procedure in cases such as these. But don't worry, you're not in any danger." The Moîrai stared at me and I withstood his gaze without blinking.

"You did not answer my question," he said.

I stood up and walked up to the transparent wall in the back of the room. I looked out and enjoyed the view of Nova Roma. "Didn't I, Ohtlinell?" I felt the Moîrai's gaze on my back. "We've been looking for answers for decades and were given none." I paused and took a deep breath.

"Nova Roma is magnificent, don't you think? As are all new cities in Eridu." I turned and squinted. "As the old ones were, and are no more... Billions of lives ended like that," I snapped my fingers, "in a few seconds. They were given no mercy, but I hear their screams even today. They ask me for a reason. The real one." I stepped forward to confront him. "I intend to provide them with an answer. The answer that even the Keepers negated me."

I gestured the wall to dilate and the guards stepped in. "Accompany the Moîrai to his quarters."

"How can you do this? You are a Keeper, one of us." Ohtlinell's thoughts resonated in my mind.

I replied at once in the same way. *"I'm the Keeper of Eridu, Ohtlinell, and this is only the beginning."*

The guards grabbed him.

When alone, a lateral wall dilated and Manfred stepped in. "Thank you." He nodded. "Yes, this is only our first step."

I sighed. "The next ones are crucial."

"We will not fail." Manfred smiled.

Chapter 6 – Herding the Flocks

The Bridge Stations had reached the maximum alert condition. In a week time, Eridu's own Fleet constituted the only traffic authorized within the Kuiper Belt. We had no chance to succeed in an open war against the whole Moîrai's Confederation. We were no longer at a disadvantage, as for the technology we had in common with the Moîrai, but their numerous allies would have made the difference in the case of a full, open confrontation. We had, though, one advantage, if it worked...

⁂

When Eridu became the sole producer of the neurotrophic drug used by interstellar pilots, some fifty years before, and the process rested under our strict control, the first human interstellar pilots received the training to join the Confederation's routes.

Pilots in symbiosis with their ships achieved a different state of consciousness—a fact well known within the Confederation—but the tests we conducted with our pilot

Cadets revealed something more, something not even the Moîrai could have foreseen.

The scientists called it a *weakness*. In the Council, we saw in it a *feature* to use at our advantage, instead; we welcomed its discovery as a godsend.

At first, the news raised an alarm among our researchers. The Chief Scientist of the SIPHI—the Space Interstellar Pilots Human Initiative—called for an urgent meeting with the Council.

That day, I met with Manfred on my way to the summit. "You don't have any more details, do you?"

"I'm afraid not, Dan." Manfred shook his head in disappointment. "I've read the same report as you did, but the Chief Scientist sounds seriously worried. His words were 'if this is leaked, Moîrai might shut down the whole Initiative'."

I stopped in front of the Council Room and prevented the wall from opening. I took Manfred aside. "This is serious. Who else is aware of it? Whatever this is..."

"The entire scenario and its implications are known only to the two lead scientists and their teams; both are here today."

"Have a complete profile of anyone even only slightly involved with the research, and raise the disclosure level of all reports to 'Council Only'."

"It's done already." Manfred smiled as I signaled my approval by letting the wall dilate.

When I opened the session, the Twelve didn't hide their worries, so I invited Manfred to describe the measures he had put in place to contain any possible leaks and security breaches.

The researchers involved with SIPHI had been under constant surveillance from the beginning, and the two Chief Scientists had been escorted to the Council complex as soon as they raised the issue and called for the emergency hearing. The fact they did so implied they, too, understood the dangers.

When we allowed them in, their expressions suggested the fear of the unknown. They scurried to the hearing table, glancing around but avoiding eye contact. They produced all diagrams and evidence of their findings and had all the Council's attention. The scientists concluded their report without coming to their personal conclusions, as if they were in a hurry and eager to drop a weight too heavy for their shoulders.

"Did you disclose any of this to your collaborators?" I asked.

"Only those who need to know, sir." The Chief Scientist turned to search for me before answering and—this time—his eyes met mine with understanding.

I looked around at the other members of the Council as everyone probed the mind of the two scientists, as they'd learned from me the way we did with the Keepers. The scientists told the truth, and their worries were ours, too.

"We understood immediately," the Chief Scientist continued, "that if we disclosed these results to the Moîrai, they would have taken the results of our tests as a serious flaw in the security of any interstellar travel." He paused. "And they would be right."

"Could they find this weakness themselves?" Manfred bent forward from his seat.

He looked straight into Manfred's eyes. "Hardly. They would need to know what to look for, and where."

I intervened. "And we will make sure no one will ever know." Both turned toward me. "You will continue your work under complete secrecy and scrutiny. And you will need to refine your discovery, and make it perfect."

Manfred nodded. The two scientists shared a mutual, puzzled look. "We're afraid we don't follow you, sir."

"You will soon."

I concluded the meeting, dismissed the two scientists, and worked within the Council on the first steps of what would become our most powerful weapon.

⁂

On Bridge Station One, Commander Anton Sage waited for our arrival. Samuel accompanied me, and our shuttle had just docked and we were at the bulkhead separating the vessel from the station. When it dilated, Sage saw us coming through the corridor and his voice revealed a pitch of worry and excitement at the same time. "Sir, Admiral." He lowered his head. "Welcome to Bridge Station One."

I fixed my eyes on his for a second as I kept walking. "Anton, I'm glad to see you upbeat, but I sense something's troubling you."

Sage exchanged a glance with Samuel before adjusting his pace with ours. I noticed he was a second too slow with his reply. "No, sir... It's just because of the wait. We sent the orders an hour ago on the privileged channel, overriding the priorities of all others—"

"And?" Samuel interrupted him, bending his head toward him.

Sage didn't seem willing to reveal what troubled him. "Nothing. We're waiting, but nothing's manifested yet on our sensors."

"I wouldn't worry too much about that," I said. "Are all Stations ready?"

"Yes, sir," Sage replied at once, and this time his voice didn't show any hesitation. We reached the Control and Command Center hall.

The officers and the staff on duty at that moment exuded the same mixture of preoccupation and eagerness I sensed in Anton, but I was pleased to notice it didn't affect their efficiency.

Permanent virtual panels showed the status of the other Bridge Stations so that any action, if needed, could be coordinated without delays and overlaps. The procedures to follow, and the actions they would trigger, had been simulated under all possible scenarios, examining all variables. When I asked Samuel about it, he reassured me. "We simulated even the impossible ones, Father."

A murmur among the staff signaled our presence had been noticed, but the brief fog of distraction was quick to dissipate and people resumed their tasks.

I stepped aside from our small group and put on the Palladium; Manfred and the other members of the Council had reached their assigned Bridge Stations as well.

"It's an important moment, maybe the most important one of our history." I wanted to greet them but allowed myself only those few words of introduction. *"Manfred, is the Fleet ready?"*

Manfred looked around at our fellow members for their last confirmation, then he sighed with relief. *"Yes, ready to intervene at once; all Stations report the pilots' units are also deployed according to the plans."*

"So be it." I shivered thinking of the extermination suffered by our race in the past and that had culminated in my daughter Hope's death.

"For the Third Loss!" everyone exclaimed and lowered their heads.

"Father!" Samuel rushed to me.

I turned and noticed that two Stations had acknowledged a number of wormholes forming.

"They're coming." A smile rose to his lips.

I glanced at the report screens. Vessels from our fleet converged to those locations. An alarm sounded the dire warning that wormholes' creation interested also the space sector of Station One, and the crew reacted like clockwork; the cruiser vessels received the exact coordinates and fighter units swarmed toward the exit points in attack formations.

The space fabric trembled where the wormholes opened and stars faded as the tunnels revealed their singularities in the space-time continuum. With multiple flashes, ships of all kinds emerged from hyperspace.

All Stations sent the incoming ships the same communication, in all known languages: "You have violated Eridu's space. Disable all defensive and offensive capabilities of your vessel. Resistance will mark you as hostile. You will be stopped with extensive use of force. Lower your shields and prepare for Eridu's Inspection Teams' boarding procedure."

I gave a last glance at the members of the Council—still connected with me through the Palladium—and lowered my head, then I dismissed them all. "There is no way back now."

⁂

Joshua waited patiently in his cockpit. In turn, his eyes controlled the activity of all sensors, the connections to the Bridge Station and with the mother cruiser ship. Caressing the commands with his hands, he set all weapons—one by one—to release the maximum energy, even at the cost of reducing the effectiveness of the defensive shields of his fighter.

He alerted the storm he commanded using the private, encrypted channel. "Get ready, guys. Stations confirm incoming traffic. Maximum offensive configuration."

"Aye, aye, sir." The voices from his squad leaders acknowledged the orders and confirmations came from all the other units.

Space had always had a magnetic effect on Joshua. Ever since his years at the Academy, that was where he wanted to be, commanding a fighter squadron and flying with his bravery.

A buzzer resounded when his unit received the coordinates assigned to his storm. Joshua acknowledged the transmission from the mother ship and yelled, "Let's go!"

The fighter jumped ahead as the first flashes from a wormhole tunnel blanched, for an instant, his field of vision, before the visor and the screens reacted and filtered the increased luminosity. The fighter's systems probed the incoming vessels for identification and to detect any hostile activity as the storm split to surround them and converge on their position.

He locked the weapons on the foreign ships. In the cockpit, the tactical panels showed the acquired targets while the storm got ready for its deadly welcoming.

From a protected rear position, the larger Eridu cruisers bolted the tug beams to prevent the hostile vessels from attempting any kind of maneuvers. Overwhelmed, one by one the ships lowered their defense shields and Eridu's transporters left the cruisers for the Space Marines to board the captured units.

Everything proceeded as hoped and with no incidents until the first military battleships jumped out of the wormholes.

⁂

Alarms and orders bounced off all duty stations like a multitude of steel balls in a pinball possessed by the devil. The adrenaline rush jolted the heartbeats of every Station One's crewmember to a pace that would have slaughtered any human from before the Selection age.

One of the crewmembers in the bridge, with his eyes riveted to the panels floating in front of him, yelled. "Hostile military vessels. Offensive measures detected. Acquiring targets."

The information from his dashboard filled the central main panels with a crescendo and we all could see the details of the danger we faced. A medium-sized flotilla of Huitzilin vessels showed up on the screens—a rather bellicose race in the Confederation. Hawkish but unreliable allies of the Moîrai, they always pushed for a more direct confrontation against the Kritas and their Alliance and aspired to a more prominent role in the organization. Of all the races in the Confederation, the Huitzilin could constitute a serious problem.

Sage's comment revealed his surprise and worries, shared by many. "We don't have pilots within the Huitzilin!"

To my satisfaction, though, Samuel had already established a direct communication channel with the Fleet squadrons closest to our sector, but the countdown for their interception with the new threat showed we didn't have much time.

The Station system sent the Confederation's standard *declare-friend-or-foe* code and the reply—from the translation of the clicks and hisses that made up their language—didn't mask the implicit hostile attitude of their race.

"We are on a rescue operation following a distress signal from Huitzilin vessels skyjacked to this star system. Do not interfere!"

Samuel turned toward me with a muted question. My reply surprised me as well. I enunciated my order with a cold voice. “Take them out!”

Chapter 7 – Silent Rumbles of War

Our Fleet dealt with the Huitzilin interference with staggering surgical precision and suffered no losses. They didn't expect our immediate reaction or its lethality. From the surrounding sectors, our dispatched battleships launched a wall of antimatter seeker-torpedoes that crumbled over the enemy vessels. The Huitzilis froze in space before reacting with evasive maneuvers, but it was too late. The Brigde Station defensive units—mainly fighters and small cruisers—swarmed out to attack the scattering enemy ships. Our Fleet obliterated the Huitzilin vessels with a show of massive firepower and lack of mercy. In all, the battle lasted only a few seconds.

The incident, though, proved beneficial, as other sparse foreign military units realized they would have met the same destiny and be reduced to particulate matter and dust bound to accrue the overall mass of the Kuiper Belt. They lowered their shields and the Marines took control of them. All human pilots aboard non-Eridu ships had reached our system and performed their expected duty without hesitation. Thousands of military vessels, and a thousand times more of civilian ships, fell into our hands.

Aliens from all races in the Confederation—with a majority being Moîrai—increased the numbers of the ones already hosted in our AIDAs, back on Eridu.

The news of what happened in the solar system reached the farther stars in the entire galaxy, stunning as a shockwave caused by the collapse of a neutron star.

We filed a complaint with all races in the Confederation for violation of our space sovereignty and—as a consequence—we announced the interruption of any delivery of Fusion, the neurotrophic drug we produced. That act alone constituted a major threat to everyone. Officially outraged, we declared Eridu space off limits to all traffic until the incidents were examined thoroughly and every case settled independently with the concerned races. We were determined to leave everyone without a clear understanding of what had just happened and of its cause.

The Keepers and the Moîrai Supreme Council of the Wisest requested my presence in Protusa on several occasions, invitations that I refused multiple times before they realized the meeting had no chance of happening on their terms.

The Kritas Alliance's political pressure, and their vetoes against the initial resolutions put forward by the Moîrai to resolve the crisis, worked in our favor and bought us precious time. Our intelligence revealed the Kritas harbored a dream of bringing Eridu and the humans into their Alliance, and wanted to seize the opportunity.

The disbelief and the finger pointing with which the galaxy received the news of the incidents, and our subsequent 'reactions', gave us the chance to test our discovery during a welcomed pause of the events and to get ready for a confrontation. The pause, though, didn't last long.

⁂

A Moîrai vessel announced its arrival to our Bridge Stations. The wormhole opened far from our sphere of influence, at some two hundred million kilometres from the Kuiper Belt.

The lone ship emerged from the tunnel and stayed there, motionless, with no replies to any of the Stations' communication attempts. The vessel was not a menace per se, but its appearance was disturbing nonetheless.

Samuel had ordered the Fleet to keep its position and to monitor any activity the Moîrai ship should undertake, but I asked him to report to me at once.

The connection through the Palladium rendered Samuel's presence in my quarters atop the Council Tower. The light of the sun made the walls glitter as much as Marina's memnosphere did from its pedestal in the center of the room. The biocomputer kept all her memories and thought processes alive for me, recombining its molecular bonds like the synapses of a brain. With time, I started to be able to connect its burst of lights with the kind of thoughts and words that it pronounced with Marina's voice, anticipating them, even.

Samuel gave me an intent look. "Father, what are we supposed to do?"

"Good morning, Samuel." I frowned. "I believe I know what this means. Can't you figure it out?"

"Emissaries from the Supreme Council?"

The sphere twinkled as if Marina giggled at his words. Samuel glanced at the biocomputer.

The sphere flashed with intensity, "Alaston," and succeeded to capture my sight, too.

"I need to talk to him." I paused, distracted by the interruption. Then I looked back at my son. "I've not given up on the Moîrai, and he could be the only chance we have to avoid the worst."

"How so?" Samuel said.

I hesitated to reveal more, but becoming aware of the Keepers' role now wouldn't help Samuel. "Alaston is very influential and has ties within the Moîrai's Supreme Council."

He crossed his arms. "I don't like it, Father."

I smiled. "They won't attempt anything. They would've sent the entire Confederation fleet instead if they wanted to."

"I'll make plans for your arrival here, then." Samuel nodded.

I removed the Palladium that encircled my head. Nothing would be the same any more; for better or for worse, change was rushing toward each one of us. In that moment, only time would reveal what it would bring to us, and to Eridu. "What do you think, Marina?"

The memnosphere in the middle of my office twisted and shivered as if it was laughing. The sparks that announced Marina's voice sent shadows and reflections on the walls, but her words didn't show any amusement. "Would anything I'd say change your mind?"

"Probably not."

I stood up and went to the transparent wall. Looking out at Nova Roma, my old memories told me I lived on an alien planet, but my heart and my mind screamed it wasn't; it was the world I helped to create.

"Your reasons are the right ones, Dan, and I understand what drives you. The only question I'd have is whether they're necessary, too."

I uttered a grunt and turned away from the scene of the city extending to the horizon. I looked back at the sphere. "If I wanted to have a Moîrai's kind of opinion, I would have called for Ohtlinell." My voice sounded harsher than I wanted, but it was too late to take my words back. The sphere dimmed and didn't reply, as if Marina had taken offense.

"I'm sorry," I said after a moment. "It was a thoughtless remark."

Some bright sparks reached the sphere surface. "The way I know you, you never make thoughtless remarks." The sphere's light trembled like a flame. "You're about to take a journey that can end in several destinations. I'm not sure you'd like many of them."

Even as an artifact, Marina had a way of looking deep into me and seeing things that I had yet to discover. Sometimes she avoided disagreeing openly. The last time she did that was the day before her death. Then, after we recovered her body, the Moîrai recorded her mind processes in the memnosphere. I tried to smile at the thought, but my lips tightened.

"Do you believe in destiny?" I asked instead.

The light inside the sphere grew in intensity. "I can't answer your question, but look at us now. Is this the destiny we were to share?"

My heart sank. "I grew bitter, Marina. I'm not sure anyone would like to feel what I fee, and share the burden of what I'm determined to do. I'm changing, and I don't know where it will lead me."

The wall reflected lights and colors from an overactive sphere, but the room fell into silence.

⁂

The Moîrai vessel seemed vulnerable, but I recognized it as a heavy battleship class the Keepers used for perilous and stealth missions. Alone, it could easily have destroyed the Huitzilin squadron we just defeated when it appeared on our space, and do that without effort.

Our probes couldn't detect any other presence. On the bridge, the voice of the fighters' squadron commander confirmed what our systems reported. "Space sector's clear." The screens showed the fighters spread into a protective cocoon around our cruiser and the Keepers' vessel. "Deploying in the buffer zone now."

"It seems you are bound to surprise me even more, Dan of Eridu." Alaston's thought reached me at that precise

moment. *"And you are taking precautions as if I came to you as an enemy, instead of as one of the Brothers."*

I smiled and took a deep breath. *"Welcome, Alaston. I expected your visit."*

Next to me, Samuel looked at my frown and understood. "Father, is he..."

"Yes." I squinted my eyes at him. "Alaston's here."

"Greetings to your son," Alaston said. *"I sense no intention to harm coming from you. I hope you can sense the same from me, Dan."*

The crew on deck awaited instructions, and Samuel interjected again. "Father, what are your orders?" He insisted on receiving instructions I wasn't ready to formulate yet. The answer came to me from the Moîrai.

"If you agree, I'd board your ship, with Mênis, too."

I snorted. Two of my mentors together. I hadn't seen Mênis since Samuel's cadet years at the Space Academy when we received the first vessels to build Eridu's fleet. Moîrai and humans had walked together on a long journey and our paths were now in peril of splitting for good. Would we look at each other still as friends in the future? Alaston brought me back to the present. *"Dan? If acceptable, a small unarmed shuttle will take me and Mênis to your cruiser."*

"Agreed," I replied, and on those terms, I gave instructions to Samuel.

A small shining rod left the Moîrai vessel's starboard side. The rod grew bigger against the uncertain darkness of our future in the galaxy. Our probes confirmed two Moîrai were aboard the shuttle and that it was an unmanned vehicle. Nothing to raise suspicions; nonetheless, all units had acquired the shuttle as target as soon as it left the mother ship.

In a few minutes, the rod reached the Eridu's cruiser in the front entry bay. We let it wait and kept the entry closed. A more detailed scan took place to examine the shuttle and its passengers. Our vessel released roboprobes that swarmed to its hull and glued to it before activating. On the bridge, tech scientists and weapons specialists received a flood of data about the vehicle and xenobiologists verified the bioscans of the two Moîrai aboard. The blueprint of the shuttle filled the screens, flashing to a new perspective each time different elements were analyzed and cleared. Alaston and Mênis's vitals received the same bruteforce scrutiny from the probes and our scientists, as the shuttle and its infrastructure continued to be inspected.

I waited for everyone involved in the safety procedure to confirm the absence of any danger or threat.

"Congratulations, Alaston and Mênis," I told their minds. *"Our doctors here signal you're in great shape, too."*

"I hope the humans are now reassured. We come in peace, Dan of Eridu." Alaston's thoughts didn't show any hesitation.

That was the second time he addressed me with my title, something we refrained from doing among us. I took the event as the sign that Alaston chose to be cautious and approached the situation we humans had created as venturing into a dangerous and uncharted territory.

"And in peace, I welcome you." I grinned.

The cruiser's beam-tractors pulled the shuttle in as the front of our ship dilated into a landing bay. The rod crossed the force field that maintained the integrity of the internal atmosphere, protruded its landing gears, and touched ground as our military personnel surrounded it.

Our welcoming wasn't one I'd like for myself, but I didn't want to interfere with Samuel's dispositions—once he gave the orders—and certainly not in front of his officers. I nodded and prepared to receive my guests.

⁂

Together with Samuel, I waited for Alaston and Mênis in my quarters. The far wall rendered the outer space as if there was no obstruction separating the vacuum from us. Lights were dim, and I had the floor reabsorb all existing furniture. This was not a courtesy visit and I wanted the bare nudity of the room reflect the message that no obstacles and no barriers had to be raised to prevent words of truth to be shared with the Moîrai; a clean room, and clean minds.

We stood in the middle when I sensed the Brethren of the Keepers approach. We let the wall dilate and the guards escorted Alaston and Mênis inside.

I addressed the guards. "The Moîrai are welcomed guests; you can leave us now." Samuel nodded and the guards left; the wall coalesced behind them.

"Greetings, Dan of Eridu." Alaston ignored Samuel's presence.

"We thought we would have met with you alone," Mênis said instead.

Samuel stiffened and was about to give voice to his feelings, but my hand reached his arm. They would have taken it as a sign of weakness if Samuel replied to their explicit disrespect.

"There was a time when a Moîrai's words were for all humans to hear." I stared at Alaston.

"We carry a message intended only for Dan of Eridu," he replied, and added—at a mental level—*"and to a Keeper."*

I replied in the same way. *"Let it be so."*

"What you have to say concerns all humans." Samuel couldn't hold it any longer.

"Dan of Eridu will share what he will decide to share." Mênis looked straight at me.

I turned to my son, nodding. "Samuel, don't take offence. We'll be gracious hosts to the Moîrai."

"But—"

"Samuel, please." I interrupted him.

Samuel took a deep breath and lowered his head. "As you wish, Father." He left through the dilating wall without deigning to look at the Moîrai.

"You raised him well." Alaston lowered his head.

"He honors me as did all those who aren't with us anymore." I gestured to seal the room.

"You sound different than the last time we met," Mênis said. "We were not prepared for the latest events. Eridu is cause for lots of concerns."

"Eridu's my first and only concern." I gave him an oblique look.

Indeed, we all looked different from the first time we met on the planet I called Earth then, some ninety years before. I had been humbled, befuddled, and wary; in the night, they looked like gods to me, their skin gleaming as from an internal light and their oval dark eyes impenetrable as if cut in obsidian. Now we were standing on an empty hall aboard a battlecruiser of the powerful Eridu's Space Fleet, with the open space visible at my back. Face to face, I saw gods no more. "So, what is the message from the Supreme Council?"

Alaston exchanged a glance with Mênis, then stepped closer. "Dan, the humans are on a dangerous path, and many in the Confederation are listening to the old refrains from the Kritas and their Alliance acolytes."

I smiled. "They are gravely mistaken, and naïve, too. I'm sure you and the Wisest must know the Kritas are ready to open their arms and welcome us to their Alliance...if only I gave them the sign." I sensed both Alaston and Mênis stiffen; I had marked a point. "The path we are on is the one the Moîrai imposed on us."

"How could you say that?" Mênis lashed out.

"How, Mênis?" I smiled again. "And yet, I remember you admitted you weren't sure there was conclusive evidence we humans were rushing toward the self-destruction that started the Selection process. Am I wrong?" My words met with silence. I looked around in the empty room and waved at the bare walls. "And what happened instead? Nothing! We expected the truth, and what you gave us is a cover-up at best."

I walked up to him and my words hissed with anger. "You suspected someone in the decision process knew about using humans' cells to produce the pilots' drug. And well before the Selection started." I snorted. "Did he force the decision and destroy our entire civilization for the drug?" I glanced at Alaston. "And what about that puppet of Ekahau? Where is he?" I turned my back on them. "And what did he reveal to the Supreme Council that not even the Brethren of the Keepers can help me find out?"

I walked toward the transparent wall and looked at the stars, thinking of the civilizations they harbored. I looked in the direction I knew Protusa was when I spoke again. "The message from the Supreme Council of the Wisest has to be one of a full disclosure of the events and with detailed responsibilities of anyone involved in the Selection." A cold determination filled my heart and I let the Moîrai feel the reach of its depth. "I want Ekahau and everyone else to receive a just trial in Eridu. I'm not interested in hearing anything different than this."

I wasn't surprised when I heard the faint breath of the wall dilate and the Moîrai leave. Their silence confirmed my suspicions. No words, no thoughts, nothing else could silence the screams of billions of humans losing their lives and not knowing why.

The wall dilated again and Samuel rushed in. "What did they say?"

"What they didn't say is even more revealing." I gave one more glance at the blinking spots in the Universe.

The Moîrai's shuttle rod undocked and sailed toward the Keepers' vessel. I turned to meet my son's eyes. "Samuel, prepare for war."

Chapter 8 – Gluing Words to Words

Minds and hearts fought for supremacy that day. The right thing to do might not be the most rational one, nor is it always wise to go where the heart leads. But what the Moîrai could not factor in, in any meaningful way, was the powerful combination that arises when the mind and the heart agree.

Nova Roma's summit with the Council of the Twelve kept an entire planet on its toes for days. We received all the experts' reports, the whole range of options and outcomes from scientists and from the highest military ranks; little by little, we made our minds meet our hearts.

Destiny is not trumpeted to a crowd; it likes best to be made behind closed doors. We discussed for days in the Council hall, under its imposing dome. On the last one, before we rendered our final assessment, I turned the dome transparent again and let Nova Roma's lights shine through. We saw the world and its thriving life, and sensed through that sight the responsibility we had toward our race. "Shall we come to a decision now?" I asked everyone after a moment.

"What will happen when everything is over?" The member of the Twelve who represented the Far East regions had asked everyone, but his eyes were fixed on me.

My nostrils dilated when I breathed. "Nothing will ever be over. There will be changes, and their effects will last for eons." I stood up and stepped into the middle of the circle. "We knew what we started had a chance of leading us to this. We know the price we may need to pay so that no one will ever again have to endure what the race of man has endured." I looked at each member in turn.

"Perpetrators of the most heinous crime will not escape their fate, or what we've accomplished together so far would be in vain. We will not sit inactive and condone the slaughter of billions."

The sun rose at that moment and the dawn's purple clouds, stained with red brushes, came to life and shed their golden light on Nova Roma below. I glanced at the sun and smiled at how silly sometimes we are to notice these things in the direst instants. Yet, maybe it marks what humans are—the ones capable of feeling the necessity of the unnecessary in our lives.

One by one, the Twelve rose from their benches. "For the Third Loss," one said, and the others repeated, "For the Third Loss."

⁂

We spent days in that hall. No one left—except for brief pauses—and no one would have been able to focus on any other chores. Around the circular walls, floating panels kept everyone informed on details of all ongoing operations while each had their own dashboard with their respective competencies and responsibility under control.

The assembly gathered representatives and leaders of all military branches, Eridu's internal affairs, and the scientists who briefed the Council of the Twelve with the discovery of the unforeseen side effect arising from the combination of human genes and Moîrai. It was like being in a war room, and, indeed, that was what everyone felt. We had absorbed the last details reported by each in turn and prepared for the worst.

"How long can we resist?" Manfred asked. The eyes of everyone checked the latest reports from the Bridge Stations. Like flies attracted by a flame, our eyes kept returning to the screens that would reveal the moment when the firestorm would engulf us if our scientists proved wrong and failed the crucial test of real events.

Samuel replied with information now everyone knew by heart. "If the plan fails, we will be able to keep any invading force from reaching Eridu for fourty-eight hours, considering the balance of forces in an all-out assault." He paused for a second, and glanced at me with a half-smile before he bent his head like his mother used to do. I had to close my eyes as memories jumped at me from the remote recess where I kept them. With pain, I sent them back before they obfuscated my reason.

"Of course," he went on, "Eridu's Fleet will evaporate in the effort. Then, it will be the turn of our ground forces. Give or take, another thirty hours before Eridu will have to capitulate to the forces of the Confederation."

I looked back at my son. "And what is your assessment in case our pilots should instead succeed?"

Samuel took a deep breath. His answer was crucial for our success and for everything not to be a vain exercise of uncontrolled madness. "I'd say we could resist for two full weeks; hopefully, one or two days more, even."

"Those two days might make the difference." Manfred went on to question the two scientists who made the whole plan worth considering years before. "Are we confident the neurotransmitters are active by now?"

The Chief Scientist cleared his throat. "Well, the activated astrocytes have the ability to respond to almost all the neurotransmitters we embedded in the drug molecules and, upon activation, release a multitude of neuroactive molecules, which, in turn, will influence neuronal excitability." He looked at his fellow scientist, who nodded with a smile. He smiled back. "Noxious signals will be followed by an action potential carried by nociceptive—or pain sensing—afferent neurons in the dorsal horn of the spinal cord. At this stage, the Glioblastoma Multiforme of enhanced Grade VI will have started to spread causing cranial nerve disorder, and extensive areas of necrosis and hypoxia."

The two scientists freewheeled with scientific details and left us way behind. I watched them in awe for a few seconds. "The tumor growth," the Chief Scientist continued, "will cause a breakdown of the blood–brain barrier, thus opening the way to the nanoparticle-mediated delivery of neoplastic enhancing molecules to further spread the tumor."

"Hold on, hold on! We don't follow you! What are you talking about?" Manfred erupted and slammed a fist on the table. "You're not here to teach a lesson and impress your students."

The scientists blushed and would've replied, but Manfred hadn't finished yet. "We are risking annihilation as a race. Stop patting yourself on the shoulders—we'll have time to honor your research if any of us gets out alive from this!"

Manfred stood up, rested his hands on the table, and bent forward toward the two scientists, now at loss of words. "Will your research give us the surprise factor to win this war?" His voice echoed in the room and a disturbing silence followed his question.

The Chief Scientist's face recovered its natural color. He stared back at Manfred, and his answer was simple enough to make everyone resume breathing. "Yes."

I sensed Manfred probing the scientist's mind before he took his seat again.

"Thank you, Dr. Stoner." That was the first time I called the scientist by his name. He straightened up when he heard his name coming from my lips. He turned toward me, his eyebrows raised, and I sensed from him the growth of a pleasant surprise.

I smiled and he relaxed even more. "Can you show us—in more accessible terms—what the Moîrai pilots will face? Please."

Stoner nodded and his face shone with gratefulness. "The astrocytes are star-shaped cells in the brain. They are glial cells, from Greek name *γλία*, for glue. They support, protect, feed, and are vital to neurons' synaptic capabilities. The specific high-grade glioma, or brain tumor, we triggered is extremely disruptive and will undermine space pilots' operational functionalities in a short time."

"Okay." I raised my hand as I sensed the uneasiness surging again in all the others. "How short?"

"Well, because of the ability of astrocytes to communicate with their neighbors, changes in the activity of one astrocyte can have repercussions on the activities of all others even when they are quite distant from the original astrocyte."

I smiled. "How short, Dr. Stoner?"

He looked at me, pensive, for a brief moment. "Within twenty, twenty-five days from now. I'd wish to be more precise but—"

I raised my hand again and turned to Samuel, who frowned. "I couldn't promise that, Father. We'll resist until the last ship is operational, but if we face the entire Confederation, not just the Moîrai forces, within that time period, they will crush all obstacles and invade Eridu."

"Stoner." I faced the scientist. "Could the Moîrai and the Confederation recover their pilots after the symptoms have started?"

Stoner shook his head. "The glioblastoma we created will cause headaches, nausea and vomiting, seizures, and cranial nerve disorders as a result of increased intracranial pressure. Moreover, the glioma will always grow back even after complete surgical excision. They'll be able to keep the pilots alive, but not have them resume their tasks. For that, they would need us."

"Thank you. This is reassuring." I stood up and declared the assembly formally over. I waited for all the guests and experts to leave. The Twelve were worried; we risked losing everything. "We survived and flourished through times of murky chaos," I addressed them. "Let's not change course now. Stand resolute against all enemies." Then I stared at Manfred. "I need to buy us time with the Moîrai. Get Ohtlinell to my rooms. This is when he'll play a useful role for us."

⁂

I concentrated and felt Ohtlinell approach from afar, escorted by the guards. I let him feel my presence, too. His reaction came at once. *"I am coming as a Keeper, and I hope to find a Keeper to welcome me."*

"As a Keeper I called for you."

A few minutes later, the guards requested permission to bring in the Moîrai. The wall dilated. "The Moîrai Ohtlinell, sir." The officer escorted Ohtlinell through the wall and left at my signal.

"Thank you for coming at once."

The Moîrai coughed—with the guttural sound they make when laughing. "A kindness I would have not been able to refuse, Dan of Eridu."

I smiled. "Please, have a seat. You may tell this room is sealed, and my words are for the Keepers and the Supreme Council only."

Ohtlinell lowered his head and opened his palms to me as he sat down.

I lowered my head in turn. "I've received a visit from the Brethren of the Keepers, together with Mênis." I paused and let the news sink in for a second. "They didn't ask about you, and I think I know the reason."

Ohtlinell didn't comment. From that point on, his eyes never left mine.

"You reached Eridu not long after I started to push within the Keepers to know of Ekahau's revelations or confessions, and his whereabouts. I need to discover who was involved with him." I stared at him. "And you had a mission to accomplish here."

Ohtlinell sealed his mind for a brief instant and reopened it right away, but it was long enough for me to notice his reaction and confirm my suspicions. Better than a full confession, and that allowed me to push even further. "Supreme Council members swear to protect the secrecy of the Keepers at all costs, and their oath has never been violated...so far."

The Moîrai stiffened. "What are you implying?"

I ignored his question. "The Keepers' efficiency rests as well on its secrecy and mythical aura that the organization enjoys within Moîrai's society."

Ohtlinell shifted his weight on his seat. "You are a Keeper yourself, Dan of Eridu!"

I grunted. "Indeed I am, and the Supreme Council sent Alaston and Mênis to convince me to desist. That means only one thing." I relaxed on my seat and sensed Ohtlinell's inner trouble mounting, even if he was now trying to shield all of his emotions.

"A traitor sits in the Supreme Council and must have threatened—successfully I have to say—to betray the Keepers' secrecy at its roots if the investigations on Kritas' involvement on Eridu went any further."

"The human has lost his mind!" Ohtlinell stood up and clenched his fists. "How dare you to suspect one of the Wisest of the Moîrai?" His voice raised.

"Sit down!" I charged my words with the full extent of a mental blow, stronger that any Keeper had ever experienced. Ohtlinell stumbled back from the impact and dropped his jaw.

"Sit, please," I repeated. Befuddled, the Moîrai complied. He shut his mind but his action gave me the pleasure to force his mind open, like thrusting a blade into an oyster and cutting the bivalve muscle with ease. Ohtlinell's hands trembled in the vain effort to resist the mental squelch. His shoulders sank.

"I have a message that you will deliver verbatim to both the Keepers and the Supreme Council." I focused my thoughts to the equivalent of a bar of incandescent metal, and then used both words and mind. *"The humans are prepared. We broke the seal of death. We see what cannot be seen and hear what cannot be heard. The mad will fall. The end is the start, all things are apart, for the Son of Man comes to seek and to save what was lost.*"

I used ancient words that narrated the myth of the Keepers. I didn't need to add more—the message had roots millions of years old. The Moîrai understood the menace and his voice trembled, betraying his worries. Bent on his seat, he raised his chin to look up at me. "Not even a fool would pronounce these words in vain. What have you done, Dan of Eridu?"

"The mad one in the Supreme Council will force the Moîrai to come here alone to discover it. He will not tolerate interference from other members of the Confederation, and the son of man will show who's the one corrupted." I stood up and let the wall dilate. The guards outside were ready to escort Ohtlinell out. "Now go. You will be given a shuttle to reach Protusa."

"A shuttle? With no pilot? Are the humans mad? How will I ever reach Protusa?"

My lips bent into a cold smile. "This, too, is part of your message, and it will not be ignored."

⁂

On Bridge Station One, Anton Sage had the small shuttle ready to welcome the Moîrai. A small unit, conceived for star system internal trips only, waited for its passenger.

"You are condemning me to a certain death." Ohtlinell faced me when we'd reached the assigned bulkhead. Then, he added for my mind alone, *"A Keeper never harms another Keeper."*

"You face no harm," I replied, unheard by the others. "Remember my message, word for word, for the Supreme Council." I turned to Sage and Samuel. "Is everything ready for the transport?"

Samuel tilted his head forward and Sage confirmed. "Yes, sir. The Moîrai will reach his destination as planned. The shuttle will be at the required sector coordinates ten minutes and twenty-seven seconds after undocking the Bridge Station."

Ohtlinell gave me an incredulous look. *"If your words are true, your message will be heard."*

I opened my palms to the Moîrai and lowered my head. "Accept what fate binds you, as we humans did. As relics of the past, we rise again."

The bulkhead dilated. Ohtlinell lowered his head for a long moment. After we exchanged a last, intent look, he turned and boarded the shuttle.

On the main deck, we watched the shuttle drift away from the Station before the boost of its main engine ignited. The engineers on deck coordinated with the Station's pilots' unit.

The wormholes every interstellar pilot is able to create come thanks to the symbiosis with the ships. The technology was at the base of the Moîrai prowess and gave rise to their dominance in the galaxy. After years of research, the anomaly our scientists discovered—and that affected the altered genes in human pilots—was instead our greatest achievement. Joined into a super-entity, human pilots created the space-time singularity, and maintained it open to its destination, without the need to have an interstellar pilot onboard the ship making the journey. If we were to prevail, the galaxy would see the emergence of a network of interconnected gates, with hubs and leaf destinations growing like neurons in a brain with new filaments and connecting synapses. The vision lingered still in my mind when Samuel exclaimed and brought me back to present times. "There!"

On the main screen in the bridge deck, in front of the shuttle, the space-time fabric faltered. The continuum distortion emitted, at first, a brownish-red glowing that intensified into a blinding, absolute white hole with fuzzy, vibrating borders and source of intense diffraction. It grew and engulfed the unmanned shuttle; we saw it vanish when it entered the wormhole that closed right after with what I could only describe as an implosion of dark light. The stars shone again as if nothing had happened, and yet...

A roar of shouts and applauses came from everyone on deck. A wave of triumph and exultation reached me from all the Twelve connected through the Palladium. We had just witnessed the future, and the galaxy had to get ready to witness the humans rise again as a flaming Phoenix.

Chapter 9 – Xrusé

At a space sector far away from the planet cradle to the Moîrai, Xrusé, the crew of the first Moîrai vessel to reach the singularity space deformity observed the phenomenum with curiosity first, and then reacted with suspicion and increased alarm when they realized the nature of what they were witnessing. The terse communication back to Xrusé said nothing and everything at the same time. "It's a wormhole formation of an unknown nature."

The past days had prepared the galaxy, and the Moîrai Supreme Council, to the eventuality of a direct confrontation between the two leading coalitions—the Moîrai Confederation and the Kritas Alliance. The news from Eridu led the Wisest to believe that the ultimate treason from the humans had only one meaning—the Kritas mingled with them. The Kritas saw in the events a breach in the tightly held Confederation and the chance to gain the supremacy if they succeded to bring the humans within the Alliance.

Before the shuttle carrying Ohtlinell emerged from the wormhole, a Moîrai squad of interceptors received the order to converge at once to face a probable hostile, yet unidentified, force. The interceptors were prepared to repel a treacherous attack from the Kritas and their Alliance.

Their befuddled commander had just established a direct communication link with incoming lethal groups in support of that which had just appeared on his tactical screen, but the wormhole opening grew before the vessels had time to scatter in their hemisphere formation. "The singularity is enlarging; the characteristics are not recognizable. The gravity wave fluctuation does not allow any confirmation of the presence of a large body mass entering our space-time frame."

In retreat, stronger and with larger vessels, the support groups sped up to reach the same space sector at once. A resounding voice reached all units at once. "Here is Cit Amoxtli, in command of the operations now. Are we facing Kritas forces?"

The voice gave no credit to the initial assessment of the interceptors' commander. His jaw dropped, and he cracked the articulation of what would've been a human's elbow. He hesitated for a moment before replying to his superior in what he hoped was a matter-of-fact, monotonic voice, deprived of any stress-revealing notes.

"We do not have confirmation of the presence of a large body mass traversing the singularity." He repeated to confirm his previous assessment. He had just finished saying the word 'singularity' when the wormhole's opening billowed and emitted a high level of electromagnetic radiation in the red and infrared wavelengths.

"Something is happening now!" He raised his voice. "All units on maximum alert. Prepare offensive response."

Diffraction rings marked the outer boundary of the wormhole; visible light from all stars around imploded into the opening as if they'd been engulfed into a flash of darkness. Then, the small shuttle from Eridu emerged in Xrusé's controlled space sector.

⁂

Ohtlinell reached the orbit of the Moîrai home planet within minutes after his shuttle entered the landing bay of the main Moîrai vessel. He mentioned a few names that cut short any questions from the Moîrai military, even from the commanding officer, Cit Amoxtli, and a communication link was established right away with the Supreme Council of the Wisest. Ohtlinell called for an urgent crisis assessment meeting in the capital, Protusa.

The landing area, in the middle of the Council's towering structure, had been emptied at once. Inbound traffic had been diverted and the sky, deprived of the common view of many flying vessels, seemed like an ill omen to Alaston, Mênis, and the other Keepers who waited on the central esplanade.

"There." Mênis pointed to a single bright spot high above their heads: a transporter had just penetrated Xrusé's atmosphere.

"Welcome. Dan of Eridu sends you." Alaston reached the mind of his fellow Keeper Ohtlinell when the vessel initiated the final landing approach.

"Greetings, Alaston. His words are troublesome, but even more is how I reached Xrusé," Ohtlinell replied.

"You will share his words with us Keepers first," Alaston said, and Mênis and the rest of the Keepers lowered their heads and showed their palms to him in agreement.

The transporter landed and Ohtlinell disembarked. Without a word, the group crossed the northeast bridge and strode under a huge ark that bore complex geometrical motifs and ideograms; humans might have mistaken them for hieroglyphics.

The main hall was silent; only the gigantic statues of the Wisest of the past witnessed their entrance. The small procession didn't slow their pace and the steps on the stone floor resonated under the sky-high, sanguine vault. The giant, metallic double-doors—threshold to the disguised Keepers' presence in the Supreme Council—turned on invisible hinges. Inside, the Keepers already present joined and followed, widening the group as it advanced.

Dan had been the only non-Moîrai ever admitted to the Brotherhood, and in their inner Sanctorum, the same question harbored all minds: had his induction been premature?

Being the Brethren of the Keepers, Alaston felt he bore the responsibility, as he had been the principal proponent of that decision. The Moîrai aimed at turning the humans into their most valuable ally. So far, everything had supported and justified the original plan, but the recent events put the humans under a different light; a light Alaston was afraid would ignite an unstoppable fire.

They reached the deepest recess of the Keepers' dominium within the Supreme Council, the Sanctorum. No sound of voices echoed in the hall. No one but Keepers ever walked through the wall that dilated in front of them, not even one of the Wisest.

The wall coalesced when the last Keeper crossed the threshold into a place the memory of the Moîrai race considered a myth.

To foreign eyes, the scene of thousands of Moîrai entering the Sanctorum in complete silence would have been incomprehensible. One by one, in tight circular rings, the Keepers donned their Palladium and closed their eyes. Their bodies left the stone floor, lifted by a force field that interacted with their brainwaves. The field created a living sphere with the Moîrai's bodies, their bodies swiveled and their heads pointed to the center where Alaston, the Brethren, and Ohtlinell, the messenger, floated. All their bodies twisted in a wonderful ballet.

The other Keepers' minds fused through their Palladium into a single consciousness, and the three separate entities shone at a mind and spiritual level.

Alaston started the conclave. *"The messenger brings the words of our Brother, Dan of Eridu."* An irritation shivered the Keepers' entity when *It* 'heard' Alaston pronounce 'Brother'. From that reaction, Alaston understood that the *It* entity was infuriated with the human. Alaston suppressed the thought that *It* was right in its judgment.

In the middle of the sphere, Ohtlinell's body spun, and he repeated words that left no doubts as for their intentions. *"The humans are prepared. We broke the seal of death. We see what cannot be seen and hear what cannot be heard. The mad will fall. The end is the start, all things are apart, for the Son of Man comes to seek and to save what was lost."*

The sphere wobbled. *"These are not words of a Brother to his Brothers,"* *It* said.

"The Brother Dan has been seeking for words coming from his Brothers, and received none." Alaston's mind shone in the center of sphere. *"Many expected those to come from the Wisest."*

It remained silent and waited.

"We waded through treacherous fogs," Alaston continued. *"Fogs whose sources perturb us even more. What the Selection revealed, should we condone it...still? The most revered oath is to maintain the secrecy of the Keepers at the cost of life. Are we afraid to reclaim this price?"*

It was thrilled, and the Brethren's words infused *It* with a revamped sense of the meaning of the Keepers' role among the Moîrai. The sphere contracted. *"But he refused to listen to them when they were delivered."*

"There is more to share," Ohtlinell interrupted. *"How I reached Xrusé..."* He paused to let his word gain weight, then went on to describe the new wormhole creation and how the shuttle made through the whole trip without the need of a star pilot aboard. The sphere grew larger as if *It* wanted to distance itself from those words and their implications. Ohtlinell pretended not to notice. *"We cannot lose their trust; we cannot lose the humans, now more than ever."*

It struggled with mixed feelings. The sphere made of Moîrai bodies trembled; the multi-personality entity fought an internal battle before it found the words. *"How this can be? We tried and we did not succeed. What is in humans that we do not know? What if they join the Kritas now?"*

"Are the humans dangerous?" Alaston asked, and the question had the sphere wring closer to him. He answered

his own question without hesitation. "*Yes. Are they capable of the most terrible and the most admirable deeds? Yes. Do they deserve annihilation for this?*" The sphere pressed in even further. Alaston waited a second for the sphere to come to rest. "*They surged back from their ashes more than once in the past; it would be foolish to wage war now!*"

The sphere expanded with eagerness, as a lung that fills in with air after too long moments of deprivation. "*Yes, it would be foolish...*" *It* said, and the last word ended as in a whisper. "*The Kritas would bring their weight in and ignite a fire capable of burning the galaxy for eons.*"

"*Thus, we know how to counsel the Wisest, and how to give directions,*" Alaston concluded.

"*Yes, we do know how to counsel and how to give directions,*" *It* repeated.

⁂

Protusa woke up to turmoil. In the early hours of the morning, the still-dark sky filled with traces from military vessels flyovers in formation and support units leaving the spaceport well before the Moîrai star reached the boundary of Xrusé's horizon.

Transporters laden with troops lifted in silence all through the night right after the Supreme Council had formalized its decision. In high orbit around Xrusé, a Moîrai fleet assembled to deliver on the orders it had received only a few hours before. The time of the departure was imminent.

Mênis stopped his vehicle when in view of Alaston's private residence, on a hill not too distant from Protusa's north suburbs and far from the Supreme Council. Thanks to his ties with the government, and his influential position in the process that led to the Selection in Eridu, he received indirect warnings of a shocking pronouncement before the envoy from the Supreme Council of the Wisest and government agents broke into his house to arraign him.

The accusations the Wisest made public later on were explicit, and Mênis had been lucky he hadn't had to hear them from the voice of the arresting officer. The Keepers and their network had been declared enemies of the Confederation.

He flew low and had programmed a broken route with improbable waypoints to deter any possible followers. He landed his vehicle behind a rock formation; from there, he checked the surroundings for suspicious activity but couldn't detect the presence of anyone in the vicinity.

The cusps and the roofs of the residence reflected the glow from the center of the galaxy, rife with stars and nebulae. Mênis risked donning his Palladium to further probe with his heightened senses. Alaston wasn't awake, but at least—Mênis sighed—he didn't seem to be in danger...yet.

He hesitated for a moment, then jumped out of the small vessel and rushed to the boundary of the mansion to send Alaston a distraught mental warning. The residence recognized him as an authorized guest, and a part of the perimeter wall dilated into the inner court while it alerted the lord of the premises.

"Mênis?" Alaston's thoughts reached him and made him sigh with relief. *"I sense you fraught with...fear? What happens to you?"*

"We all are in danger. We do not have time to discuss. Can you leave at once?"

The inner wall dilated and Mênis entered a main entrance hall. Outside, security units from the Supreme Council were converging on the area.

Fully awake now, Alaston stood busy with a number of floating panels in the hall. "What is going on, Mênis?" he asked without lifting his eyes, guiding his hands dashing through the panels.

Mênis followed his gaze to discover a series of outdoor scenes beyond the residence's perimeter. Security vessels were landing, bearing the crest of the Supreme Council; guards rushed out and took position. In a few seconds, they surrounded the residence.

"Wisest, help us!" Mênis exclaimed.

Alaston glanced at him. "On the contrary, I believe the Wisest vowed our demise, but they underestimate us Keepers." Alaston gestured toward the wall and a stem emerged and blossomed into a control panel.

Alaston entered a series of commands while Mênis stared at the Brethren of the Keepers with eyes widened into an alarmed question.

"Follow." Alaston touched his arm.

Mênis let Alaston lead him deeper inside the residence while a low frequency sound, more like a dull vibration, animated the entire building. A floating panel preceded

Alaston as they walked and Mênis watched him check diagrams and activate unknown symbols.

Alaston sensed the doubt burning in his companion's mind but didn't stop to interact with new evanescent shapes. "I am preparing our way out and a welcome for our visitors."

At a junction, the stone floor dilated and revealed a steep, descending narrow corridor. The panel seemed animated by its own will and descended into it, followed by Alaston. "Come." He turned to Mênis. The floor coalesced after their passage.

"We need to warn the others," Mênis said, but Alaston smiled. "Everyone now knows what needs to be known." A rumbling from above gave Alaston's last words a sinister meaning. "Someone has just received the Keepers' warm welcoming." The corridor ended into a hangar; a fast Keepers' fighter vessel waited.

The trembling increased in intensity as they took place in the cockpit. A round, luminous circle opened, revealing a gallery pointing upward. The shuttle lifted and dashed at full speed.

They emerged amid flames and rumbles. Mênis looked back at the receding ground below. Scorched remains of the residence fumed, most reduced to a flattened and vitrified surface glowing hot in the twilight of the new day. No sign of the Moîrai security personnel—their smoldering vessels melted still in the intense heat and radiation that emanated from the debris that was once Alaston's home.

The fighter turned and gained altitude. Mênis captured a last image of the rock formation where he had left his vehicle. It was melting into a bubbling pool of lava formation that drifted its way down the gentle slope.

In the meantime, in the highest Xrusé stationary orbits, the last troops' transporters docked to their mother ships. Heavy armored personnel debarked and joined the rest of the ranks. They didn't know yet their destination, but were ready to inflict a mortal blow and perform a surgical removal of any threats to the Moîrai leadership.

Chapter 10 – Si Vis Pacem

The Fleet was ready. Troops were ready. Humans at all levels were ready to face any possible scenarios, and yet no one really expected what we were about to face.

I can't say I hoped for peaceful negotiations, reminiscent of the ancient organization of the United Nations. It wasn't very effective then; it would've done no good to us with current events. Who knows, though? Maybe discussing with an alien logic would have been more conducive for all parties to find a common ground than ever in the past.

In my quarters in Nova Roma, Samuel reported what our scouts confirmed. The Moîrai had mobilized. At best, we had only hours before a first wave would attack Eridu's space-sphere. I received the news with incredulity. His intelligence operation had been risky, and our agents acted with bravery to give us that information.

So soon. I guessed I gave too much credit to Alaston and the Keepers. I stood up and went to look at the thriving city and our fledging new human race.

"Father?" Samuel deserved to hear at least some comments from me. I had no words when Samuel finished describing the last details of the operation.

Nova Roma was full of life, at every moment of the day, and its nights never slept. *"As the old Rome."* I sighed.

"Father?" Samuel called again.

I half-turned, and spoke over my shoulder. "You've done a great job. I suppose everything's in place?"

"Yes, Father. Shouldn't we expect a possible message from the Moîrai?"

I pivoted on my feet and faced my son. "A message?" I frowned. "They bring no message. They're coming for a second invasion, that's the message. Take them, Samuel. Take them all."

⁂

All Bridge Stations raised again the alert to maximum level. To unaccustomed eyes, the hundreds of officers on the huge main Operations Deck would look efficient, sharp, and quick to react to the flood of information that flew off the floating panels, too fast to be retained and understood by one of the old humans. To an unaccustomed eye...

Sage noticed the brisk movements were not just because of efficiency. Both men and women were less talkative than usual. A misplaced word here, or a gaze that drifted for too long away from the dashboards, would have a cost no one could afford that day.

He turned his eyes around and nodded to his second in command, who seemed lost in thoughts. "How's the pilots' vitals?"

"As expected, sir." He felt Sage's piercing eyes as if they physically violated his. "We are ready, sir," he added at once without blinking.

"We have to be. Fusion supplies?"

"Everything's under control, sir. All sectors are covered. We completed the pilots' units extensive training—"

"Did we train them for this? To face the entire Moîrai fleet invading?"

He hesitated. "Not exactly, sir, but—"

Sage grunted. "Stay alert. Keep an eye on our Fleet liaisons and keep everyone busy."

"Aye, aye, sir!" He snapped to attention and second-guessed himself for a moment.

"I have to meet now with Admiral Amenta at the FCC." Sage turned to leave the bridge when his second called out. "Sir?" His lips were tight. "Will we make it through...sir?!"

Sage forced a smile. "Of course."

With its dimmed, reddish lights, the main hall of the Fleet Coordination and Control contrasted with the crisp luminosity of the Operations Deck, or the OD, as people called it. Sage felt like he had left the brightness of the day for a somber, everlasting night, engulfed in a bloody nightmare. He waited for a second to let his eyes adjust.

Every person in the hall focused on military tasks. The entire zone of Eridu's direct influence in space—up to the Kuiper Belt—camped in the middle of a spherical representation of the solar system. The Bridge Stations and each space Fleet unit had their presence marked with different symbols and shapes. All around, other monitoring units—manned by low-rank officers—dealt with narrower representation of different space sectors but with growing details so that the flow of information remained at the highest no matter the size of the area under control.

Samuel and other high-ranked officers swarmed around and within the large central space-sphere. It allowed interaction with all units, from larger battle groups level down to the individual ships. Sage never made it past the training needed to achieve that kind of focus. He sighed with a pinch of regret as he watched the officers fly within the sphere, supported by its force field as if they were in a no-gravity zone.

But the regret lasted only for a moment; the responsibility those men had now was what he always feared and wished to avoid. How could anyone take decisions that could lead other men and women to death? The ability to order the certain death of the few in exchange for the life of the many—how could anyone make such a decision?

He stood there, staring at the staggering ballet, and waited for Samuel to notice his presence.

In the middle of the sphere, Samuel had an eye on every sector and every movement in space. His mind evaluated with eagerness the same scenarios that made Sage shiver in retreat. The space pilots' units controlled all areas probing for impending wormhole formations, and areas changed color and intensity in correlation with their threat level. The pilots were the first and most important layer of defense around Eridu; knowing Moîrai tactics, no space sector was immune from an imminent attack. Eridu's first-strike fighters, supported by heavily armored mid-cruiser ships with the greatest offensive capacity, kept slaloming in and out of the locations where our pilots felt a disturbance in their continuum.

Samuel had instructed them to react to every false positive as if each was the main point of penetration of an expected, hostile Moîrai fleet. With a grain of sadness, he had issued the orders to fire first and ask for intentions later, and warned everyone that Eridu was now at war.

He shared his attention among all sectors and intervened when necessary. Relentless, he showed the same obstinance and inspired personality his father had.

With the corner of his eye, he noticed Sage at the entrance of the Control hall, but didn't let the event divert his attention and waited for a moment when the space-time fabric paused and all gravitational ripples subsided.

Typical of Moîrai offensive procedure, they engulfed the target with thousands of false wormhole creation attempts to exhaust the target's resolve and determination, undermine its tenacity until the moment the real strike would deliver a massive concentrated blow with highest chances of success.

The space-sphere seemed to calm down, the colored threat-areas faded. Samuel snorted; the Moîrai acted, following the book. His eyes met with Sage's. He nodded at him. After a flip in mid-air, he drifted toward the floor. "Anton, what news brings you here?" He tried but couldn't smile when he touched ground near his friend. "An attack is imminent." He pointed back at the space-sphere. "The pilots are kept busy by the Moîrai's decoy measures."

"Don't worry 'bout them," Sage said. "They're in great shape, though their evolution scares me; even more since they've been able to fuse their minds together into a...hybrid?"

"We must dare, Anton, and dare again. They're our only hope. If they succeed, we won't have to suffer from the first blow."

"If they succeed." Sage turned his gaze away.

"What's going on, Anton?"

"Thousands will perish, Samuel. I can't get my mind around this."

"Thousands? Maybe millions."

Sage sighed. "Indeed."

Samuel stared at him. "Look, my sister's now dead, and billions died before her. We're not the cause of all this." He searched for some reaction in his friend's expression in vain. "Maybe this war will open the way for a long lasting peace, instead; even when adding the Kritas and their acolytes to the equation."

Sage nodded, but it seemed only a mechanical reflex. "You're certainly right. I better go back to the OD and make sure everything's ready."

Samuel tried to catch a glimpse of his eyes in the brief instant before his friend turned to leave, but failed. He watched him walk away, head bent as if he followed an invisible stripe to guide his steps; his back curved as if he carried a weight.

As soon as Sage went through the dilating wall of the FCC hall, Samuel signaled one of the officers to approach. The man listened carefully, replied in a whisper, then nodded and left the hall.

"Admiral," a voice called out. Samuel set aside his worries and turned to glance at the main sphere. The space sectors blinked and glowed again; the Fleet had resumed its dance.

⁂

In the Bridge Station, the tension of those moments made people walk with a brisk pace. Not far from his destination, the Operations Deck, Sage stopped while in the main corridor. Personnel came and went—his people—and they didn't have time to glance at him. He looked around, and everyone seemed to him eager to face the moment when many would find death. Sage didn't notice that someone else wasn't in a hurry, like him, and kept his pace and stopped when he stopped.

He gathered himself again, covered the short distance to the entrance, and waited for it to dilate instead of walking through it at once, as usual. The noises, the sounds, and the animated discussions met him at the threshold. He felt them like a barrier and it made him shudder; he took a deep breath and stepped on through. Once inside, he accelerated his pace to reach his command station, centrally located on a raised level and visible from everywhere in the vast hall.

His second in command stood in front of the main dashboard and saw him approach when he reached the footbridge. His eyes took a last glimpse of all Bridge Stations' statuses. "Sir, an attack is imminent."

Sage frowned; he didn't like the sparks of excitement in the officer's eyes when he said 'imminent.'

"It's going to be ugly." His voice sounded harsh.

"Sir?" The officer raised his chin with a jerky movement.

"Nothing." Sage dismissed the question with a hand wave; instead, he reached his swiveling chair at the main control center. The floating panels covered all details but Sage wanted to hear it from him anyway. "What's the status from the Stations and the pilots' units?"

"All systems go, sir, and the pilots—"

"Very good." Sage interrupted him. "You're dismissed now. Thank you."

"Sir? What?" His head jerked as if Sage had just slapped him.

"You may go!" Sage didn't raise his eyes from the dashboard and bent his head sideways with a huff. The officer hesitated for a moment and shifted his weight. Then took a couple of steps backward. "Aye aye, sir." Turned and left the main station. Sage glanced at him to make sure he was leaving.

Down the footbridge, the officer crossed and saluted a fleet colonel he didn't recognize, but was too puzzled to pay attention.

The alarms shrieked at that moment. Alerts flashed, coming from all other Bridge Stations, too; for the first time, the pilots' unit had raised the confidence level of an attack beyond the ninety-five percent threshold and located the continuum disturbances into three separate space sectors.

Sage watched his hands tremble as if they didn't belong to him; drops of sweat beaded his face. He felt everyone ran blindly toward death, once more insensible to the humans' race mortality.

⁂

"This is it, lads!" Joshua yelled on the Command Comm channel. "Three sectors. Ours is assigned. Full thrust!"

The fighter's chemical booster kicked in its high acceleration impulse followed with only a few seconds delay by the ion thrusters. Joshua felt his g-suit fight against the tremendous acceleration. He checked all reports from the Bridge Stations, but they had yet to send information on the composition of the enemy. He led a large interceptor group, but no matter how large it was, the Moîrai foes could have them outnumbered. "Request enemy's ID."

"Proceed to destination, Captain." The calm voice of a liaison officer from the Bridge Station grated on his nerves.

"Request ID of enemy forces!" Joshua yelled. "For the Loss' sake, guys!"

Afar, the space-time disturbance had grown visible to the naked eye, and it carried the fear of the unknown.

Joshua eyes widened and his lips opened in a stunned slot; the disturbance was the largest he had ever seen.

The entire group sped up to meet with the incoming might of the Moîrai's military power. In their cockpits, the men silenced all exterior thoughts and put a damper on the surge of the survival instinct. That day, many discovered the real meaning of courage.

The tactical group mission panel filled up with unexpected new information, and the orders had to be executed at once.

⁂

The FCC smelled of sweaty humans under the influence of an adrenaline rush. More than humans, to be precise, but there were none left to compare them to the past. They were the present, and they were fighting to be the future, too.

The space-sphere in the middle of the hall showed the entire Eridu's fleet split to reach the three areas where the wormholes' creation had accentuated. The pilots declared them the location of a simultaneous attack launches. The central one was the largest; huge, it could only mean a massive attack, as if the entire Moîrai fleet were to erupt from the widening wormhole aperture. High above the ecliptic—the plane containing most of the planetary objects orbiting around the Sun—the wormhole would have provided the enemy vessels with a clear path toward the inner solar system and Eridu itself.

Two smaller singularities, at opposite locations on the ecliptic, obliged the Eridu's fleet to split, have the Sun in the middle, and juggle with the trillions of fragments, icy bodies, and dwarf planets of the Kuiper Belt.

Samuel, flying inside the space-sphere in the FCC, coordinated the defense plans with his officers, checking on each of the main groups' formation and verifying the timing of the wormholes' expected eruptions.

The agitated voice of a rank officer broke his concentration. "Sir, the pilots report the three areas will open within seconds from each other, sir." The countdown showed the wormholes would regurgitate their load of lethal foes in the next minutes, sparkling out as flares in a full moon night.

He faced a problem with no hidden variables. Splitting Eridu's forces in three main intercepting groups risked spreading the fleet too thin, leaving them outnumbered at the two opposite disturbances opening right then at the Kuiper Belt. "It's not right. It's not right!" Samuel burst.

"Sir, the gravitational waves from the main area don't lie..." the same officer insisted.

Samuel spun inside the space-sphere and turned toward the voice. He tightened his lips and stared at the floating panel one of his officers pointed to.

In a low voice, the officer continued. "We need to send most of the Fleet to counter their main arrival coordinates, sir."

Samuel closed his eyes, took a deep breath and held it in for a second, then let go all the air through his open mouth in a feral way. He activated the high priority channel to communicate to everyone in the FCC. "Code priority zero!"

The officers froze, hearing the announcement of a priority level that overrode all previous directives.

"Divert all units from the high-elliptic target. Split the Fleet into two main groups."

"Sir..." an astonished officer muttered, his eyes now fixed on the massive gravitational signals from the soon-to-be neglected area. He blanched.

"Execute!" Samuel yelled. On the space-sphere, pilots' activity still concentrated on the giant wormhole formation to counteract the arrival of a massive Confederation offensive. "Pilots' units on the new targets. Now!"

⁂

On the Operations Deck, the order request for the pilots' intervention on the new targets made everyone scramble for confirmations. Sage didn't react. He watched—as if in a trance—the new Fleet orders on the floating screens and the coordination request for the pilots' units to expedite the redirection. He turned his sight away from his dashboard and rubbed his face with both hands. He then joined hands as if he prayed to an absent divinity.

The rest of the OD personnel, in unison, coordinated the new course of action with their Fleet counterparts; the Bridge Stations now needed only Sage's final authorization to execute.

Not far from him, on a footbridge, two military security guards had joined the Fleet colonel. He whispered on his implanted communication-link device. "Sir, Commander Sage is inoperative; requesting permission to intervene."

Samuel's response allowed no room for interpretations. "Remove him from command!"

The officer gave the guards the go and walked up the footbridge. The guards ran to the command station and, one guard on either side, gripped Sage's arms. Under the incredulous eyes of the station's personnel, the colonel addressed the distraught prisoner. "Commander Anton Sage. I'm Colonel Chris Telle; you're relieved from duty."

He looked down at the crowd that had gathered right below the elevated platform of the commanding station. His eyes stopped when he recognized Sage's second in command and yelled, "You. Ratify the order. Divert the pilots to the new coordinates. Now!"

All personnel in the Operations Deck stared at their new highest-ranked operative, still unsure of how to react to the unexpected twist in those critical moments. He nodded in phase with his breathing, then straightened up and hollered at the people who stood as frozen on the commanding station floor. "Get back to your dashboard and let's block those Moîrai." He turned around and took a deep breath. He placed his hand on the nearest dashboard. "The order is ratified!" The last words erupted as if liberated from an oppressive weight.

Colonel Telle smiled and whispered to his implant, "It's done."

In the outer space, the Moîrai wormholes' disturbances on the ecliptic opened.

Chapter 11 – First Blow

Samuel breathed out when he saw the pilots' units fulfill his latest order, but stared at the growing wormhole above the ecliptic. On the central space-sphere, the wormhole resembled a dark maelstrom whose equatorial diameter now reached over a hundred kilometres.

He looked around at all his officers in the FCC—well-trained, dedicated, efficient, and committed to their tasks without hesitations—so why was he assailed by second thoughts?

What if he was wrong? What if everything was true and he stared at the massive entry point of the invading assault? Because it was *indeed* from there that thousands and thousands of enemy vessels would have swarmed out free from harm now that the bulk of Eridu's own Fleet had already left the space sector under his orders. What if he had just condemned his race to annihilation?

He only had to wait; only a few minutes before doom, or before salvation. The new strategic operation unfolded and the point of no return was long gone.

The space-sphere had no more bright areas, no pulsating sectors blossoming everywhere, but only three, steady and menacing, and the entire Eridu Fleet converged to be present only at two of them. A cold shiver ran down his spine, but as his father taught him many times—*"...control your emotions, Sam"*—no one in the FCC could see anything but a resolute, determined Admiral, Samuel Amenta, Commander in Chief of Eridu's Space Fleet.

His heart missed a beat; the wormholes showed their tunnel singularity.

⁂

The first line of Eridu vessels prepared to sustain the initial waves of attacks. Small fighters, in a triangular shape, fast and lethal units derived from the same Moîrai vessels that constituted the first delivery of the Eridu's Space Fleet squadrons. In the rear, larger and larger vessels piled up with stronger defensive and offensive systems.

To the flanks of each Eridu squadron were the latest addition to the Fleet, the ships known as the "Alliance of Death," from the French word that stood for wedding band. In their empty center, the ring-shaped vessels created powerful bolts of high-energy antimatter heavy particles. The bolts inflicted devastating damage on their targets. These vessels were part of Eridu's last decade of covert preparations, and this was their first appearance on a space battlefield.

The outer ring of the wormholes' singularity areas bent the space-time; the stars, visible from beyond that region, elongated as if they dripped into the rings and then faded when the tunnel enlarged.

The humans' vessels targeted the tunnel's opening and fired all at once. At the same time, the pilots' units opened their own tunnels to match the Moîrai's and trap the incoming vessels.

From the opened wormholes, a multitude of flashes signaled the appearance of each of the Moîrai vessels emerging at full speed, with their defensive shields raised, scattering in all directions like a firework's stars explosion. The haphazard maneuvers showed clearly they expected a hostile reception.

Eridu's vessels' weaponry blasted against the enemy defensive shields; some of those collapsed under the impact and the vessels vaporized against the subsequent massive firepower, scoring a full hit. With a smaller scale, the gases and debris from the silent explosions of a doomed vessel matched the fireworks display of the emerging enemy ships.

The part of the Moîrai ships that instead emerged straight off the hyperspace tunnel found another wormhole opened right in front, waiting for them, and disappeared within with no hope to escape.

The battle raged with the expected fury, even if only a few seconds had elapsed since the Moîrai's wormholes vomited their loads. The "Alliance of Death" formations, farthest from the center, attacked with concentrated antimatter bolts the outer boundary of the swarming enemy vessels.

The jetsam from the initial explosions reached the front line of the Eridu small fighter class units. They yanked fast to avoid the largest fragments, some as large as the fighters themselves, and let them shatter with no harm done against the shields of the larger vessels behind.

Fighter classes from both sides appeared to be in equal numbers after the decimation the Moîrai suffered from those trapped in the wormholes.

In those initial seconds, there had been little to no fire coming up from the Moîrai, who seemed taken aback by the Eridu actions and the matching wormhole that gulped many of their largest battleships into a ravenous, black abyss. The event dented the enemy arrogance as some of the Moîrai ships fell out of their hitherto plan, and in some areas struggled, outnumbered, against the humans.

The effect of the surprise, though, didn't last long and the first counterfire from the Moîrai blasted through the frontal fighter line of Eridu's Fleet, creating crimson, magenta, and golden, white flashes where once were a fighter unit.

Joshua and his group approached the largest Moîrai formation off-center, at a fifty degree angle with respect to the flight path the enemy followed, with the intention to make them split and turn them into an easier prey for the smallest but faster Eridu ships, but those were still some ten seconds from the interception.

Right above those units, from Joshua's point of view and in the tactical screens, midsize Moîrai "Penetrators" units approached fast—vessels with heavy defensive capabilities whose principal tactics was to get deep inside enemy groups and release antimatter torpedoes in an exploding, all-directions massive burst. Joshua let his groups get a little closer, then assigned the targets on the tactical display to the "Alliance of Death" units. "Get those bloody penetrators down now!" he yelled.

He dove his ship down with the highest acceleration, followed by the rest of the squads, while spiraling at the same time to avoid blaster traces from the Moîrai. The group sped at maximum impulse to put the pursuing enemy vessels in the Penetrators' intercept course and give room to the "Alliance" vessels to release their bolts at the same time. The Moîrai Penetrators scattered in all directions and only two received the impact of the antimatter guns. A blinding flash accompanied the instantaneous conversion of mass into energy, and two wrecked Penetrators spun away out of control in the universe, leaving a dilating trail of gases, crystallizations, and small debris.

Eridu's fighters regrouped, stronger with the arrival of Joshua-led vessels, and shaped into loosened wedge formations as they attacked.

They split head-on with the leading front of the Moîrai attack units as Joshua's group released their concentrated blaster fire blows against the enemy's frontal protective shields. The Moîrai ships diverted most of their energy to their front to absorb the immense impact of the heavy Eridu's cruisers' blasters, but weakened their rears, exposed now to the fighters that swerved their way back to pound those weakened defenses with their blows. The tactic worked, but not without casualties in the melee that ensued against the incoming Moîrai fighters.

Joshua yelled on the squadron private channel, "Keep an eye on those fighters! Don't stop weaving." The battle intensified and moved deep inside the Kuiper Belt while the

"Alliance" ships pounded—unrelenting—on the fugitive Moîrai Penetrators and prevented the resumption of their offensive.

Joshua saw the warning of an incoming hostile group on the tactical floating screen. He yelled as he yanked hard the controls, "Watch those bastards!"

White blaster pulses came toward his squad from the Moîrai ships in a tight diamond formation. They had just emerged from behind a large mass of icy concretions that were spinning dangerously close to each other in unnatural orbits. The Moîrai vessels had used their tractor beams to push the debris together to form a natural shield and swung the rocks over and around them at the last moments to fire on the scrambling humans.

Joshua shouted, "Break up! Break up!" but the rest of the squadron had already seen the blasters' flashes and scattered while releasing a cloud of passive antimatter mines. The mines reached the darting icy rocks and a colossal spike of energy ensued from the matter annihilation that damaged the navigation systems of the closest vessels, Moîrai and humans alike. Some crashed without control against each other, others into Kuiper's rubble like shrapnel from a bursting bombshell.

The rest of the enemy vessels had recovered from the initial shock of the lethality of the humans' welcoming, and the squadrons' channels filled with agitated bursts of communication. "Blue angel, blue angel, bandit on your six." – "Knocked out! Five for me!" – "Red leader hit! Red leader hit!" – "One more for the Loss" – "Ayeeeh" – "I lost my shields; I'm bailing out!" It never stopped—the rambling rumblings of communications from the different units. Short bursts of light revealed little events of death in a much larger battle.

⁂

The officers in the FCC followed the clashes that took place at the two ecliptic entry points. Samuel waited for the moment when the largest of the three wormholes would reveal what had traveled through its singularity tunnel.

When the space-sphere showed the quasi-simultaneous opening of the two wormholes in the ecliptic, soon followed by the human pilots' ones, shouts erupted. They turned raucous when the hostile ships emerged at high speed from the tunnel—many with no trajectory deflections—only to enter an instant after into the pilots' wormholes and vanish from the space-sphere. The officers jumped from their seats, and threw their arms up in the air, screaming.

Samuel smiled at the officers and they pumped their fists at him, but the battle was not over. Eridu's fleet had to accomplish a costly mission—delay the Moîrai until the brain cancer affected their pilots and made them erratic. Then the mission could be declared accomplished, whatever the cost in human lives.

The battle was pursued with the remaining Moîrai in punitive expedition. A more detailed estimate showed the enemies outnumbered the humans with a two to one factor, but their moment of disarray had allowed Eridu's Fleet to score the first victories. The thrill of those successes lingered on still, but the officers returned to their duty stations to support the Fleet with tactical and strategic intelligence. The largest Moîrai wormhole kept growing, and nothing would have stopped whatever came out of it.

Samuel walked closer to the central space-sphere and let the force field grab him as he crossed the activity threshold. He drifted up, farther away from the ecliptic plane, and stopped face-to-face with the wormhole.

He felt he glared into an evil, black eye with fuzzy, wobbling boundaries. Samuel sensed the fearsome weight of the unknown, and he shivered. The ultimate destination of the humans' wormholes was a secret known only to the Eridu's Council members. Samuel frowned. Why not share with him? Why did his father insist on keeping that a secret? Where did they send the Moîrai ships?

Chapter 12 – Burning Bridges

Towering over Nova Roma, Eridu's Council stood proud. Its buildings and towers were facing the most important moments of its short but intense life as an institution.

The news of an imminent first battle reached the planet faster than the wind from a solar eruption. Even the aliens at the AIDAs—the Aliens Interim Detention Areas—received word that the worst scenario had happened; the humans were at war.

The Council held regular closed sessions, but there were still more pressing decisions to make about the wormholes and the Moîrai's fate.

The Council Member from the former Australasia region was about to conclude her speech. "As far as I know," she raised her eyebrows and her voice, "no Moîrai ever showed compassion! Why should we be lenient with them?" She sat down. A murmur of approval marked the general sentiment of the Council.

"If I may say..." Manfred stood up. "If I may say, this is not the time for blind revenge, but to reach an agreement on the most favorable course. De facto, we are at war, and the Council should take every reasonable precaution to increase our chances to secure a victory." He sat back. His words received the support of a silent, mental clapping from our fellow members.

I listened all day to the discussions among my fellow members. My son Samuel would soon face an aggression of an unprecedented hostility and he would need all our help to make sure his efforts were not in vain. The Council hesitated between an all-out war effort and a last, ultimate attempt to come to an agreement with the Moîrai.

I raised my hand and sent a mental request to have the right of speech. All eyes were on me.

I stood tall, as was the custom in the Council before addressing the others. "I can only praise everyone's effort and dedication." My gaze crossed the sight of each member and acknowledged every one. "You deserve my most sincere congratulations." The members lowered their head. "You've uncovered all possible scenarios and exposed the positives and the negatives of each. For this, I am grateful." I knew something not known to the Council; the news was unexpected, as was the messenger. I stepped aside from my seat, walked down the few steps, and reached the central podium.

"We are at war." I placed my hands on the lectern. "But we knew well this would come. The Supreme Council of the Moîrai has decided to ravage the very foundations of the Confederation, the glue that held everything together for millennia." I paused. The members looked at each other, confused, trying to understand from the immediate neighbors whether they knew anything.

The murmur rose, both at physical and mental level. I raised both my arms. "Patience, patience." One by one, the finest men and women in Eridu focused their attention back on me. The Council, with some effort, regained its composure.

I paced my words. "Your curiosity deserves to be satisfied." I glanced at the floor. "I'm the Keeper of Eridu, and I revealed to all of you our path and our values." The Council Members bent forward on their seats when I pronounced the word 'Keeper', as if they tried to achieve a greater intimacy with my thoughts than the one they had already.

I raised my eyes. "You've been chosen because of the values and the principles the Keepers stand for, that you share and stand for, too. Through me, you are part of the Keepers as well."

The representative of the area once known as the United States, Christine, a black woman, stood up with measured movements, and others followed her example, but I hadn't finished yet; I gestured to them to take their seats again. They glanced at each other, hesitating, but they complied, and I waited for a few seconds before resuming.

"As you know, the Brethren of Keepers himself came the other day to bring a message on behalf of the Supreme Council. You also know he didn't have the heart to deliver it. His struggle was difficult, as was that of the Keepers." I took a long breath and held it in for a moment. "But you shouldn't hear this from my voice. These times will be remembered. These are the times that will justify our existence."

I turned and let the entrance to the Eridu's Council Main Hall dilate. All eyes turned toward the opening wall, to the figure advancing in the corridor and crossing the wall's threshold.

A brief commotion started when the members recognized our visitor.

"Dan, what is this?" Manfred gave me a worried look. Others stood up and leaned forward. Surprise, disarray, and alarm, all mixed, and with a different blend for each member; I could see clouds of passion emerge from their ranks like vapors from a raging vent. I concentrated to see the waves of feelings the members had trouble controlling and hiding from me. They exuded emotions like molasses through a sieve.

With a long, steady pace, my guest advanced. Our eyes met and his thought reached me. *"Thank you, Dan of Eridu."* Ohtlinell joined me on the central podium.

The Keeper lowered his head and opened up his palms toward the Council Members. Everyone stared back, mouth agape. I felt their incredulity and skepticism, but I believed Ohtlinell's words, I believed his recount of the events in Protusa, I believed the betrayals and the dismay. I believed.

I used no words; it was time to reveal Ohtlinell that I wasn't the only human versed in the Keepers' path, so I sent everyone my thoughts. *"Members of Eridu's Council. Ohtlinell is a Moîrai, but a Keeper, too. I'm a Keeper and a human. Remove all of your barriers to the Keeper so that the Keeper may recognize himself in us."*

Ohtlinell turned to face me; his jaw dropped and his head bent to one side. He stared at me for a long moment. *"Indeed, Alaston is right. The human is an incessant surprise."*

Manfred was the first to react. *"I sensed the Keeper while he spoke to Dan of Eridu. I was present. He described impossible things to believe; therefore, he must be telling the truth."*

"And yet I didn't feel your presence!" Ohtlinell's gaze jumped to inspect Manfred, and then came back to me. *"The Keepers, the most valiant, are trying to reach Eridu right now. But not everyone was lucky, or fast enough."* The Moîrai's thoughts trembled, as if he stuttered. Images of destruction and killing, the merciless chasing of the Keepers through their hiding places, the round-ups, the recounts of the tortures, the tales of the ones rescued, and the pain for the ones lost forever.

The Council fell into a grave silence when Ohtlinell concluded. *"Not everyone will make it. The ones who rebelled are now pariah among the Moîrai, and their names are revealed."* An immense sadness, the strongest ever I felt in a Moîrai, invaded Ohtlinell's mind. *"Indeed,"* he looked at me, *"there is a mad one sitting among the Wisest."*

I stepped forward. My eyes met in turn with each member's and I addressed the Council with a stern voice. "I can read in you that any previous hesitation has vanished." The Council waited for my final words, some nodded. "So be it; our star, the Sun, will take care of the invading forces." We had reached unanimity.

⁂

In the main Bridge Station, the Fleet Control Center walls absorbed all sound reverberations and culled noises at birth. Officers concentrated on their dashboards, each dealt with the level of details their rank and expertise allowed them. After the initial moments of joy and sentiments of triumph, the gruesome reality of the battles manifested only one possible outcome: Moîrai's ultimate victory. Eridu's Fleet did its best to slow down the enemy advance, but only so much could be done against forces much greater in number. The violent battles had left the Kuiper Belt behind. The conflict moved closer, within Neptune's orbit. Yet, the kill ratio favored Eridu, and the work done at the FCC accounted for much of it.

"It's opening now!" An officer yelled just below Samuel, who floated, inert, as if he were hypnotized by the giant, third Moîrai wormhole. In a long, interminable moment, the tunnel opened up, ready to vomit the forces of doom and thwart the efforts of all humans.

The space sector filled with thousands of flashes and the first vessels appeared. Samuel trembled and a frisson ran along his spine. 'Father, forgive me,' he thought, and closed his eyes, crushed. Even with his closed eyelids, he felt the multitude of flashes on his face. In that moment, Samuel felt death could not give him peace, and got ready to endure the entire Universe's condemnation.

At the same time, two other wormholes opened close to each other and appeared on all space-spheres. The officers who monitored all wormholes' activity in and around the Eridu's sphere of influence believed they experienced an anomaly; unexplainable with their knowledge, but an anomaly nonetheless. The gravitational waves' disturbances pointed to a single area of interest, and an extremely unstable area, too; space travel theory suggested that all operations would have been difficult to the extreme, if not impossible, for space pilots to initiate a wormhole formation, or trigger the opening of a singularity tunneling there, in those conditions.

"What is *this*?" one lieutenant said, and gestured to highlight and expand the area under his supervision. He turned to grab the attention of his nearby colleagues. "Are you getting the same?"

A tense voice came out distinct from the group: "Unbelievable." No one dared to turn to see who had spoken. The lieutenant nodded and got back to his holograms and floating screens; the 3D rendering of the space sector showed a bright section labeled 'Sol', and two wormhole tunnels grew at a mere distance of ten million kilometres from the star at less than a third of the radius of Mercury' orbit.

The space-sphere filled with thousands of ship symbols, the Moîrai emerged from the singularities at full speed and reached the Sun's corona in less than a second to receive the full impact of the furious solar plasma.

Free electrons, protons, and hard X-ray radiations degraded all systems aboard, and the star attracted the vessels unable to break its gravitational grip at such a close range. At first, the Moîrai pilots tried desperate measures to fight the inevitable, but soon the ships lost all maneuvering capabilities.

Inside the vessels, the temperature rose to tens of thousands of degrees in a short time; at least, when it started, death inside the ships ran swift through all locations. Spontaneous combustion consumed all organic material; the air itself ignited.

The ships' external structures ionized, then the atomic bonds broke and protons and neutrons detached from the nuclei. The vessels dematerialized, their existence became doubtful even in the eyes of the Universe.

At the microscopic level, the events that took place in the Moîrai vessels made the process of natural evaporation as cool an event, in comparison, as a breeze in the polar regions of Eridu. The bulk of the enemy expedition became part of the dance of the excited particles that constituted the plasma of the Sun.

The Fleet officers shivered; they were military trained, and Moîrai officers at the Space Academy had trained many of them. Dying from a torpedo in space, collapse from a close explosion, or being hit by a blaster on a battlefield on an alien planet had been always in the mind of every Space Cadet. Their brain and their minds had categories for those deaths, but which category could hold the loss of life as they'd just witnessed?

"Sir, sir!" Someone pulled his uniform.

Floating in the space-sphere, Samuel resented the intrusion and twisted. His brow hardened and he tightened his jaw. He strained his eyes to recognize who was there and why his face beamed in the subdued light of the FCC.

"Sir? The wormhole." The officer pointed behind Samuel's back.

"What?" Samuel muttered.

The officer raised his eyebrows. "You were right, sir."

Samuel turned and glanced at the symbols that flooded the area that had been occupied only moments before by the wormhole. Ships, in the thousands, but the units had been identified as large commercial transporters with no offensive capacity.

With their tractor beams, the ships kept together thousand tons of inert materials, rocks, icy concretions, maybe small asteroids, too. The overall mass, as detected by the probes and the pilots' units, should have convinced the humans that the entire Confederation fleet was attacking. It was indeed a diversion, and the Moîrai had come alone.

Samuel breathed out hard.

Chapter 13 – Dysfunctional Reunions

Two days had passed since the assailant forces swarmed out of their wormholes, and Eridu's Fleet showed the first signs of faltering. In the FCC of the Admiral's battleship, Samuel watched the front line advancing inexorably closer to Eridu and shook his head. He managed the battles as they spread, various squads and groups chasing each other with implacable determination.

The sheer numerical superiority of the Moîrai more than counteracted the field advantage the humans had, and he only delayed the front line's move past the Kuiper Belt.

He sighed. The crushing, pincer assault put in action by the enemy required a sacrifice beyond the humans' capabilities to stop the invaders. He cringed each time his units turned into wreckage and littered the space as the battles progressed. Behind the front line, only twisted vessels, human and alien bodies—or tiny parts of those—dust and debris forever scattered, forever abandoned.

In space, a battle is silent; there are no rumbles and no explosions that can be heard from a distance. The crude, devastating reality of death, of killing and being killed, didn't allow for aural distractions, and only multi-colored flashes and ephemeral flames accompanied each loss and each defeat; and the flames died out the instant they were born. Vessels burned from the inside, though, as rotten bodies battered by a deadly fever.

Samuel rubbed his chin and felt the rough contact against the growing beard. In the last few hours, the Moîrai had launched several attacks against the Bridge Stations, all repelled for now, though they couldn't resist much longer.

It was clear to him that Moîrai tactics had only one primary strategic target, the invasion of Eridu. Their skirmishes against the Stations prevented Samuel from deploying additional forces elsewhere to counteract the enemy's main objective. With time passing, the front line moved even faster as the strength of Eridu's fleet dwindled. With his eyes riveted on the space-sphere, Samuel remembered he promised the Council fourty-eight hours before the inevitable capitulation.

A silvery and growing layer showed the expanding Moîrai-controlled space; in that moment, it touched the orbit of Saturn. The silver tentacles surrounded the shrinking blue area that marked the sectors still under human control and menaced Eridu itself.

Samuel knew only time separated the Moîrai from Eridu and their complete victory. The enemy attempted further wormhole creations once, when they reached within Neptune's orbit, but interrupted the process as soon as they detected Eridu's pilots had been able to match their efforts.

The Moîrai didn't try any further risky maneuvers and proceeded by methodic, necessary steps and cautious incursions. Considering how the war proceeded, the logic for them was not to risk additional losses against a new wormhole creation technology they knew nothing about. It wasn't in their genes to force the events when everything else, step by step, worked to their advantage. They knew they would have conquered Eridu in the next few hours. What's a couple of days for a race counting its history in eons?

"The communication with the Council is live, sir."

Samuel turned toward the voice and nodded to the communication manager. He drifted down to the floor and exited the shrinking space-sphere of Eridu's influence.

He smirked as he walked toward the room to meet with his father and the other members of the Council. In his mind, he wondered why they called the meeting now, when he never missed sharing every detail on the status of the war. With a sigh, he thought there was nothing he could do any better, or anymore.

In the meeting room, the eidolons of the Council's members awaited. Samuel's father stood in front of them all. Entering the room, Samuel didn't greet anyone, and didn't say anything, either. His father's face was impenetrable and didn't show any emotion or worries. He didn't remember ever seeing him like that.

"Good day, Admiral," Manfred said. Not his father, he noticed—Manfred welcomed him first. He lowered his head. "I salute Eridu's Council, but I don't understand the urgency of this meeting." Samuel stared at Manfred for a second. "Councilor, my presence is needed elsewhere."

Dan stepped forward. "Samuel." His son turned his head then stepped forward to face him with his whole body. "There are new developments. This is the reason for the meeting."

"It must be of an extreme importance for the Council to interrupt my mission here." His tone mounted, showing the tension he was enduring. "You all know every distraction can have fatal consequences now."

Dan squinted his eyes. "We can't give details of the request, Samuel, but indeed, we're here to have you create a distraction."

"*What?*" Samuel snapped.

Dan sighed; there wasn't the time for a father-son confrontation. "Manfred, please, give the Admiral the coordinates."

"Wait." Samuel raised one opened hand to stop Manfred's intervention. "Father," he stepped even closer, "we are holding with everything we have. The morale is fading fast and I can't do much about it. The Fleet is committed to the ultimate sacrifice and you come here to ask for a *distraction*?"

"Samuel, it's vital." Dan stared at him. "The Fleet needs to drive the Moîrai away from a precise space sector, and pilots' units will have to ignore any wormhole activities in that area."

"This is madness!" Samuel threw his arms up in the air and turned away.

"In a sense, you're right." Manfred moved in to face him. "Let me give you the exact time and coordinates, Samuel."

Samuel stared at him for a long moment, then closed his eyes and his shoulders sagged. "What do we have to do?" The others in the Council nodded and interrupted the communication.

"Son. Trust me," Dan said. His rendering faded and Samuel remained alone with Manfred.

In the meantime, beyond the range of Eridu's probes, other vessels emerged in space and gathered at three times the distance between Sol and the Belt.

⁂

In Xrusé, the Keepers fled and hid however and wherever possible. Citizens in the capital Protusa had witnessed an unprecedented witch-hunt. The Supreme Council of the Wisest denounced the existence of the mythical Keepers, how they infiltrated the highest position of the Moîrai society, and formally accused them of treason. Only thanks to the collaboration of good Moîrai, they said, the Wisest had finally acquired enough evidence and detail of the underground organization, feared by many and loathed by others. Their dissident and vicious activities could now be unveiled at last and the sect dismantled, the Wisest revealed.

Keepers' names circulated and were shared via all channels. Everywhere, Moîrai were put under investigation based on the slimmest, unrelated suspicions; anyone alleged to be in collaboration with the Keepers was apprehended and disappeared. Everyone suspected their neighbors and their relatives. The Wisest fueled fear and paranoia.

After their fortunate escape from Alaston's residence, while on the run, Mênis and Alaston managed to warn other Keepers, and so the chain of mutual help and alert enjoyed a few hours to develop before the Wisest launched—publicly—the organized hunt.

In a few frightful days, many succeeded in reaching the base on the floor of the main ocean of Xrusé. At least that one was a well-kept secret not even the Wisest knew about. When they arrived, the base harbored a number of early escapees, but they didn't reach ten percent of all Keepers in Xrusé.

With Ohtlinell, who happened to be already at the base when everything started, Alaston and Mênis ran a crisis unit, trying to save the largest number possible of Keepers and organize a breakout operation in the shortest possible time. Time was running short, and they needed to leave Xrusé.

In an adjacent large laboratory, a dedicated task force of Keepers tried to account for everyone in the Brotherhood.

"Most are missing." Mênis shook his head as he cheched the latest results on the floating screens above the central desk. "There is no way yet to know precisely how many hide in safety, or whether they have been captured, killed, or worse."

Alaston listened, pensive. The room had been sealed, but he set the wall between them and the laboratory to be transparent from their briefing room. He stood up and moved closer to the wall to observe the activities. Watching his Keepers busy and resourceful calmed him down.

"How foolish I have been," he thought. *"How did I fail to prevent all this?"* He neglected the weak signals, and yet they should have told him something wasn't normal in the Supreme Council; their veiled inquisitions and the questioning about Keepers' motivations, the unprecedented motion the Supreme Council approved with unanimity to have all information concerning the Keepers' organization shared among all Council members—for better security, they claimed. He touched the wall for a moment before he turned.

"What are you implying, Mênis?" Alaston asked.

"I mean Keepers will be tortured, of course, to extort detailed information on the organization's assets and its complete membership." Mênis shifted his weight on his seat, unable to find comfort.

Alaston lowered his head. "If this is the case," he looked at both, "even this base will soon be discovered. We will be trapped, with no other solution than fighting for our lives."

Ohtlinell dropped his jaw and his eyes widened. He leaned forward over the floating surface that reported live data being collected on Keepers' whereabouts. "I cannot believe your words. The Wisest will not—"

"You have not seen their determination at his residence." Mênis interrupted him and indicated Alaston to his right. "We barely escaped death."

Ohtlinell gazed at Alaston, but no words came from the Brethren of the Keepers. He lowered his head and understood that Mênis wasn't inventing things. "What do we do then?"

"You go back." Alaston stared at him. "To Eridu."

Both Mênis and Ohtlinell looked at each other in complete bewilderment.

⁂

The Moîrai in command of the flagship received details from all units under his orders. From the simulation of a million scenarios, the battle's predictions left no doubts, and—he reasoned—for sure, they also had the advantage of the latest new battleship. Even if most of the technology was shared between the two races, the humans couldn't possibly match his best vessels. But his patience was running out.

Moîrai's confidence kept rising, but the humans fought hard and with cunning expertise; on many occasions, they'd been able to prevail even when outnumbered.

"This is taking too long." The commander slammed his fist on the dashboard. "Blast them out of the way!" he shouted in the bridge deck for everyone to hear.

The human fighters alternated rapid incursions with concentrated fire from their mid-sized units, while the largest cruisers pummeled the Moîrai counterparts from a safer distance.

Even if the admission disturbed the Moîrai, their small fighters units had proved less capable than the humans', and there were those ring-shaped vessels. He always thought it was a serious mistake to share practically everything with the humans, and those vessels were the proof he had been right. He stood up and slammed his hands on the railing surrounding his station. *"Beware of humans!"* he thought.

His units pressed on and gained space, but it was too slow. Then, a voice from the deck called for his attention. "Commander!"

On the main screens, the humans had regrouped and started to withdraw from the sector. He grinned. "I can see that. Be careful. They're a treacherous race," he warned. "All units, maintain position."

The Moîrai didn't follow the retreating vessels at once, so the humans sent a swarm of antimatter torpedoes in their direction. They fired a last salvo of blaster, sent all energy to their fore shields, and left the sector at maximum acceleration.

On the leader ship's bridge deck, the human maneuver caused guttural sounds of exultation among some of the officers. "They are in retreat!"

"Cowards," the commander thought. He laughed. "The enemy stumbles before our might." He supported the cheers erupting on deck, but he lowered his voice to address his chief military scientist at his side. "What are the chances of an ambush?"

The scientific officer didn't raise his eyes from his instruments. His hands and fingers danced with the floating symbols above his multiple dashboards. "With the intel available to us, the risk of a trap is less than one percent, Commander." He looked up with a grin.

"Comfortable." The commander stretched his neck, then pulled himself up to his full height and declaimed, "Hunt those brainless rats!"

Under his command, the entire Moîrai assault group chased the fleeing human ships at maximum impulse.

Aboard the escaping vessels, the human commanders watched the Moîrai's maneuver and smiled.

⁂

In the FCC of Bridge Station One, Samuel observed the events in the space-sphere rendering. Eridu was dangerously close to the front line. He obeyed the Council, even if Manfred refused to provide him with an explanation. *"It's a matter of life and death, Samuel,"* Manfred told him before interrupting the communication link.

The operation met with success. His units evacuated the space sector that needed to be freed and the Moîrai followed, after only a few moments of hesitation. *"Maybe that's how my subordinates feel when I assign orders but can't share the reasons,"* he thought.

A few metres away from him, the leading officer of the squad monitoring the wormhole occurrences had maintained a permanent liaison with the pilot units and voiced his worries.

"Sir? The pilots are detecting a multitude of space-time singularity activities in the sector, sir."

Samuel stared at him and glimpsed the glitter of his concerns. "Let them be." He sighed.

The officer nodded, but his lips tightened; he couldn't stand Samuel's gaze and didn't react to the order.

"Enact pilot diversions. Initiate the round-up!" Samuel added with impatience.

"Yes, sir!" The officer jolted.

A few seconds later, all sectors blinked with a massive amount of singularities appearing and disappearing at random. *"Whatever is coming, it better be to our advantage,"* Samuel thought.

The vacated sector flickered as thousands of tiny flashes littered the space-sphere. The probes detected the creation of additional new wormholes that blossomed right in front of the emerging ships. After a moment, that Samuel felt as eternal, the ships, hesitant at first, jumped into the new singularity tunnels and their symbols disappeared from the space-sphere. The wormholes closed. The officer glanced at him, but Samuel pretended he didn't notice. He wouldn't know what to answer to any question, and went back to the central space-sphere.

Much farther away in space, unbeknownst to the parties at war, a stealth gathering of space ships took note of the peculiar fluctuations of the space-time. Unnoticed, they advanced at minimum impulse to investigate. Curiosity, but opportunity as well, led those ships. With black hulls against the black depths of space, like a nest of scorpions, they advanced.

Alarms shrieked from multiple sources. From the various duty stations, the officers shouted orders directed to the units under their control, the dashboard flickered with a sense of madness and urgency. Samuel dashed through the space-sphere, ripped from his thoughts by the claws of his most troubled fears; the Fleet had just received a major blow and retreated a million kilometres toward Eridu, chased by Moîrai battleships. *"I knew it!"* he thought, and damned his weakness before the Council. "I knew it!" he lashed out, aloud this time.

He drifted down as fast as the force field allowed him and ran as he touched the floor toward the tactical units controlling the sectors under a massive assault.

"Sir," the nearest officer in charge saluted him, glad to see someone ranked higher would deal now with the situation. "Our withdrawal from the sector has weakened our positions here, and here." He expanded the space representation to get more details to appear, and highlighted the various areas and the group units involved as he spoke. "We dispatched reserve units to reinforce fighters' group Thirty at these coordinates. The Moîrai are concentrating their effort at the weakened locations."

More sectors had turned red in the floating rendering and additional vessel symbols showed the increased presence of hostile units and the subsequent loss of command in areas previously controlled by the humans.

"Group Thirty held with help from additional destroyers, but this adjacent sector..." The officer paused to look at Samuel. "Sir, we didn't have enough reserve units close by. They arrived too late and the Moîrai created a breakthrough." The timeline of the recent events showed the disappearance of entire humans squads from the quadrant and the inflicted losses.

"I see it's contained now." He rested one hand on his shoulder. "Well done." His voice didn't reveal any emotion.

"It is, Admiral. But all those people...and the reserves..."

"I know, Captain." Samuel nodded. The petty officers, up to then bent over their dashboards and floating screens, turned their heads; all eyes were on Samuel. He glanced at everyone and sighed.

"We are not supposed to win. We are here to buy time and give Eridu a chance." His voice betrayed resignation.

"But sir, how long can we keep doing this?"

Samuel turned toward the voice and half-smiled. "What generation are you, Captain?" Samuel thought the officer looked young, even for a new human.

"I'm a third, sir."

Samuel sighed. "Only a third." He nodded. "For as long as we're able to. If we fail...nothing will matter anymore." He noticed the young captain clenched his jaw, and some of the petty officers stared at the floor.

"We're gonna make it!" Samuel said with renewed enthusiasm. He looked at all those men and women, of the third, maybe fourth generation. He thought of his youth, of his mother, Mary, and his half-sister, Hope. He felt a knot tightening in his throat. He cleared his voice. "You need to believe. Just don't give up; not yet."

⁂

The sky in Nova Roma showed a spectacle that kept all eyes riveted to the event. Never before had anything this risky been attempted. A wormhole opened in the outer space, but large and close enough to the planet to be visible from the surface.

Aboard the vessels escaped from Protusa, the Keepers admired the humans for this prowess, but many felt apprehension and, in some cases, fear.

No escape mission ever would be so grandiose and so foolish in the future as the one they were about to accomplish. Yet, no escape had ever been carried out with no real plan, no certitude, and no knowledge of how it could end in the mind of the escapees. They put their lives in the hands of the humans.

Maybe only Alaston nurtured faith; he waited, confident, for the tunnel singularity to open and re-enter into the physical space.

Time spent in the hyperspace tunnel—the subjective time, that is—was always the same; no matter the distance, no matter the actual time interval as experienced by anyone in an external reference system in the physical space-time.

Many Keepers worried the humans might hold them indefinitely within the singularity. Who knew, even dissolve the wormhole and let it collapse. What would have happened to them then?

But these weren't worries that troubled Alaston. He trusted Dan—in spite of everything—and Ohtlinell had no doubts that the human still harbored the Keepers' principles and values unaltered—*"There is no hatred in him. I never sensed such a strong hunger for doing what is right in anyone's mind,"* Ohtlinell said after his amazing return to Protusa from Eridu.

Dan had sent him. *Was this not—per se—a signal?* Alaston reasoned. Wasn't Ohtlinell himself, and his journey, the real message from Dan?

Alaston lowered his head and waited with patience for the tunnel to open. No reservations haunted his mind.

⁂

I looked up at the sky. The Council members, and Ohtlinell, had joined me on the large terrace atop our tallest tower. The moment didn't require any comment; everyone stared at the growing, shimmering freckle well above the horizon.

The Fleet, and the army in Eridu, received orders not to intervene, not even to escort the arriving vessels to their assigned destinations at the various spaceports.

The whole planet awaited with trepidation the opening of the wormhole. I was sure that no one slept on Eridu in those moments. I wasn't alone in thinking that this further arrival of the Moîrai on Eridu would mark our rebirth. This time, these Moîrai didn't come as invaders, they came to seek protection and shelter. But they were Keepers and would have to follow the lead of us humans.

Chapter 14 – No Time to Heal

Death can be fascinating, as life is. The invading Moîrai forces had almost reached Eridu. Our Fleet was only hours from its capitulation. We waited for the miracle that would have altered the fate of the war. From my terrace on the highest tower of Eridu's Council in Nova Roma, bright deformities and vivid luminescence, at times, marked the night sky, to diffuse some time later. Flashes of death for some, moments of renewed hopes for others.

The day before, we declared the highest alert all across Eridu: ground troops, the Fleet reserves—kept for a last desperate defense—civilians, everyone prepared for the ultimate battle. No one, anywhere on the planet, mentioned surrendering or considered capitulation a possibility. If the Moîrai wanted us, they would've had to fight every man in every city, in every ditch, in every corner of the planet. This time, they wouldn't find a powerless race they could have culled in one night.

Our Fleet fought through its last moments, and soon, if the second part of the plan didn't kick in... If the Moîrai made it to Eridu, whether or not their pilots lost their mental capabilities—as expected—the event wouldn't change our ill fate anymore.

Next to me, Alaston gazed at the battles between our races that made Nova Roma's sky glisten and announce our doom. "How awkward life is. Do not you agree, Dan?"

"How so?" I replied as another glittering explosion blossomed above us. More lives vaporized, humiliated, lost. Maybe one of our ships, maybe one of the Moîrai's.

"I remember another time and another terrace, in Protusa." His gaze went through our city. "Nova Roma looks a bit like our capital, do not you think?"

I turned to look at him and I sensed sorrow. For us? For the Moîrai? I couldn't tell, and I didn't reply.

"You do understand why we cannot intervene, not yet, at least." Alaston stared at me. "If the news that the Keepers—or what is left of us—are here in Eridu reaches the Wisest..." He paused. "They would not try to conquer Eridu and put humans on their knees. They would come to destroy the planet."

"I know."

Another flower of light grew in the sky. "We need to leave, unseen. Humans need to win this battle, and not just for their sake." He stared at me. "You need to win for the Moîrai, too."

I withstood his sight and didn't blink. "Nothing will be as it was. You understand this?"

Alaston lowered his head. "I will be the last Brethren of the Keepers." He raised his gaze again and opened his mind to me. No barriers into his knowledge, no obstructions into his thoughts. *"The Wisest have lost the way. They plan to invade Kritas' Alliance after Eridu's war. The whole galaxy as we know it will burn."*

A large explosion marred the horizon and the sky with a stretch of the color of a bloodstain.

I sighed. "They are getting closer."

⁂

The Moîrai acted as bloodhounds closing in on a wounded prey. The battlefront closed in to reach Eridu, and the Fleet had conceded the Asteroid Belt, and then Mars, to the assailants. Both belligerents suffered massive losses. In the Bridge Stations, no one talked anymore. In silence, officers and petty officers attended their duty to support the last, still-operational units and watched impotently as their numbers dwindled. They didn't have much to do now other than waiting, or registering further advances of the enemy fleet. Every additional hour required the sacrifice of many lives.

The units deployed to defend the Stations had decided not to down their arms. They would fight and die as all other vessels and crews did. Moîrai only had to try approaching the bases and would have suffered even more losses.

Samuel received communication of this resolution by his Commodores. He hadn't the heart to try and change their minds. The Moîrai were bound to score a complete victory. All was lost. In the FCC, the space-sphere now showed Eridu surrounded by the Moîrai forces; it was large enough that Samuel could distinguish the continents.

For the first time in those two days, he dared to give in to his feelings. He could have verified it for himself, but it was now too painful to endure the unknown. "Lieutenant," he called.

A young officer stood at attention. "Sir!"

Samuel considered he might have been from a fifth generation. *"Our last one, maybe,"* he thought. "What about Captain Joshua Amenta?" He sighed as soon as he asked the question. All first generations were known by the family name of their mothers only. *"We lost the genetic memory of the last male spared humans,"* he realized.

The lieutenant checked on the floating screen his belt created in front of him. His hands moved swiftly for a second before the answer showed up. "His group is still active, sir."

"What about him?" Samuel held his breath.

The lieutenant glanced at him. "He's alive, sir."

Samuel nodded and released the breath he held until then.

⁂

What was left of the human Fleet retreated tens of thousands of kilometres at each clash. Joshua stopped counting the number of friends lost in battle. The ship's vital-support system kept him awake and fed, but he stopped nurturing hope for what would be the end they were rushing to.

"Who cares!" he thought while targeting the next Moîrai destroyer. "Target acquired. Antimatter torpedoes launched. It's on you guys!" The antimatter torpedoes created a fraction-of-a-second vulnerability inbetween the instant the Moîrai shields collapsed and the moment they fully restored.

He pulled hard and deflected a few blasters' shots before the combined blows from the human cruiser ships in the rear powdered the enemy.

The Fleet had found this vulnerability early on, right at the beginning of the conflict, and kept inflicting damage this way to the Moîrai who had yet to find how to counter the lethal human tactic.

Joshua looked at the gauges. His fighter's energy level approached the moment when he would've needed to dock and recharge. Soon it would be matter of either bursting blasts to the enemy or keeping the shields charged to deflect their hits.

There was only one problem to deal with—he had nowhere to dock safely. All units, even the largest ones still active in the fight, now struggled to fend off death at each moment.

"How's your energy gauges, guys?" Joshua asked on the squad's channel.

A moment of silence followed, then a voice answered for all those still alive. "You're kidding, right, Capt?"

Some others shared a nervous laughter on the intercom when one of the fighter pilots lashed out. "Well, I knew it was a mistake missing the Evasive Maneuvers lessons!"

"Aha, but she was a hottie, Glenn, and—"

A bright flash and a weird, brief cracking noise interrupted the communication and killed the laughter and giggling that still lingered on in the intercom.

"Fuck!" Joshua shouted. "Regroup, regroup!" A few Moîrai ships had just broke through and targeted them.

The battle pursued with ever-increasing violence, the Fleet conceded ever more space to the enemy, and Eridu appeared on all vessels' tactical screens.

⁂

In the FCC hall, officers bowed in their seats. Many dashboards had been turned off. The floating screens showed Eridu and the battle now raging just beyond the Moon. The Fleet line of command was gone and the last groups kept fighting to the death on their own. The Moîrai—incessant—kept hammering the remaining fighting human vessels.

The central space-sphere showed a giant Eridu, the Moon, and the incoming doom less than a million kilometres away.

Tired and demoralized, Samuel kept observing, waiting for the miracle to manifest itself. Something had gone wrong—maybe they were all wrong; the genetic trap had worked already but the Moîrai found a way to keep their space-pilots healthy. It didn't matter much now, and the last human vessels would rip open, explode, and disintegrate under the heavy fire of the Moîrai fleet. Then it would be all over.

They were decimated, and the valiant sacrifice of the entire Eridu's Fleet meant nothing.

"Sir, we received a secured connection with the Council. In the briefing room."

Samuel nodded to the technician. "Thank you."

His father's eidolon waited for him. Samuel watched the wall coalesce behind him in an effort to delay the moment when he had to admit his failure. He turned and faced his father.

"Samuel." Dan appeared as resolute as ever.

He lowered his head. "Father, I failed you, and I betrayed us all."

Dan shook his head. "There's time still. You're still alive and we are not done yet."

"The Fleet is no more!" Samuel exclaimed and redressed himself.

Dan smiled at him, as a father, and bent his head to one side. Samuel thought of his mother and felt his eyes to swell with tears.

"For as long as we can still fight, we have time. We shall fight whatever the cost. And if they make it here—"

Samuel broke. "Father! It's over. The last vessels are being destroyed as we speak." He hesitated. "And it's Joshua's squadrons out there!" He said it and felt as if a weight had been slammed on his shoulders. "I cannot save him!"

Dan exhaled hard and his shoulders collapsed. He didn't expect that, he wasn't ready for that. Until then, he hid the knowledge—the certitude—that Joshua would die with the others, and mourned him already, in a sense; instead, he was still alive! "Joshua." Dan brought his right hand over his mouth, and clenched it. He shut his eyes, sobbed. "Annah," he said, and shook as his grief took over.

Samuel watched in awe as his father gave in to his emotions. Dan took a deep breath, opened his eyes and implored, "Don't let them kill you, Sam." A different man stood in front of him, broken.

"Father..."

"If the Moîrai should land, you will have to take everyone with you and flee. The Keepers are here and will join you in time." Dan paused to let his words sink in. "Alaston will teach you and the others. Don't give up, never give up..."

Something happened in Eridu, because Dan whirled to look elsewhere, out of the scene rendered in the Bridge Station briefing room. He faced Samuel once more and crossed his hands on his chest. "I love you, son."

Before Samuel could say anything, the image froze and faded. A moment later, Samuel was alone again in the room.

"Flee?" he thought. *"When everyone here wants to fight?"* Words whirled in his mind—the Keepers, Alaston, Moîrai, humans, his father.

He connected the dots, the space-sector to evacuate, and the multitude of fake wormholes. So that was it, as his father thought. *"There was a conspiracy, and it betrayed the Keepers as well."*

He understood better his father's last words. He had to confer with his officers; he filled his lungs with a long breath. There were still a lot of things to do and to be put in place.

⁂

"We're done," Joshua thought. He should have been scared, yet he accepted his fate without fear...almost with expectation.

"Status check," he asked in the squad's channel.

The few remaining fighter pilots replied in turn, with monotonic voices. No emotions colored their words. The other units shared, on the floating screens, their damage, the undermined functionalities, and it became obvious that they were unfit for another spar against the Moîrai vessels.

The Fleet—the remnants of Eridu's pride—regrouped within the Moon's orbit. The Moîrai, for reasons known only to them, waited for the last ships to retreat, stop, and regroup. They were no longer a threat to them, a few thousands broken vessels. The space around them was marred with dust, particulate, and emissions of various gaseous elements that oozed from spiraling wrecks and froze into a glittering dust.

From his cockpit, Joshua saw no longer a Fleet, but rather a space ships' cemetery, a field of wreckage ready for metal recycling. He sighed.

"Amenta?" a voice called him, one of the other few squads captains still alive.

"Neufeld? Is that you?"

"Yeah. The one and only." He snorted. "Listen, we can't support you in further attacks now. We're broken. My units can either maneuver, fire, or charge the shields. Can't do more than one thing at the same time."

Joshua snorted and peeked at the tactical screens. "We're sitting ducks. What are they waiting for?"

On the displays, the Moîrai had arranged their vessels in a sort of bowl-shaped formation, covering a large space in front of the humans' squadrons, blocking any possible escape maneuver, and had each ship targeted. Joshua had the onboard artificial intelligence compute the probabilities for the few scenarios still available to them. Its voice sounded harsh in the cockpit, as if Joshua had asked something too obvious for the synth-brain to waste an answer for.

"Escape scenario, zero percent success probability; chances of survival, zero percent confidence level. Invasion delay scenario, fourteen minutes, ten seconds; repel scenario confidence level, zero percent. Combined attack scenario, zero percent success probability, zero survival confidence level. Surrender option—"

"Oh, shut up!" Joshua interrupted the litany with a brusque smack on the dashboard. "Heard that?"

"Yeah. Same thing over here, Amenta... Listen, we've discussed it with the other squads, too. No one wants to surrender."

"I agree."

"This is what we propose..."

Joshua communicated the plan with the units under his direct command. He smiled as everyone agreed without a second thought; no one hesitated.

"All right. There's nothing more to share. From this moment, all units are on their own. Do as much as you can. It was an honor, the best two days of my life."

"Aye, aye, Capt" – "Good luck, everyone" – "You bet" – "See you on the other side"—and more made Joshua fight hard to retain his emotions.

The tactical alarms resounded. "Moîrai on the move!" he yelled. The enemy units advanced at minimum impulse, converging toward the human vessels and toward Eridu.

Joshua swiveled the fighter to face Eridu. The planet camped majestically, occupying the whole view. *"I'm lucky,"* he thought. The Mediterranean Sea, his homeland, and the Nova Roma territory were barely visible, but they were there! He breathed hard.

"For the Third Loss!" he shouted on all channels, to every squadron and every group. Shouts and screams from everyone on the channels repeated those words and any last sentiment of fear and doubt were put aside and forgotten.

The human units jumped forward at once, as one single body and one single mind, at maximum impulse. Then the ships shut down the engines and ionic thrusts. All units transferred the rest of their meager energy from the defensive shields to the offensive system. They fired all at once, all residual torpedoes, and the furious blasts depleted their last quantum of power and caught the enemy by surprise. Shouts of joy and rage marked every explosion in the Moîrai ranks.

"For the Third Loss!" still echoed in Joshua's ears as the reaction fire from the Moîrai reached the humans. The first lines exploded at once; furious debris scattered in all directions and impacted against the units in the rear.

Joshua smiled. *"We're all together now,"* was his last thought before the blinding impact of a Moîrai battlecruiser's blaster hit his ship.

⁂

The fireball as seen from Nova Roma grew and tore the sky apart. Those who watched it trembled. Many cried. They knew what it meant. People hugged each other and sobbed.

All over the planet, the sirens wailed a mournful sound. A long, steady note traveled across all cities, broke through all barriers, and shattered somber hearts.

Loudspeakers instructed all citizens to reach the nearest underground facility, hundreds of metres below the surface, without any delay. Easy instructions to follow, but were the hardest ones to abide by and accept for they announced the doom, the defeat, and the loss of many lives.

Alarms resounded in all military facilities and spaceports; troops prepared for this, but everyone hoped the moment would never come. The first units to scramble moved swiftly, certain to meet with death.

Before entering the shelter admission points, those who could raise their eyes one last time to the sky saw a fireball that was already fading, and so was their hope for the future. The sirens kept screaming and the sound rippled between the once-proud buildings.

The sky had sent its message and the sirens' cry reached even the two-thousand-metre tall Council towering over Nova Roma. When the fireball appeared, I knew I had seen Joshua's death. Tears dried already, and my heart had stopped beating with compassion. It shrank so many times in grief and grew back each time smaller, but now didn't recover. I felt my heart become a dense, heavy stone in my chest.

"Dan." The memnosphere flickered as Marina called me. Hearing my name disturbed me.

"Dan is dead, Marina. I'm no more. What remains of me is a shadow; there's no more life left for Dan."

The wall dilated. Manfred and Alaston entered.

"We need to go soon." Through the transparent wall, Alaston glimpsed at the sky.

I didn't turn; I didn't need to. "I know. I warned Samuel, and I'm sure he'll be ready when the Keepers reach him."

I felt Manfred's sorrow and accepted his silent embrace, but didn't react.

"Why don't you come with us?" Alaston continued.

"I won't leave Eridu." I turned and faced both of them. "Not now, and not while humans are still fighting."

"You should go, Dan." Manfred approached. "You'll be more useful with them. The Council will lead the resistance. They're all in safe locations and—"

"Safe locations, Manfred?" I said. "I won't go to any safe location. A shuttle is coming to take me to the spaceport."

"This is madness!" Alaston exclaimed.

"Madness?" I lashed out. "Don't come talking about madness to me. There's no madness in Eridu. I suggest you fix your eyes on Protusa."

Alaston lowered his head and showed his palms to me. "I am sorry, Dan of Eridu. It was not my intention..."

I walked up to them. "The time has not come yet for me, and I'm done with mourning. What is necessary will be accomplished. Now go, both of you."

They lowered their head and stepped back. I let the wall dilate. On their way out, Manfred stopped and gave me a last look. "For the Third Loss." I nodded and he left.

A dull thud from the terrace announced the arrival of my shuttle. I sealed the room.

"Marina, have you nothing more to say?" I glanced at the memnosphere.

"Maybe because I would have words for Dan, only." Her voice seemed so real. She was now, with Samuel, my only tie with a world sometime—in the last years—I doubted it ever existed.

"Have you replicated yet?" I asked.

"Of course. You'll find me wherever a memnosphere is." The sphere sparkled. I nodded. *"How real can she be?"* I marveled always, but I missed her physical presence; also that had been denied to me.

"Fine. I need to go."

"I know...and if a Moîrai gets in here, don't worry, I know what to do."

I sighed. Marina, how I missed her.

On the terrace, the shuttle dilated bulkhead waited for its passenger and a crewmember came running when she saw me. "Sir! We need to go at once!"

The sky showed bright spots and traces where the Moîrai ships violated the highest layers of our atmosphere. They indulged in a slow descent. *"Tasting their victory,"* I thought. The Nova Roma spaceport scrambled its fighters and the now-visible Moîrai ships grew in number and in size as they prepared to counter our last airborne defenses. I walked toward the shuttle, stepped in, and took a seat.

"Sir," the pilot welcomed me on the speakers. "It'll be a fast ride, sir. I hope you don't mind abrupt maneuvers, if needed."

I smiled. "Not at all. Let's go."

The shuttle left the tower with a jerk and sped toward the spaceport. Some hundred kilometres above us, the battle started and Eridu witnessed its last heroes face their destiny.

Chapter 15 – Reversal of Fortune

The shuttle touched down without incident on one of the landing areas reserved for the Fleet.

Fighters were still scrambling to intercept the Moîrai and make them pay a high price before they reached Eridu's soil. The first clashes stained the clear blue of the early day and white filaments netted the sky when debris burned, consumed by the friction with denser strata of air.

We witnessed the final gasps of bravery from the Fleet crews to support a desperate plan for victory and got ready to confront the Moîrai on the ground. The menacing enemy ships exchanged fire with human squadrons scrambled from all over the world. Their numerical superiority gave no room for any other plan than preparing for a bloody guerrilla war on the surface.

⁂

The space deep blackness spurred into multiple colors from the beautiful yet lethal burst of energy as the antimatter torpedoes annihilated the last resistance.

The Moîrai fleet commanders smiled with glee when the last human ship splintered from a silent internal deflagration and then exploded. Its debris bounced off the defensive shields, harmless.

The descent to Eridu presented no more obstacles and a vulnerable planet floated on their screens. They sent a communiqué on the successful operation to Xrusé and the main military leader of the expedition prepared to dispatch a vessel back to Protusa to announce the victory in person and provide the Supreme Council with details of the operation.

"Crazy creatures." The Moîrai chief commander watched the fringes of the last exploding human battleship from his bridge deck. "Courageous, but crazy! That was not necessary."

"I agree." His second reached him by the side and lowered his head. "They have yet to learn, but they will." The tone of his voice didn't mask a pinch of derision. "Crazy bastards, indeed."

The commander snorted, erupting in the harsh coughing sounds typical of a Moîrai who laughed loudly.

"Prepare the fleet for the invasion. Today, I want to walk on Eridu."

From afar, stealth like a pack of wolves, a third group of space ships got ready.

Eridu's cities and continents appeared vivid on the screens and as inviting as the most precious crystals in the galaxy. "*Nothing can stop our might now,*" the Moîrai thought. He caressed the moment when he would have received the reward for his success and his military wisdom from the ruling power of the Supreme Council.

The fleet started its descent, while—aboard—heavily armored ground troops and assault vehicles completed the last checks to debark and engage the humans on their soil.

"Maybe the Kritas were right, after all." He turned to his second officer. "Humans bring instability to the galaxy and their presence undermined our resolve."

The second lowered his head in agreement. "Yes, but now we will do what was necessary from the beginning."

They exalted each other and relaxed, as any other military mind would in similar moments with the enemy at their mercy.

When the fleet approached a hundred kilometres from the surface, the tactical groups alerted the incoming threats of more small fighters from ground bases and in manifest offensive attitude. Soon after, the humans opened fire.

Enraged, the commander yelled on the bridge. "Destroy those rats!" The Moîrai forces commenced to wipe out the last oppositions.

A new set of alarms—unfamiliar because of their rarity—lit up, unnoticed, on the monitoring screens of the interstellar-pilot's vitals. The ship jolted, as if its navigation system malfunctioned, and the commander stared at the navigation officer but didn't make any comments.

The officer bent his head in surprise, but the ship regained its course right away. He cleared his voice. "Accounting for the fleeting interference from the remaining hostile vessels, sir, our estimated touchdown will be in six time intervals, sir."

"Everything is going to be smooth now," the commander thought. The resistance from the humans had been tougher than anticipated but, in the end, it was just a manageable threat. The Moîrai smiled; the campaign was not at risk anymore.

Another jolt from the ship made him reach for his dashboard to keep his balance. His eyes pierced the navigation officer's back. "What now?"

"Our rear shields, sir. We have just absorbed a major blaster hit."

The Moîrai dropped his jaw, baffled. The tactical screens filled with hostiles at an approximate distance of a few thousands of kilometres. "Where did those come from?"

The black vessels had only then exited their stealth mode and opened fire. They seemed to rejoice at every blaster hit, shivering with a thrill. The swarm of the antimatter torpedoes they sent had only a short ride to go, then they created holes in the Moîrai forces.

They despised the Moîrai. What an occasion the humans created for them; the remains of the Moîrai's fleet was so damaged that it would easily succumb in the face of a fresh horde of hostile forces.

As a Moîrai would have said, it was necessary for them to take part in the events now.

The befuddled Moîrai commander stared at the tactical screens.

⁂

The Fleet officers and the rest of the personnel of the Bridge Stations welcomed the escaped civil crews from the inner Traffic Control Stations. Shaken, they had seen the rage of the war go past them and feared the worst. Some units received indirect damage, but they suffered only minor losses. Before their departure, they had to wait for the first chance when the battles raged beyond them and left at maximum impulse toward the Kuiper Belt and the far main Bridge Stations.

Samuel arranged for the evacuation procedure; the operation progressed with efficiency even if managed by morale-broken Fleet crewmembers.

In time, Alaston established communication and sent instructions; soon, the humans would board their spaceships and leave the Stations' infrastructure to avoid whatever destiny the Moîrai loyal to the Supreme Council had in mind for them.

Samuel sat alone in his sealed office, waiting for the Keepers to arrive. He had one churning thought in his mind that agitated all his emotions and made him eager to leave as soon as possible: revenge! *"Whether or not the Keepers will support that."* He made himself the solemn promise that one day he would march on Protusa.

He frowned when he heard the heavy thumping footsteps of someone running in the corridor just outside his quarters. The wall announced the arrival of a lieutenant from the tactical units.

"I gave instructions not to be disturbed." Samuel opened the communication link but kept the wall shut.

"Sir! We need you at the FCC." The officer sounded hysterical. After a deep breath, Samuel let the wall dilate.

When Samuel arrived at the FCC, the space-sphere reproduced in real-time the ongoing battle around Eridu. The officers were bent on their dashboard working fast on the floating screens.

Samuel gave a quick look at the scene. "Are you in contact with the Keepers?" By then, everyone knew about the existence of the Keepers, as the secret was no more. Now Keepers meant rebels in most of the officers' minds.

"Yes, sir. They carried out evasive maneuvers and passed through the Moîrai forces while in stealth mode. They confirmed the rendezvous with the Stations as planned, sir."

The information from the battle had been analyzed multiple times already, but the evidence was unmistakable; Kritas forces now engaged the Moîrai in battle around Eridu and the violence of that new conflict left no doubt as to their intention: to obliterate their archrivals.

Samuel shouted to the communication managers, "Get me Alaston at once!"

"Samuel, this changes our plans." Alaston's voice was charged with a renewed enthusiasm. "I never thought one day I would have welcomed Kritas battleships attacking our fleet." His voice, though, had lost the brilliance that accompanied his first words.

"How's that possible? And where's my father?"

"I left him a few hours ago in Nova Roma. He was heading to the underground Fleet Command Center there. Your father is resolute to battle every single Moîrai who sets foot on Eridu." Alaston paused. "The folly of the Supreme Council gave the Kritas an opportunity too good for them to pass. I am surprised they did not send a larger task force."

"My father trusts you, and I've known you since I was born. But I won't hide from you how uncomfortable I am with this."

"I understand. I hope you will soon change your mind."

"What do you mean? ... Alaston? *Alaston!*" Samuel yelled in vain at the fading projection of the Moîrai.

He snorted. "All tactical units! Full report and double those damned duty stations!"

⁂

On the spaceport tarmac, the shuttle crew and I strode toward the entrance to the Fleet underground facility when the unexpected happened. Those around us shouted and pointed at the sky. We stopped and looked up. The enemy had stalled, as if they were unsure of how to proceed.

Our remaining units kept fighting, but the Moîrai stopped hunting them down, seeking to destroy them. They hesitated and their descent momentum slowed to a halt.

Then, the shining vessels of the Moîrai fleet turned and retreated, gaining altitude and leaving!

Thus, not everything was lost. We ran to the underground FCC facility and its officer in command, a Commodore, greeted me. We crossed a series of barriers and checkpoints as he led me toward the main hall. The Commodore briefed me with a barrage of information his staff had been busy collecting. "The Moîrai are under attack and suffer already from heavy casualties." He paused.

I probed him and he wasn't hiding any information from me. "Who?"

"It took some time to identify the aggressors, but it is certain now; they're Kritas, sir. I'd say the balance of the battle is still uncertain, but it's a massacre up there."

We walked at a brisk pace to the center of the FCC operative hall. "This is excellent, but I sense there's more." I looked at him and the Commodore hesitated for a split second. He glided his sight away from me and stared at the group of analysts and officers we were about to meet with.

"Indeed, sir." He cleared his voice. "We've noticed a strange behavior in the Moîrai maneuvers, but we can't tell what that is."

"Finally!" I thought. "Don't worry about that." I couldn't refrain from having a cold smile develop on my lips. "Is Eridu secure?"

The Commodore raised his eyebrows, glanced at my own smile, and frowned. "For the time being, sir."

We stepped onto the main command platform. "There's one more thing, sir." He stopped and forced me to turn around to face him. I bent my head to the left with a measured movement. "Yes?"

"The Keepers, sir. They disappeared from all tactical screens as they were reaching the Stations."

My smile widened.

⁂

The Keepers' fleet attained ordnance in-range with the enemy. Invisible to both belligerents, they waited, immobile, and observed. Behind them, in retreat, the task force Samuel had arranged from the units defending the Bridge Stations was ready to provide support. Their auto-targeting systems had been instructed to make no distinction between Kritas and Moîrai vessels. Both were to be considered hostile.

The systems shifted the focus on the most threatening targets in turn, the ones that would have constituted an immediate danger as soon as they'd left stealth mode and engaged them in combat.

Alaston and the other Keepers waited patiently for the moment when their offensive capabilities equaled at least the number of possible targets, or exceeded them, even. There was no need to rush—not necessary per the Moîrai philosophy—as long as the conflict maintained the current balance and the hostile units kept slaughtering each other.

While he supervised the ongoing battle on the displays, Alaston realized that there were no alternatives given what he knew. Not acting and not intervening to change the course of the events would have plunged the galaxy into an unlimited conflict well beyond the theater of a single star system. In that perspective, they would have had to decide on the best way to engage and collaborate with the humans.

"There is time," Alaston thought, and then focused his attention on the flow of information and predictions over the battle's outcome that kept changing in his dashboard panels.

The Keepers' units had surrounded the limited space sector around the conflict when things started to look up for the Kritas.

On the bridge deck, the tension mounted. The Keepers' personnel, devoted to the tactical assessment of the battle, could neither understand nor interpret the latest data. The confidence level of all predictions dropped to increasingly unreliable levels until all calculations lost any meaning and alarms blinked on all dashboards. Without any apparent reason, the actions and the coordination of Moîrai groups and units became impaired.

"This makes no sense," Alaston exclaimed; he stood up and called for a double check. Next to him, the timeline analysts rushed to work on old and new data, but everything pointed to the same previous conclusions. "There are unknown factors in play that invalidate all probabilities," said one of the analysts.

"I can see that, but why?" Alaston said.

"We detected that Moîrai vessels have stopped firing in the middle of a clash or are floating inert while the Kritas destroy them. In other cases, units have left the protection of tight formations and fled at full speed in random directions; some ended up in the middle of Kritas groups..."

The analyst dropped his jaw and gave a blank stare at Alaston.

"Sir," interjected another. "The erratic behavior seems to increase. We cannot factor in valid parametres anymore for any reliable prediction, but the Moîrai units have lost cohesion."

In haste, Alaston conferred with every tactical group commander; he put on his Palladium and called for an emergency assembly.

The major task force leaders confirmed the same results. Alaston asked the question everyone had in mind: "Shall we stay in stealth mode until the Kritas finish killing all of the Moîrai?"

The Keepers looked at each other through the Palladiums; then one decided to reply for everyone. "You are the Brethren, and as such, you have the final say. But we have been chased, captured, tortured, and killed. The Keepers are our only nation and our only people now." He lowered his head and opened his palms to Alaston, and so did, in turn, each one of them.

Alaston's arms shivered; then he lowered his head and presented his palms to the assembly. "So be it. We will attack after the last Moîrai vessel is destroyed."

They waited and Alaston watched the Kritas enjoy their butchery, though the time for their retribution was nigh. He ordered the targeting systems be reprogrammed to disregard the Moîrai vessels, especially when none seemed to be capable of anything but unpredictable behaviors to the point of succumbing to friendly fire.

For many of the Keepers, the battle was disconcerting, and Alaston noticed that a few lowered their head, refusing to keep watching the brutal scenes shown on the tactical displays. He walked to a point in the bridge where everyone could see him and activated a communication link to all units. "This is a defining moment for us Keepers. We saw our Brothers betrayed and hunted down in Xrusé, captured, maimed, and killed. Was it a friendly fire that took them from us? No! We are pariah now, and Eridu's Keeper has called for us. This is where our allegiance stands."

Heads rose again. The Kritas units, in a much lower number since the start of the murderous battle, became the target of an overwhelming set of weaponry. The probability of a swift cull increased with each passing moment, but Alaston waited for the last Moîrai vessel to be destroyed. Then, the Keepers would engage and attack the black Kritas vessels with no mercy. It was a necessity, just as necessary was for him to monitor—until the last ship—the slaughtering of what remained of the Moîrai forces sent to invade Eridu.

A Kritas battlehip hit the last Moîrai vessel and Alaston saw it fracture, rip open, and then disintegrate in a last, huge, mute explosion. Nothing distrupts the silence in space, not even the death of thousands of beings in a massive explosion. The Kritas units halted to taste their victory; torn parts, gases, and debris flew away with fury.

"Now!" Alaston ordered the attack. The Keepers' vessels emerged from stealth and had the Kritas trapped in a gigantic death chamber made of thousands of battleships.

The impact of massive antimatter weaponry shook the space-time fabric and annihilated all enemies in a huge, blinding release of energy.

Chapter 16 – Through the Ashes

Sirens screamed again, but this time people gathered in squares and chanted. They hugged and cried, but no one glanced at the sky in fear. What remained of Eridu's Fleet reserves—side-by-side with the Keepers'—flew over all continents and traced the skies with garlands and swags of vapor trails.

I watched the manifestations of joy from afar and felt everyone's euphoria, but couldn't join in the jubilation. I felt nothing—no, I felt a primitive cold as that of a heart that had never learned compassion. The world reacted as if we had won the war and all was over, but we only went through a battle; moreover, we made it only at the last instant, and thanks to the Kritas' unexpected but timely intervention.

Worldwide, the Council rejoiced with the people. Indeed, we had avoided the worst, but we had paid a tremendous price and the Council had to mourn the dead.

I stayed away from all official events and the communiqués cited my grief for the loss of Joshua as the reason. I carried a cruel destiny on my shoulders. When a child is born, the process of a separation that lasts a whole life starts. My grandson...the son of my daughter, Annah—all too soon. His death came too close to the one of my daughter, Hope. The only thing my mind could think of was that the work was not yet over.

Throughout the subsequent weeks, Keepers kept arriving from other corners of the galaxy, and they related the misery and desolation the crews experienced when they had to traverse the debris from the battle's killing sectors and the ashes still trapped in our planet's gravity well. Shooting stars traced Eridu's night sky, and nights became a vivid memento to the ones who were no longer with us.

The Confederation came close to the brink of a deadly war against the Kritas Alliance. The brain damage interstellar pilots suffered spread panic, and the hysterical fear of an inexplicable pandemic ran for months in the galaxy. Yet, no one connected the symptoms with Eridu's events, or Fusion, the transgenic neurotrophic drug we produced.

We knew which race received our modified molecules and what would have developed in their pilots' brains. We had undermined the offensive and defensive capabilities of many races more efficiently and with more lethal consequences than the combined number of antimatter weaponry from all civilizations. We created for ourselves the time buffer we needed to rebirth after the deadly confrontation with the Moîrai.

We regrouped, and the influx of space ships from the Keepers—de facto, a nation within the Moîrai nation for millennia—recreated in record time Eridu's capability to launch a large offensive campaign. 'Damage to the extreme' is what I had in mind, and the words echoed in the crude void of my soul.

From my office in the highest tower of the Council, the world seemed not to have changed at all. It was as if nothing ever happened, but too many mourned their dead. The gangrene that infected the Moîrai Supreme Council constituted a real threat, and the Keepers' presence in Eridu helped to make people aware that more had yet to come.

The news of a pandemic affecting the interstellar pilots became our alibi to justify the AIDAs as quarantine centers. Our official news reported that Eridu's scientists were the first to uncover the risk of an epidemic, but didn't have a cure yet. The quarantine measures the Council adopted months before were justified in light of the panic and how fast the pandemic spread to the rest of the galaxy.

We humans had to stay the course, and our race would never concede to the incoherence dictated by fear. Races in the galaxy limited their contacts with others to prevent contagion, and travelers discovered the reality of quarantine centers mushrooming everywhere in the various star systems.

The perennial tension and the cold war status between Kritas and Moîrai created a status of paranoia, and their mutual efforts to cover up the recent events raised the pathological secrecy in both of their camps. It reached such new heights that the knowledge of the carnage of Eridu didn't leak beyond the highest levels of their respective governments—a carnage that their politicians wiped off the memory on the altar of opportunism—and it played to our advantage.

I stood in front of the transparent wall of my office and grinned at the first stars twinkling in the early evening sky. I thought of all those innocent civilizations and of the moment when Eridu's fleet would appear in Xrusé's sky.

The memnosphere shimmered and sent reflections dancing around on the translucent walls. "What are you thinking?" Marina's voice asked.

"Of the future. Why are you asking?" I said in a low voice.

"Because now I worry each time I see you pensive. I always fear you're torturing yourself." She paused. "I'd like to be able to read your mind as before."

I let out a long sigh. "How many years, Marina?"

"How many...since what?"

I turned toward the sphere. I wasn't in a romantic mood and knew I'd never feel that way anymore. "Since you died." My voice sounded harsh and bounced off the walls of the room I kept free from any amenities.

The sphere looked as if it were alive, an alien being that twisted and shone with a tremulous light as a reflection of its thought processes, but didn't reply at first. After a long moment, Marina's voice broke the silence. "Why are you asking me this?"

I imagined Marina. I remembered her as a vibrant and dramatic young woman; in my mind, I saw her once-beloved eyes trembling with tears. "How many years?" I repeated in a firm voice.

The sphere emitted a flash. "Ninety years, seven months, fourteen days, six hours and twelve minutes. Do you want the seconds, too?"

I snorted. "Then it's about time, and I endured everything for too long. Show me when Joshua was a kid; show me Annah, and Mary."

The sphere flashed from within. A three-dimensional scene replaced half of the office, a scene from Civita. Our terrace, Mary played with little Joshua and Annah watched, her blue eyes beaming with love.

I clenched my jaw. At that moment, the unnatural cold that took up residence in my heart pierced it and blasted through it frozen needles that met no blood. I clenched my fists and resolved that nothing would ever stop me.

⁂

We closed Eridu's space-sphere to all interstellar traffic; in exceptional cases, we allowed ships to reach selected heavily guarded rally points beyond the Kuiper Belt. Any commercial transaction and negotiations took place there, without crossing the Belt, and monitored by a large battleship deployment. We turned the Kuiper Belt into a curtain of steel.

In a matter of only months, the galaxy saw the birth of pirates, outlaws that profited from the times of uncertainties to make profits from the loots of captured commercial vessels. The same groups acted as pirates in certain sectors and sold security services in others. To traverse remote sectors, frequent travelers along those commercial routes controlled by rogue groups bought their 'insurance policy' to protect their cargoes against the risk of being looted by those same 'patrol squads'. A lucrative business.

The political climate saw the Kritas blaming the Moîrai for everything, and the Kritas intervention around Eridu convinced the Moîrai and their Supreme Council that their archrivals were behind the whole mess.

Some influencial Moîrai feared the humans again. *'Tíme Dánaos'*—'Beware of the Greeks', said a human long-gone culture some two millennia before. In the remote past, galaxy civilizations looked with apprehension at what the humans had been capable of all along their troubled history. They scrutinized us, they observed us, and planned for our annihilation; they wanted us extinct, and they almost succeeded. They crushed us down into our own funeral ashes, but through the ashes, we will rise again.

The Eridu's Council met again in high secrecy. We knew how considerable was the effort we asked of mankind, especially after the suffered losses, but Eridu and the human race responded. The operation details were known only to a small group of chosen individuals, each responsible for some crucial aspects of the overall preparation and plans.

The giant phoenix still camped on the Nova Roma main spaceport, and our plans received the code name of "The Rise of the Phoenix."

The Council turned the auditorium into our operational control center. The highest qualified fleet personnel worked there in turns to ensure an uninterrupted process, and nobody left the Council compounds for any reasons. It became a citadel, with its own internal services. The members of the Council supervised any external communications on a 'need-to-know' basis.

The walls of our meeting hall showed the information coming from every branch involved, military to civil alike. The countdown to the 'GO' moment didn't give a time, but the percentage of readiness. We monitored every level in the chain of command with a mental fever that flirted with paranoia.

The Council accepted Alaston with full membership, as a peer. The move raised a few eyebrows, but what the Keepers had done during the Battle of Eridu—as people called it—helped to smooth out any wrinkles.

That day, the agenda dealt with the future military chain of command of the combined forces, Keepers' and humans'. Manfred stood for a full control in the hands of Eridu's commanders. "With all due respect to the Keepers." He looked at Alaston. "Without you, we would not be here, but without us, you would be nowhere." The Council members took the same stance without hesitation.

Alaston didn't react; he understood Manfred's position. A bit surprised, I saw him lower his head and show his opened palms to Manfred.

I perceived a mental blink and saw Christine's mind light up. The Selected from the NorthAm regions rose from her seat. She commanded respect; when everything had started ninety years before, she faced more unrests, vandalisms, and threats from rogue groups than anyone else in the Council. Those same rogue elements had joined later on the Kritas' attempt to foment an upheavel in Eridu.

What Marina and I had confronted around Civita paled in comparison. For a moment, the final battle against the Kritas in their subterranean base in the old Pennsylvania occupied my mind, but then I heard Christine speak.

"Members of the Council." She let her gaze pause on each of the Twelve. "Brethren of the Keepers," she said when her eyes met Alaston's. "Dan of Eridu." I lowered my head.

She knew how to play with pauses. "These months have proved our strength and the resolve of our men and women." A flux of mental approbation emanated from the members. Christine smiled. "We are close to completing the preparatory phase, and I'm convinced—beyond a shadow of a doubt—that things don't happen without a reason."

I wondered where Christine intended to lead her speech to, as she kept her mind veiled. I smiled. *"Things don't happen without a reason," I* thought, and agreed with her.

"What the Moîrai did," she didn't face Alaston, but she glanced at him for a fraction of a second, "set the galaxy on a precise course that led to the recent events." She paused. "No other race would have been capable of doing what we have done." Her voice rose in a crescendo. With the corner of my eye, I noticed Manfred nod with a sly smile on his face. "No others," she went on, "beside humans are so clearly destined, have so strongly been forged, and are so prepared to take now the lead!"

My eyes widened, as I hadn't seen that coming. Manfred stood up, followed by all others. Alaston looked at me, unsure whether what he was witnessing counted as another quirkiness of being a human. I sent him my thoughts, *"I've no idea,"* and I didn't lie.

Manfred stood up and cleared his voice. "Christine, do you have a motion to present the Council for an immediate vote?"

She looked at him with a serious expression. "I do."

"Please proceed." Manfred sat back. Everyone stared at me and I mentally poked Manfred, but he ignored me.

Christine raised her right hand. "I put forward the motion for an immediate vote to solemnly proclaim Dan of Eridu as Eridu's Primum." She fixed her eyes on me and proceeded with the same tone. "Conferring him all and every power in Eridu's matters; all and every power as Commander in Chief of Eridu's Fleet and all military branches; all and every power in the jurisdiction, control, and authority over Eridu's relationships with all races, known and unknown, in this galaxy and others, as the case might be. For the Third Loss, may he be guided and lead with wisdom and justice."

Every member raised their right hand, and said—at a mental level, too—"Aye."

Alaston sealed his mind. Manfred stared at me, but the hint of a smile gave the expression on his face a shrewd look.

⁂

Security sealed and quarantined my whole quarters. In the corridors leading to my rooms, guards stood proud and with a new insignia on their shoulders, 'EP', with a flamboyant Phoenix rising from its ashes.

In my office, Marina's memnosphere refused to answer any of my specific questions about the announcement. Of course she knew, and her silence more than confirmed she had a role in all this. Nova Roma received worldwide recognition about receiving 'The Capital' title, and I—for the first time in years—didn't know how to react.

I played my role, of course, but I couldn't see where this reversed coup d'état would lead us. Emotionally, I felt emptied, and I feared what filled now my heart. The whole Council must have prepared in all its minutiae the transition of power, because everything proceeded too swiftly and as clockwork to be otherwise. At mere twenty-four hours after the resolution received the official ratification, I demanded from Manfred a complete disclosure and told him to consider that my first order as Eridu's Primum.

"What is this?" I fumed. "What was going through your mind, Manfred?" He stood rigid while I talked. "And relax, for chrissake!" I lashed out.

"Sir," he started; I looked him squarely in the eyes.

He sighed. "Dan, I'm sorry; I couldn't tell you anything. You wouldn't have accepted."

"You're damned right. You forced my hand!"

"Can't you see it?" Manfred approached. "The things you've done and accomplished, the way you seem to always find a way to turn the direst situations into opportunities..."

"Exactly. You said it. '*I seem*' to find a way."

"Oh c'mon, Dan." Manfred walked up and down my office. "Everybody looks up to you at all times; even the

Keepers, maybe even Alaston. This has nothing to do with you or your glory. This is the future of Eridu at stake, and of the new mankind." He turned toward the memnosphere and implored, "Marina, tell him!"

My eyes fixed on the memnosphere. "Of course. Marina is involved, too. I cannot believe it." I turned my back on them and looked through the transparent wall. In the distance, a small dome protected the ancient stones of Civita, the Memorial and its precious diamonds. "Marina, you knew what I'm going through now. It's not the right time."

"Dan?" Marina's voice sounded dear and coming from a past that scorched my soul. I stiffened.

"Dan," she repeated. I sighed, but kept looking outside.

"Dan." She pleaded a third time.

I turned toward my torturer. "What? What justification will you bring forward now?"

The sphere glimmered as if someone, or something, inside chuckled. "I need no excuses, dear. You've changed a lot, and you're the same old, still stubborn mule. Protest as much as you like, it's a fact now, and you know better than anyone else that this is the best way. Even with all you're going through."

Manfred's eyes jumped from the memnosphere to mine and back, as if he tried to tie a thread that kept escaping him.

I listened to her voice; unfortunately, I agreed with her and hoped justice still lived within me to keep the monster at bay as I felt it lurking for a way out, wanting to take control of my actions.

"So stop being fussy," the sphere glittered, "and listen to what Manfred has to tell you."

Manfred opened his mouth to say something, but stopped when I stared at him. My eyes burned with a light that imposed silence.

⁂

In those days, orbiting around Eridu, factories delivered new space ships without intermission. The Keepers revealed the details of their advanced cloak technology and we integrated it to our proprietary artificial intelligence developments, derived from the Moîrai memnosphere blueprints. Our interstellar pilots moved to brand new vessels and began the mental fusion with the ships' components. Meanwhile, the epidemic affecting interstellar pilots kept the galaxy in a state of emergency, and we reinforced the already strict measures regulating any exchange and communication with other races.

In Nova Roma, the underground FCC vibrated with excitement and its countless activities. The countdown to complete readiness showed a level above ninety percent, but the last metres are always the longest.

Samuel and Manfred sat to my right and to my left. We waited for the Keepers' delegation, and for Alaston. We asked for their complete collaboration under our lead.

Samuel's nervousness betrayed his youth. "What if they disagree? Alaston's their Brethren, why would they—"

"Calm down, Samuel." I locked my eyes on his. "Alaston knows we have qualities—peculiar ones the Moîrai will never develop—and there's a coup d'état on Xrusé orchestrated by the Wisest."

Manfred interjected. "Don't forget your father suspected that before it happened, and Alaston either ignored him or failed to recognize the clear signals for years. Sometimes I have the impression he barely's able to stand your father's stare."

Samuel sighed and nodded. "Okay, but what if Alaston keeps failing?"

"Alaston never rushes anything." I paused. "And yet, he never denies things when they're evident, either. The Keepers will never forgive the treachery of the Wisest."

"We'll know that soon." Manfred raised his chin when the luminous eidolons of Alaston and five among the elders of the Keepers appeared, projected into our FCC from their flagship in geostationary orbit above the Mediterranean Sea.

Their expressions didn't reveal much of their thoughts. Although we wore our Palladiums, they kept their minds secluded. Forcing a mental probe would have been a wrong first step to begin a delicate negotiation.

We stood up. The six Moîrai lowered their heads and opened their hands to us. I gestured them to take their seats; the pedestals emerged from the floor and we all sat down.

"It looks like the Moîrai have the tendency of always outnumbering us humans," I greeted them.

Alaston took advantage of that remark to set a friendly tone to their visit. "And yet, Eridu's Primum, the humans emerge victorious."

I lowered my head in turn. "Circumstances favored us."

"Circumstances Eridu's Primum had planned for," he replied, and his companions openend their palms in approval. Manfred bent forward a bit to nod at Samuel.

I decided to be cautious, though, and let Alaston choose what to say and when. "I thank the Brethren and the Keepers, and I speak for all Eridu. You are welcome here."

Alaston straightened up, and it seemed his projection glittered more. "We bring news of a decision that found no disagreement. The Keepers will support Eridu's Primum if his objectives include restoring the Keepers to the place that is theirs in the Moîrai Confederation."

I didn't need to tell Alaston and the Keepers that I intended to restore them, certainly, but limited to the Moîrai society. "It is my will also."

The Moîrai lowered their heads and rose, prompting us to do the same. "Eridu's Primum," said Alaston. "The Keepers will follow the Keeper."

Chapter 17 – Conversation of Death

The 'GO' countdown in the Chief of Staff room showed a ninety-eight percent completion and a success confidence level above ninety. The results from the analyses of every intelligence detail continued to be updated as the operation proceeded.

Samuel frowned at the numbers, even though the probability of success was high enough to dispel all reservations. The Commodore in command during that particular shift of duty noticed the Fleet Admiral's worried expression. "Sir?"

"I'm fine. The preparation is spotless, but I was thinking..."

The Commodore raised his eyebrows.

"I'm sure, back in Protusa, the Moîrai commander of the fleet was pleased with a similar figure before he decided to invade our space sectors."

"Yes, but—"

"Never mind." He raised one hand. "Find out what pieces of information we might still be missing, and raise those figures." Samuel pointed at the dashboard, then walked away to meet with his father, Alaston, and Manfred.

"Aye, aye, sir." The Commodore saluted, but Samuel had already crossed the dilated exit.

Brainstorming in one of the FCC meeting rooms, we covered all the known factors multiple times, questioning every conclusion, and I worried about the unknowns.

"For all that we know," Manfred pointed at the updating dashboards, "the obstacles to our victory are minor."

I humphed. "I'm not yet satisfied."

Manfred and Alaston sighed. They had just spent hours illustrating all details, with the support of the latest reports, assessed the status and how the steering of all operations proceeded.

"I summoned Samuel to this meeting." I felt my son approaching in the corridor. "He will be here presently."

Manfred hummed for a second. "I guess you're about to put a proposal on the table, if I know you well." He stared at me.

I smiled. "You do know me."

Alaston dropped his jaw in the usual Moîrai perplexed—and funny—expression. "I know you, too..." he said, bemused.

The wall announced. "Fleet Admiral Amenta." I let the wall dilate. "Welcome, Samuel. Please, have a seat."

Samuel greeted everyone with a nod and glanced at the pedestal that rose from the floor and blossomed up into a seat as Samuel took his place.

"I suppose," I stared at my son, "the Fleet operations are on time as expected?" I hated to put him under the spotlight, but I had to trigger his reactions.

"Father, you know better than I. And you also know what worries me."

Manfred frowned. "Worries you? I wasn't aware of any issue...." He turned toward me. "Dan? What's going on?"

"Let Samuel continue." I nodded to my son.

"Well..." He hesitated for a moment, but then he saw in my eyes my firm support. "We are on time. New ships—and old alike—are being equipped with advanced stealth technology from the Keepers." He lowered his head at Alaston. "Our interstellar pilots' fusion with the new components is well under way. We'll be ready soon."

"So?" Manfred insisted.

"So... there's something I don't like. A gut feeling."

Manfred raised his shoulders and frowned.

"I'm afraid," Samuel went on, "we're venturing with the same cocky attitude the Moîrai had when they invaded us. They took too many things for granted. What if we're making the same mistakes, here? May I?" Samuel looked at me. I gestured for him to proceed.

He stood up and manipulated the dashboard remote relay on his belt. A series of floating panels appeared and filled up with data and diagrams.

"This is the latest information available on interstellar traffic in and out of the sectors that interest us." Samuel touched a couple of the floating diagrams. "And these are the trends that present anomalies." Two diagrams enlarged in front of him.

"Interstellar exchanges and trade have dropped by over sixty percent in the last months—"

"But this was expected..." Manfred interrupted him.

I rested my hand on his arm. "There's more, Manfred."

Samuel thanked me with a nod. "Now, look at these figures." Another trend diagram emerged. "Here are all the alarms, incidents, disappearances, and cargo losses claims from the races operating in those space sectors. Who's behind it?" He manipulated the floating screen that split into multiple diagrams per sector and per race, connected to the main one.

"Trends are not uniform, but an interpolation of all data didn't allow us to point to any single race with high enough confidence level." The ones he referred to came to the front. "There is a clear escalation of incidents in these sectors," which he highlighted, "and the growth is exponential. It appears to affect all races equally, but there are a few exceptions. But, as I said, we have failed to detect a strong correlation with just one of them." The trends and reports Samuel had highlighted showed the differences of the tendencies in each isolated case.

"How did you get this information?" Alaston interrupted.

"That's classified, Alaston," Samuel replied at once.

I raised my right eyebrow and closed my eyelids for a moment. I looked at Alaston and narrowed my eyes. "Alaston, what I'm telling you cannot leave these walls."

Manfred looked at me, alarmed.

"You inducted me into the Brotherhood of the Keepers. I learned a lot from you. Now you have sworn your allegiance to me, and that means that I consider you part of me, as Samuel is, and the Twelve in the Council are."

Alaston lowered his head and kept it in that position.

"We have a special unit," I said. Alaston raised his eyes back to me. "A genetically engineered unit."

Alaston's jaw dropped. I smiled.

"There are humans in the galaxy who do not look like humans," I said. "They have infiltrated other races for years. We made them reach medium-high ranked positions in various sectors, and we have eyes and ears in the right places."

"Moîrai, too?" Alaston managed to say with the impediment of a jaw that kept dropping.

"Not yet; not in every race, but we're working on it."

"I will be forever surprised by you, Eridu's Primum," Alaston's mind spoke. I lowered my head and looked back at Samuel.

"Alaston," he said. "You have been exposed to a confidential and privileged information that is coded A+ in the Fleet."

Alaston stared at Samuel.

He continued. "It means that revealing this information will have you prosecuted for treason and punishable with a capital sentence without trial."

I stared at Alaston. "As it was for a Moîrai who revealed the existence and personal details of the Keepers."

Alaston straightened up on his seat and his jaw tightened. I took advantage of his epiphany to introduce one important message. "As it happened in Protusa, it's the offense the entire Supreme Council of the Wisest is guilty of."

Alaston stared at me. "I understand, Eridu's Primum."

"Good, we all are aware of the consequences now," Manfred said. "Samuel, I still don't get it, though."

Samuel smiled. "Organized piracy. A large-scale operation is in place. And it's a dent in the Confederation armor."

⁂

The units assigned to the tactical squad waited while docked to Bridge Station One. The departure time for the Reconnaissance-in-Force scouting mission approached quickly. The FCC had just finished uploading all the information to the squad, and their biocomputers were processing and integrating the information to the flight plan. The most probable intercept route came out of a complex correlation of events acquired in real time.

The units would follow a multi-staged wormhole tunneling creation chain and would test the Keepers' stealth technology the humans had integrated to their vessels.

Sitting in front of the OD command dashboards, Colonel Chris Telle had supervised the operations at the Station since the day he'd relieved Anton Sage from command. He nodded, pleased at what he saw. He only needed one final green light.

"Admiral." He activated the secure channel. "Everything is in place. Space Marine units are boarding now."

"Excellent." Samuel's voice sounded excited. But he then adopted a more serious tone. "We expect a lot from this mission."

"I believe the assigned commander is a fully capable officer, sir."

"Chris." A short pause followed. "I want you to lead the operations."

"Sir?"

"Your orders are being uploaded as we speak, and you will board the flagship in fourteen time units from now."

Telle hesitated; his mind revisited all he knew about the mission.

He sighed, but he was happy, too. "I will not disappoint you, sir." He looked around to make sure no one was close enough to overhear his words. "What about the line of command at the stations?"

"A civilian official is aboard the next shuttle arriving from Eridu. He's been selected personally by Council Member Manfred Neufeld."

"Will I meet him before I leave?"

"Negative." In his mind, the Admiral's reply told him the discussion was over even before starting.

"I'll get ready then."

"Good luck, Chris."

"Thank you, sir." He closed the communication and accessed his classified files.

⁂

The spaceships undocked and drifted away from the station before starting the ion thrust at minimum impulse. From the main deck, Telle looked back at the imposing Bridge Station One. Without an external reference, and in the absence of a sensation of movement, it looked as if the Station shrank as it floated alone in space. The mission involved many unknowns, and Chris wondered whether he would return, and to what. With an effort, he took his eyes away from the station and glanced at the itinerary for their first jump. He took a deep breath and smiled.

He was happy the Fleet Admiral trusted him enough to put him in the lead, but he couldn't refrain from thinking that they didn't know as much as he would have liked to, nor what they'd face and deal with.

A team of interstellar pilots supported the human spaceships. Mentally and physiologically connected to each other, they gave proof of their enhanced capabilities during the Battle of Eridu. They'd faced hostile confrontations with success, but outcomes—in the end—are dictated not by pilots, but by blasters, antimatter weaponry, and the guts of the commander of each ship, down to the smaller fighter units.

He checked again the status of every unit and of the Space Marine squads. He had read their profiles and he was reassured somewhat, but whom would they confront?

He frowned. The mission and the task force he led received the code name of 'Hekate'; an ancient deity, she had power over heaven, earth, and sea. He didn't trust deities, especially those from extinct civilizations.

"Bridge Station One to Hekate; you're cleared to go."
"Hekate to Bridge Station One. Farewell." The navigation officer turned to look at him.

He issued the orders and the ion thrust pushed the task force at maximum speed. In the distance, the pilots created the first wormholes that billowed, and the singularity created its peculiar, yet beautiful diffractive ring.

An instant before the vessels entered the wormhole tunnels, Samuel's voice resounded on the private, encrypted line. "Farewell, Chris."

The space around them disappeared and the whole Hekate mission became an anomaly in the quantic cosmology. Telle smiled.

⁂

They reached the target space sector without incident. During the journey, at each intermediate waypoint, they'd emerged within the Keepers' cloak, in full stealth mode. They profited from the sparse traffic to test the new technology and the result had Telle grow more confident about their probability of success. *"At least up to the moment we leave stealth,"* he thought.

Once out of the cloak—once they'd become traceable, that is—it was a matter of balance of force with the rogue elements they had to assess and then, eventually, convince them to be part of Eridu's larger plans.

For days, they'd monitored the sectors for a large-enough incident to intervene, but either the 'pirates'—as they ended up calling them—had reduced their activities in the areas they controlled, or the new cloaking technology wasn't as efficient as the Keepers thought and they'd been spotted.

The biocomputers marked the first few episodes with positive signatures of pirate activity and triggered the alarms, but when they reached the area, they were too late and found only debris, shipwrecks, and the remnants of a swift battle. The wait was tedious, and the missed occasions affected morale.

Telle looked at his dashboard. *"We take too long to intervene."*

"Captain!" he called out.

A tall figure approached. "Yes, sir."

Telle turned and his gaze met a young Fleet officer who stood rigid as a pole at his side. His dossier stated he was one of the best in big data analytics the Academy had delivered in the past years. "I want you and your team to reconfigure the neural connections of the biocomputer."

"Sir?"

"We'll fail in our mission if we continue this way. It takes too long to decide whether an incident is one of the kinds we need."

The captain shifted his weight from one foot to the other, then tightened his lips. He shook his head. "I don't follow you, sir."

Telle raised his eyebrows. "I see." His voice took up a colder tone. "We're not after the most beautiful mathematical solution. We're after cunning groups. They're devious, and aren't waiting for us to show up."

The captain seemed to understand and frowned. "We risk increasing the false positives by a large factor, sir."

"If we don't do that, we risk missing every single one of our chances." He stared at him. "Just do it."

And false positives they chased, for days, until...

Insistent alarms sounded on the command bridges of all units in the Hekate task force. The incident was by far the largest of any of the false positives of the previous frustrating days. The space pilots activated the wormholes and the task force jumped in without hesitation.

They emerged under the cover of the Keepers' stealth cloak. The tactical displays showed details of a major ongoing conflict. Large transporters, flanked by their own security patrols, engaged in battle with a swarm of lighter vessels, while mid-sized ships tried to tug the transporters away from their defenders.

Telle grinned. "Pilots, ready to intercept a jump into hyperspace. Wherever they go, we go!"

The units maintained a safe distance, and they watched battle reach the expected conclusion. Despite the many losses, the pirates bested their prey and captured the cargo vessels. The rogue battleships' tractor beams pulled the cargoes into a tight formation, then the bandits created a surrounding layer with their ships.

Shaking his head, Telle watched all other supporting vessels coast away from the area. In rapid succession, powerful internal explosions made their hulls tremble and inflate. Then the vessels ripped apart in massive deflagrations that sent broken parts flying in all directions. Pirates don't take prisoners.

On the deck, he heard the navigation officer announce, "Wormhole creation detected. End point acquired. All units prepare for the tunneling." Telle nodded and his confidence in the mission success received a much-needed boost.

⁂

The rogue space ships emerged from hyperspace back into the Euclidean space, followed by the Hekate task force. Telle and the other members of the crew watched in awe at the spectacle that appeared on the 3D renderings. A dying star's nebula blossomed like a multicolored flower casting off its immense petals. The pirates sped right into the nebula, and soon, cloud-like shells of gas and dust appeared in breathtaking colors and surrounded them.

Hekate followed at a distance, and its ships' sensors and probes detected an increased level of radiation that disturbed long-range communications and forced the crew to rush to counteract the interferences. From inside the nebula, emissions affected the entire electromagnetic spectrum and varied without a detectable pattern, acting as a cosmic jumble device.

The cloak must have held, because the pirates didn't change their course within the nebula or give any sign they were aware of the presence of their followers. On the tactical screens, the human vessels kept the maximum allowed distance from the rogue vessels while still in range to trace them, even with the nebula messing up with the probes' efficiency.

Telle stood on the main deck to better admire the sight, then asked the tactical crew. "What's the response from the simulations?"

The lieutenant on duty fixed his eyes to the series of floating panels and dashboards. He gestured and played with the diagrams for a moment, then raised his eyes and turned. "The environment will affect all guided systems and weaponry, sir. I wouldn't recommend engaging the targets within the nebula."

Telle agreed. "Fine. Proceed with the pursuit."

The bandits penetrated deeper into the nebula, inside more dense and opaque layers.

"Sir?" The lieutenant nodded at some new information that filled his dashboard. "Maybe you should look at this."

Telle approached. "I'll be damned." He watched the data, mouth agape. "If this is accurate...this must be one of the most ancient stars in the universe."

The floating analytics were still correlating the information of the first brown dwarf star ever discovered, but the response left little doubt. The lieutenant expanded the view. "It's probably only a few hundred million years from becoming a black dwarf, sir." He raised his eyebrows. "But there's more."

His curiosity wasn't as attracted by the marvels of nature; not far from the brown dwarf—slightly bigger than Eridu itself—the display showed an electromagnetic disturbance. "This pattern is too regular." He didn't raise his eyes from the floating display. "It's artificial, sir."

Telle gazed at the lieutenant and frowned. "Artificial?" His eyes must have been piercing, because the young officer lowered his head and didn't reply.

"It has the mass of a small moon."

"Yes, sir."

Telle moved right behind the officer and looked over his shoulder to all other diagrams and floating panels. "Is this the pirates' destination?"

"Affirmative."

"Can we track them all the way down from here?" He bent even further. His head hovered over to the right of the subordinate's head.

The lieutenant nodded and uttered, "I believe so, sir." His shoulder dipped a bit when Chris's hand rested on it.

"I don't care what you believe in, son. Can we track them from here?"

"Yes, sir!"

Telle nodded and raised his voice. "All units stop. Maximum cloak, passive attitude." Then he squeezed the young lieutenant's shoulder. "Keep both your eyes on that thing and find exactly what it is."

"Aye, aye, sir."

In the meantime, the rogue vessels and their stolen cargo continued their route toward the structure.

The humans hid for days, observing and registering all activities. Meanwhile, Chris Telle ordered a communication probe sent a hundred million kilometres beyond the external limit of the planetary nebula to open a secure channel with Eridu.

Telle's proposed course of action required him to have the authority to conduct negotiations—per the approved arrangements—with whoever was in control. The dispatch from the Council came back agreeing with his plan.

The data collected allowed classifying the type, number of vessels, and nature of the gigantic construction. Considering its huge dimensions, the structure was scarcely inhabited; the organic life forms detected by the probes were concentrated within a minuscule area compared to the rest of the infrastructure. The complex was a huge and intricate construction that someone built and hid in the nebula for a purpose that didn't match with being just a base for pirating operations. Moreover, it was the source of the radiation and the strong electromagnetic interference.

The number and class of rogue vessels traveling through the space sector weren't enough to constitute a danger to the Hekate task force. Most of the time, small convoys escorted the captured transporters and cargo vessels—easy prey for the human battleships.

Rogues came and went with their loot, and the probes identified their prey as belonging to many different races. When they reached the 'base', they all entered the complex. After a while, the pirate units left again for further plundering, with no trace left of the cargo vessels.

The space traffic went on without stopping. Although the enemy ships were clearly equipped with a great deal of offensive systems, the pirate base didn't present the characteristics typical of a military installation. It looked dark in the feeble visible light from the brown dwarf, and most of it seemed inert.

Telle planned for the next phase and set his trap. The Hekate task force deployed accordingly within the nebula and waited for the next arrivals.

⁂

The pirate facility ingurgitated prey vessels without relent, and the structure's dimensions would have made it able to harbor the largest fleet in the universe.

They didn't have to wait too long.

The bed in Chris Telle's quarters announced the arrival of an urgent communication. He opened his eyes at the vibrations and jumped off the bed when he realized why his rest time had been interrupted. The floating panel showed the concerned face of a lieutenant in the FCC. "Sir, a sizeable target is approaching."

The wall dilated just in time for him to cross the threshold and dash into the corridor.

"Brief me." He walked at a brisk pace to reach the bridge while the officer's face on the floating screen off his belt filled him in with details.

Tactical officers crowded the floating space-sphere reproducing the area sector around Hekate's taskforce. The details on the composition of the convoy that approached the nebula arrived just in time for Telle to assess the situation.

He listened to his first officer, who described the target's composition and expounded the rules of engagement and the readiness for strategy they had planned while waiting for a sizeable target.

"Arm the mines. We go for it." He grinned.

The pirates' vessels—and their captives—cruised at a steady speed toward the nebula; the mines and the human battleships waited ready to pounce like a wild beast on its prey.

The biocomputers kept updating the confidence level for the attack and simulated all possible timelines of events after the first strike; Telle and the others watched the numbers grow with increasing anticipation.

They jolted when the mines activated, all at the same instant, and dashed to stick to the hulls of their targets. Smaller antimatter mines destroyed the external offensive systems and powerful EMP blasts, combined with an intense burst of high-energy of hadrons and isotopes, disabled the systemic components of the vessels. The first strikes killed the majority of living beings aboard.

The Space Marine transporters emerged from the hyperspace cloak and docked with the enemy vessels. The side bulkheads extended to fuse to the external hulls like octopus suckers. The implacable beating of high-energy anti-particle beams annihilated the enemy hulls; the Marines rushed inside, blasting their way in against an already weakened resistance.

The attack lasted only a few seconds and left no time to organize a meaningful reaction from the targets. In the FCC, officers of all ranks burst into cries of victory under the satisfied gaze of Telle.

He raised his eyes to one of the floating panels that displayed what he considered his top priority, and took a deep breath, of pride, satisfaction, and tension release. *"No Human Casualties"* glowed big and bright in the middle of the screen.

He snorted. "Let's see who these guys are." He signaled his second in command to keep the helm, and headed, together with the Chief Scientist, to board a waiting shuttle.

⁂

The shuttle moved into a dock with the largest of the enemy vessels, next to the Marine transporters. A squad led by a staff sergeant waited at the breached hull.

"Welcome aboard, sir." The sergeant saluted when Telle showed up.

"What do we have here?" Telle saluted back as he entered the pirate vessel.

"I guess it's better you see for yourself, sir. This way." The sergeant led Telle and the Chief Scientist deep within the ship. They traversed somber corridors, and the dark structures contrasted with the luminosity that was standard in Moîrai and human spaceships. Corpses littered the cruiser's halls and galleries—bodies of different races but wearing the same uniforms.

"Mercenaries." The sergeant snorted as he stepped over one of the dead bodies. "Many have advanced equipment, but others have much less effective *spitters*." He pointed at some of the cadavers holding old, weaker blasters no longer in production. "I'd say this organization is still gearing up, sir."

Telle nodded.

The Chief Scientist gazed around and at everything. "Where are we heading, Sarge?" Without waiting for the answer, he knelt to examine the insignia in one of the dead pirates. "Interesting."

He pointed at the back of the neck of the body. A tiny socket emerged in the space between the dual spines of the alien.

The sergeant glanced, but didn't show much curiosity. "We're not far. I think you'll find things even more interesting there."

The scientist exchanged a look with Chris.

A squad of Marines guarded a large entrance at the turn of a corridor. As Telle and his party approached, one of the Marines touched a switch and the massive metal door slid up. A breeze charged with an unpleasant smell of metal, oil, and chemicals welcomed them. "Don't worry, it's not toxic." The sergeant entered the first. Beyond the bulkhead, the group faced a huge cylindrical chamber.

The scientist looked at a device that had appeared in his hand from nowhere, as if he played a sort of a magic trick; Telle had no idea where he had hidden it until then. "It's a storage unit," the scientist said after a moment. "Multiple thousands of cells." He stared at the device's floating screen. "Organic material. Analyzing that now."

The sergeant grunted. "You don't need your device to guess that." He turned and touched a few commands on the bulkhead. Lights flooded the chamber.

"I'll be damned." Telle raised his head to follow the line of rows and rows of cells filled with a translucent liquid. Corpses of all races floated inside.

"Holy shit." The scientist looked up and stopped to look only at his device.

⁂

The bulkhead sent a tiny vibration through the sole of their boots when the shuttle docked; Telle and his first officer waited for a small delegation from Eridu. A few minutes later, the dividing wall dilated, the delegation stepped in. "Admiral." He snapped to attention. "If I had been warned of your arrival, I would have prepared for a better welcoming, sir."

Samuel smiled. "No worries. My father considers the new situation of an exceptional importance, and I didn't want you to waste precious time in preparing for a welcoming." He winked.

Telle nodded, smiled back, and led the way to the meeting. The corridor walls echoed with their brisk marching steps.

"The task force's captains are waiting for us in the briefing room," Telle said.

"Excellent. With the new reinforcements, we'll be able to face this new development. Anything else to add to your last communication?"

"No, sir, but I urge we intervene before the missing convoy is noticed."

"Your prompt action showed great judgment. This wasn't anything to mull over for too long."

The briefing room wall dilated and the first officer preceded the group into the room. "Fleet Admiral Amenta." Everyone stood at attention.

"At ease." Samuel walked to the front, followed by Telle. Floating screens blossomed and covered the back wall with the mission details.

"You're all aware," Samuel addressed the whole audience, "of the exceptional circumstances of this mission." A quick glance at Telle confirmed what he needed to say next. "You're receiving your orders on your transponders now. You've done a great job so far, and the new units in reinforcement will help toward the success of your mission." The task force leaders relaxed a bit.

"Hekate has grown and is much stronger now. We could take on a Moîrai armada if we needed to..." Some chuckles accompanied his last remark.

"We will engage the rogue organization within the hour. Use the time to get to know with your new colleagues after the briefing." Samuel nodded to Telle and their respective first officers took the lead of the briefing.

On their way to the FCC, Telle sighed. "I believe this reveals a change in the alliances. It can be a delicate situation."

"Yes, it might be dangerous, but we can turn that into an opportunity; new agreements don't have strong roots and are more easily broken." He smiled.

Chapter 18 – Live or Die

The alien structure floated in the center of the FCC space-sphere. The chosen moment for the assault matched with the opening of its main docking bay to receive the next convoy.

Lights around the bay's entrance flashed intermittently with increasing frequency; the pirate complex lowered its defensive shields. The colossal opening grew larger, ready to swallow in the next convoy whose ships' symbols had just appeared in the space-sphere, aligned in formation on a straight course toward the base.

Seconds before the convoy reached the docking area, Hekate battleships emerged from within the stealth cloak. Using their tractor beams as catapults, they flung the carcasses of the captured vessels at high speed toward the entrance.

The rogue vessels didn't react in time to the fast approaching mass of debris, and panic began. The convoy scattered to avoid the collisions and the pirates opened fire on the dead ships, but it was too late. Some of the slower captured transporters didn't clear the route in time and couldn't avoid the impact with the debris. The bullet-ships burst into the transporters that exploded and centered the docking bay like a rolling avalanche. Balls of fire engulfed the area and deflagrations shook the adjacent infrastructures. At the base, the crew attempted to close the large docking bay, but the obstructing wrecks and the incurred damages thwarted their efforts.

A second later, a swarm of fighters erupted from within the base through the opening of hundreds of smaller docks, but the rest of the Hekate ships emerged from stealth mode to repel the attack.

In the FCC, the frenzy of the battle didn't affect the efficiency of the tactical support officers. Samuel and Telle supervised the engagement of the human squads into the ensuing battle.

The success of the operation rested on clearing, right away, a path for the Marines' assault. In their transporters, the heavily equipped soldiers waited for the moment to enter into action.

A burst of distress signals from the rogue base triggered alarms in the FCC. "Are you scrambling those emissions?" Telle yelled.

"Yes, sir!" The communication lead officer dashed his hands across the dashboard. "We're correlating the signals to all possible destinations. ETA four time units, sir."

Telle smiled. "If you agree, sir" he turned toward Samuel, "I'd join the Marines' second wave."

Samuel nodded.

In space, the enemy formations broke apart when they realized they were faced with an unmatchable power and resolve. Some tried to flee, but were crushed against the net of human battlecruisers, which only had to use a small number of search-and-seek antimatter torpedoes to annihilate any hope of escape.

⁂

The first wave of Marines met with the sporadic resistance using brutal force. They'd received instruction to limit casualties at all costs by obliterating any threat from any source and origin. The Space Marines accomplished their mission with impeccable efficiency and the orders gave them carte blanche in the attack. 'Brutal and swift' best described their assault tactics. The smell of ozone covered, in part, that of the melting flesh.

The Marines gained control of the area and ejected part of the debris and wreckage from the main docking bay. The second wave landed on a cleared deck and didn't require any delicate maneuvers from their pilots to touch ground.

Telle wrinkled his nose as he stepped outside the shuttle. Much of the stench of burned organic and inorganic materials still lingered, and the smell fought against the atmospheric filtering systems. He waited for a Marine captain to approach him and salute.

"You've done a great job, Captain." He saluted back.

"Thank you, sir."

Other Marine shuttles approached to land and complete the occupation.

"What's your assessment?"

"We searched, we sought, and we destroyed, sir." He paused. "The last pocket of resistance has been isolated and confined." He grinned. "That is, once they were no longer a threat, sir."

Chris's tone lowered. "You had specific instructions not to destroy everything, Captain."

The captain grunted. "For that, sir, you'll find plenty of evidence."

He nodded.

⁂

The Marines and the engineers' squads spread through the entire complex to secure the place and achieve total control. In one of the main storage areas, leaning forward at the balustrade, Samuel couldn't see the bottom of it. A breeze ruffled his hair. "Unbelievable."

"I was shocked, too, when I saw it only an hour ago." Telle raised his eyes toward a ceiling, too far above to be visible.

"Have you established communication yet?"

"Yes, but we've not revealed who we are, nor said a word about our intentions. They can't do anything but wait for our next move."

"Good. Let's find who these pirates are."

They reached the area the Marines had turned into a prison ward.

"Shall I activate our video link, sir?" The sergeant waited with his hand on the commands.

Samuel shook his head. "No, let me see them, but activate the audio only from our side."

"Yes, sir."

The floating screen revealed the sector where the captives had been confined. Samuel distinguished three different races. At the far end of the area, a small group hid behind others.

When the prisoners saw the floating communication screen blossom open, an enraged, bulky Huitzilin came out of the ranks and advanced with his characteristic hopping gait.

"You bastards. Who are you? Moîrai? You don't know what you're dealing with." A viscous spit from his scaled mouth traversed the virtual screen and splat on the wall, drifting down and leaving a yellow trace behind.

The Marines present in the hall chuckled. "We kicked them hard," one of them muttered behind Samuel's back.

"Who are you?" the Huitzilin repeated.

Samuel's words hissed between his lips and spoke the Moîrai tongue. "We ask the questions here. What are the weak Huitzilin doing so far away from their rock? Who is babysitting you?"

"Arrghh." The enraged Huitzilin slammed the wall in powerful blows with his fists. "You will pay for this, bastard."

Telle had to turn to hide a smile. The Marines were not known to keep their scorn of the enemies a secret, and Telle ignored the fingers that stood straight from many hands.

Samuel laughed. "I guess you refer to your naïve attempts to call for help. You will die of old age before anyone arrives, and the next convoy will face the same destiny."

The alien's neck pulled his head between his shoulders.

Samuel continued. "You are accused of piracy, murder, illegal exploitation of organic resources, illegal production of neurotrophic drugs, and treason toward the Confederation. This alone would be enough to authorize my fleet to turn your homerock into a homedust!"

"So I'm right." The Huitzilin hopped toward the source of the voice in the hall. "You're indeed Moîrai!" He spat again.

Samuel smiled. "You do not have the required technology to put in place this operation, nor other races in the Confederation, for what it's worth, would dare to help you..." He paused as he noticed a movement at the far end of the hall. "Who is hiding over there?"

The Huitzilin glanced toward the back. "We're no allies with anyone." His head popped up again. "We've bought the technology dearly for our own benefit."

Samuel's voice raised and slashed like a whip. "You lie! You are a mercenary and a criminal and are running a highly profitable business, Huitzilin. I will ask it one more time. Who are you hiding there?"

The alien stared at the darkened floating screen in their cell, then turned and exchanged looks with other Huitzilin. Finally, he gestured to a nearby group. They moved, grabbed the hiding prisoners from the back of the room, and brought them to the middle. An alien with limbs as large as humans' torsos advanced and stood behind the prisoners. At a nod from the Huitzilin—that confirmed his de-facto leader's role—the alien twisted and snapped the necks of the four prisoners with astonishing ease. The bodies crumbled to the floor and jerked in spasms for a few moments. Samuel exchanged a look with Telle.

"They were just technicians we hired." The alien spat again. "We're loyal to the Confederation."

Samuel grinned. "Kritas, huh? Your loyalty will be tested, Huitzilin. And it'd better lay where I command."

⁂

Further convoy arrivals stopped after Samuel made the Huitzilin—yet unaware he dealt with humans—transmit a communication to their home planet saying that the Moîrai had seized the base, commanding their leadership to a full capitulation and summoning them to the factory complex.

The Huitzilin officials complied and announced their arrival, the exact composition of the government convoy, class, and ordnance of the escorting units, and their submission statement, sent in advance as proof of their loyalty toward the Confederation.

The Hekate tasks force battleships outnumbered the aliens as they emerged from the wormholes' hyperspace and entered the planetary nebula. The tactical systems made no effort to conceal from the incoming vessels the extent of the raw power of the ordnance that targeted them, ready to obliterate every one of their units from space.

The much larger Eridu battleships forced the alien ships to pass between them in a deep space re-enacting of the Caudine forks; as per instructions, they proceeded with shields down, inactive offensive equipment, and traveled at a minimum impulse while pinged by the offensive system of the humans' vessels.

On the FCC of the Admiral's ship, the crew monitored the arrival of the Huitzilin's highest institutional core, and the fleet was ready to release a deluge of fire at the first signal of hostile activities.

Aboard the pirate factory base, Samuel and Telle sat in the main engineering deck and followed the approach from the monitoring devices. The Marine specialists had now completed the takeover and controlled and ran all operations at the complex.

"How do you think they'll react, sir?"

"They're here because they fear the Moîrai. They'll leave exalted when they'll know they can be be part of their demise."

"And the mercenaries?"

"They understand only one thing." He snorted. *"Pecunia non olet."* Telle looked at him and nodded.

"Well..." Samuel straightened up and signaled the Marine captain. "It's time to get ready for the reception. Gear up."

⁂

The Huitzilin delegation's shuttle undocked the lead vessel and covered the short distance to the factory base.

Samuel watched the tiny vehicle and glanced at the dying brown dwarf star, indifferent to the events that unfolded under its watch. He sighed. *"The good will of many, foiled by the sins of a few."* The Moîrai would face the destiny they had created for themselves.

The shuttle approached and Samuel left the observation pod that protruded from the factory structure like a peduncle supporting an inflorescence. He joined Telle and other high ranked officers in the control room the Marines had set up for the summit.

The Huitzilin's shuttle landed on the heavily guarded docking area. When they came out, they found the area teeming with soldiers in assault gear; heavy equipment still removed the debris and ships' wrecks from the recent battle, and the ozone smell told of a violent battle.

The humans shared the same equipment as the Moîrai; to the Huitzilin's eyes, they had just surrendered to the Confederation forces.

Without answering any of the timid attempts from delegates to ask questions, the Marines escorted them to a nearby enclosed hall. Marines lined up, along the walls, shoulder-to-shoulder. Their blasters, set to maximum energy release, pulsated, menacing, and ready to deliver. A ten-metre-high catwalk ran around the hall and Marine snipers pointed their needle-accurate guns at the incoming group without the courtesy of hiding the laser beam spots. In the middle of the area, metal stools waited, and looked uncomfortable by choice. In silence, the Huitzilin leadership took their places.

From the adjacent control room, Samuel's altered voice echoed powerful in the hall. The awe-and-deceive show had started. "You are guilty of treason."

Motionless on their seats, the Huitzilin listened to the list of accusations, unsure of their fate; some clacked their double jaws in the stress. Under the threat of hundreds of blasters pointed at them, and the humiliation, fear gave place to indignation, and indignation ceded the rank to resentment until rage came out.

Their High Councilor jumped from his stool. "Enough!"

He trembled and clasped his claws, and some of his frightened peers tried to make him sit again.

"You...you Moîrai! You can kill us all now. You're already killing my people." He pushed with scorn the trembling limbs that tried to calm down his fury. Unseen, in the adjacent room, Samuel grinned.

"You starved us for generations, you kept us under your yoke for too long. I despise you. We surrender and accept all your terms, but stop vomiting your arrogance on us." He sat, trembling.

"No one understands your frustrations more than we do, Huitzilin."

The hall filled with murmurs at the unexpected reaction to his show of anger. The prisoners glanced at each other, unsure of the meaning of those words.

The Marines raised their visors and guttural sounds of bewilderment came from the alien delegation. The wall dilated. Samuel, Telle, and other officers entered the hall.

⁂

On the observation pod, above the engineering deck, Samuel and the Huitzilin's High Councilor looked out at the nebula and its colors.

"The Kritas were right to fear the humans; the Moîrai tried to tame the beast, but didn't succeed." He looked at the human and squinted with his piercing red eyes. "We had no choice."

"Everyone has one; the choice to live or the choice to die." Samuel shook his head. "We've been abused, and others were ready to do worse. Besides, your agreement with the Kritas..."

"No agreement. Just a transfer of technology, and we paid them a hefty price."

"Kritas mustn't suspect anything has changed yet. When the time comes, we'll deal with them, too."

The alien grunted. "I hope the humans will show us the respect the Moîrai always denied us. Keep all your promises and the Huitzilin will walk at your side and recognize Eridu's leadership." He saw the human nod. "What shall we do with the factory?"

Samuel smiled. "Restart the production, but under the new terms; you'll sell the formula we gave you." He paused. "The Huitzilin will share our success."

The alien grinned. "As the son of Eridu's Primum desires." He turned to face him, and his two large limbs took Samuel's hands, enveloping them.

⁂

The added factors of the support from the Huitzilin's organization and their net of mercenaries changed the simulations data. In the FCC, Samuel noted with satisfaction that the confidence level grew the more biocomputers kept analyzing. "Secure the space sectors and prepare for the Fleet arrival."

"Consider it done," Telle said.

The space-sphere computed all possible scenarios; in every one, if the 'backdoor' remained closed, the human Fleet had the advantage. Both men looked at the tactical officers floating within the sphere, working without a pause to fine-tune all parametres. With his staff officers, Samuel had laid out the plans. "Chris, Hekate will be our bridgehead."

Telle nodded. "It's so ambitious, I bet no one can see it coming. How will the Keepers react?"

"Father believes Alaston will pose no objections. After all, the Keepers will be reinstated, and that's all that counts for them. For the Huitzilin, it's their only chance to aspire to a more prominent role in the galaxy."

"All right, then." They both nodded at the result of another completed simulation whose details and variables added to the growing biocomputer understanding of the war to come. Then, another simulation started anew.

"I need to go back to Eridu now, and I've nothing more to instruct you with. For the Third Loss, Chris."

"For the Third Loss, Admiral."

Chapter 19 – Council, Council Off-the-Wall

The flagship emerged from hyperspace and received the welcoming of a breathtaking view of Eridu in space—the cradle, the new hope, and the only reason to fight. The whole planet devoted its resources to rebuild the new Fleet, to seed a new future for the race of men, and to honor those who gave their life for it.

Samuel watched the descent from the main deck. As Hope once predicted, humans were now whole and were getting ready to secure their future. *"Hope, can you see us now?"*

Countless battleships constellated the space above Eridu, and more were being built in orbit. Many flashed their salute to the Admiral's vessel during its approach.

The darkness of outer space turned first into a dark blue, and then the miracle accomplished by the laws of nature gave birth to a radiant sunny sky.

Below, the Mediterranean Sea gleamed during the final descent, and Nova Roma's piercing towers became visible. Would humans write the final chapters of the Moîrai's rule?

Samuel hoped to be able to give that question an answer soon, and he could think only of one that would fit and be worth to live for.

The ship touched ground next to the Phoenix adorning the main tarmac of the spaceport. A shuttle with the Council insignia waited for him.

"Good morning, sir." The attendant saluted as he stepped out. "Eridu's Primum is waiting for you in the Council Tower."

He nodded. "Then let's make his wait as short as possible, shall we?"

The shuttle lifted above the ground, turned, and sped toward Nova Roma.

⁂

The wall dilated; I turned and smiled. Samuel entered. "Father."

I walked around the large round table to greet him. "I wanted to see you before the others." My hands held his for a moment. "Your news has been such a boost to everyone's commitment, and an unexpected lucky twist." I snorted. "Imagine! A neurotrophic drug factory hidden inside a dying star's nebula."

"The resentment against the Moîrai is high, Father. Of course, the Kritas always manage to exploit the sentiment to their advantage."

I put my arm around his shoulders as we walked to the large bay window. The spaceship traffic had increased since his departure, and I noticed my son's admiring look. I waved my hand at the scene. "We are ready, Samuel. This time, we are ready."

He turned toward me with a serious expression on his face. "Do you ever think of Mom and the others?"

I frowned.

"Hope came to my mind today. I don't know why."

I sighed. "Maybe it's her way to tell you she's beside you. You were always close."

"Is it for them we're doing all this?" He rested his right hand against the transparent wall. Before I could say anything, he grabbed my arm. "Don't worry, I'm not faltering."

"I never doubted it. And yes, I think of your mother, of your sisters, and of everyone else. All the time. You're the only one who can feel what I feel; and now, also, Joshua... But it's not the time to look backward, son. We need to plan for the future to give a meaning to our past."

The wall announced the arrival of the members of the Council. We faced the entrance and I let the wall dilate.

After the members finished their reports and Samuel answered all questions on the pirate organization and the Huitzilin, I raised one remaining issue to be addressed, and I felt again a cold grip tightening around my heart.

"We Selected do remember. You've chosen me as Eridu's Primum, as I chose you before to establish the Council." The Twelve lowered their heads, and I nodded at Manfred; he knew what came next.

"When we'll have accomplished our mission, there will be questions and there will be doubts. The Confederation will no longer exist, and the Alliance will have to cease, too." I paused. "When Eridu was our planet, the Earth, democracies were corrupted. Sycophants crowded the courts and everyone rushed for a share of glory and wealth, but no one ever took responsibility. When failure and corruption reigned, no one ever took the blame." All members stared at me, severe and solemn.

"As Eridu's Primum," I continued, "I have to accept full responsibility for everything and from everywhere it will come. There will be no place for servile self-seekers." I stood up. "But there will be shared accountability. You elected Eridu to be led by one, but the whole Eridu will lead them all."

Manfred rose and crossed his arms on his chest, his right on his heart. "For Eridu's Primum," he yelled, "and for the Third Loss."

My son stood up and did the same; one by one, all members rose. In that moment, I felt my daughter vindicated and her last desire accomplished. I had a family once, and a much larger one now. I felt each of those six billions ghosts, who crowded behind me, shout, "For the Loss, for the Loss, for the Loss." I swore their cries would receive an answer.

⁂

Hekate reached its destination, Xrusé. Covered by the Keepers' cloak, they lurked in space, close to the planet. The Huitzilin occupied the rear space sectors and fulfilled their role; the ships, convoys, and cargos entering and leaving the Moîrai space became their new prey.

After the first unexplained disappearances, the tension mounted among the Moîrai and in their Supreme Council. Those incidents, in space sectors directly under their control, were not to be tolerated for too long.

As planned, with the next convoy capture, Hekate allowed a distress signal to sneak through the scrambling filters. Soon after, a patrol left Xrusé—a small squad of ten cruisers and about fifty fighters set route toward the coordinates the intercepted communication originated from.

Chris Telle set the trap together with the Huitzilin. "Let them chase your units into quadrant twelve–twenty-two–sixteen." The battleships waited there for their prey.

In the FCC, the space-sphere rendered the chase as it happened. "The Moîrai have confirmed with Protusa they've detected unfriendly units, sir."

Telle kept staring at the space-sphere. The data from the engagement arrived en masse and showed the offensive systems of the Moîrai ships acquiring their fleeing targets. The biocomputers digested and learned.

"I admit it, the Huitzilin are brave," the first officer commented.

Telle glanced at him. "You overcome your fears when your hate takes the lead."

In space, the Huitzilin ships twisted and jerked to avoid a full hit on their stern defenses. The blasters lit up the shields at each hit. The Huitzilin couldn't play that game much longer.

"Send squads one, two, and three to intercept."

"ETA in four time units, sir."

"Assuming the Huitzilin last that long," Telle thought. "Warn we'll cover them with our cloak field as they enter the quadrant. Activate seeker-torpedoes and keep the encrypted channel open with the intercepting squads."

"Yes, sir."

While in the Keepers' stealth field, the intercepting cruisers moved within range and acquired the targets. The Moîrai dashed to attack the 'pirates'.

"One time unit, sir."

"Set the Huitzilin on a steady course. Now!"

Aboard the Moîrai ships, the maneuver was unexpected, but no one spent time to analyze the quirkiness. "All targets acquired." On the flagship deck, their commander quivered with the anticipation of a quick and easy victory. "Fire!" but the Huitzilin disappeared from the Moîrai's tactical displays.

At the same time, fifty huge battleships emerged from the cloaking field, and their shields absorbed with ease the blaster hits.

The Moîrai ship's tactical screens showed a swarm of seekers torpedoes plunging into them from the rear and the front.

"Torpedoes!" the shout resounded on the deck. They scrambled in all directions as a panicking flock of birds while—at the same time—the intercepting human squads emerged from the stealth cloack and fired their blasters. The battleships reached the range of their tractor beams, and trapped the enemy ships.

The Moîrai commander's jaw dropped and ordered the first officer, "Signal our surrender."

The officer gave him a blank stare and his words killed all hopes. "Sir, we lost all communication links!"

The officers watched the shields grew weaker and weaker under the onslaught of blasts as the internal structures groaned and twisted until the torpedoes reached their vulnerable targets. Matter and antimatter met, and death came with a massive burst of light.

The humans' FCC space-spheres reported the casualties and captured additional important data from the battle.

⁂

In Protusa, the last communication from their small task force acknowledged establishing contact with an outnumbered bandit group of inferior ship classes. Then, the squad vanished without leaving a trace.

"How is that possible?" The question, shouted with rage, echoed between the ancient walls of the Supreme Council of the Wisest. They probed the mind of the bewildered and recently appointed Moîrai Fleet Commander. "Our disappointment in you is growing, Ekahau."

"We cannot say." Cit Ekahau Tum lowered his head and opened his palms.

The One—who had seized control of the entire Council—captured Ekahau's mind as a feral cat would grip a prey in its fangs. He trembled.

"Which means you act without acquiring full knowledge, first!" He tightened his grip.

"No!" Ekahau's knees bent before he managed to straighten up again. "There are elements that are beyond the knowledge I can achieve."

"Is that so?" The grip tortured him. "And what do you suggest, then, to repair the damage you cause us?" The last word hissed the same venom that blemished The One's soul.

"Uhh." Sweat pearls glittered his temples, but he resisted the temptation to swipe them dry. "There can only be one answer; the same one we have faced for eons—Kritas!"

"Ah, Kritas, our improbable allies. The ones you believed to have melded into our larger plans."

"Yes. The ones *I* have brought in!"

The pride's somersault didn't buy him much. *"You shall fix this!"* The raging Wisest snapped his mind and a blinding pain made him fall to his knees.

"Go to the Kritas! Take with you whatever forces your limited knowledge suggests to you and mend that which your ineptitude has caused." He scorned him. "And make sure to have sane pilots onboard."

The Council members left Ekahau shaking on the old stone floor. No one dared to look at him as they followed The One.

⁂

The probes intercepted troublesome signals coming from the planet. Xrusé was in turmoil, and the number of encrypted messages had risen to unprecedented levels.

"Sir?" the first officer called. Telle raised his gaze. "You better have a look at this. Something major's happening in Xrusé."

The knowledge-puzzle still missed many tiles, but the main picture was clear.

"The Supreme Council is sending military-grade ciphered comms all over the planet," the first officer said, "and troops are moving in to space ports. Sir, it seems like a large-scale mobilization is taking place."

He nodded. "Get me the Fleet Admiral. I'll take the link in my quarters."

"Sir? Kritas are mentioned a few times."

Telle left the FCC.

In the briefing room, Telle spoke to Samuel's eidolon. "No, Admiral, there's no trace of any reference to Eridu or us humans."

At first, Samuel didn't reply. Telle noted the unusual hesitation. "Sir, if I may... I think this opens up an opportunity for us."

"I know what you're implying, but we have to keep into account the treacherous nature of the Kritas." Samuel blinked.

"It might play to our advantage, sir; nothing hurts more than a reliable enemy when you crumble."

He nodded. "We need to be sure. Spare some scouts, send them to the Kritas' system...and stay hidden. Prepare the mission. Whatever we discover, we're ready. I'll join you for the last details."

"Aye, aye, sir." Telle saw Samuel reach for the transcom bulb; the image froze, then faded.

The mission involved a high risk. FCC simulation responses estimated a fourteen percent failure for the minimum acceptable scope. Risks were at the lowest if only the fastest and the smallest units in the Hekate task force were assigned to the mission. For some officers, the estimates came hard to manage and accept. "It's a suicide mission," they exclaimed.

The best composition for all scenarios troubled the officers—a small number of one-man fighters with the support of an interstellar pilots' unit and nothing else. We had to find a way to involve the Kritas in the events, not appear as a threat, and insinuate in them a sense of opportunity. The biocomputers insisted that assigning the most vulnerable vessels to the most delicate mission for the war ahead was the only way to lower the risks of a failure. Telle didn't like it much, as he had to ask for volunteers, but he had to admit it made sense.

The latest data on the Moîrai mobilization created the background for all possible scenarios the scouting squad would face. The destination, the Kritas' Alliance and their homeworld, added unknowns to the complexity of the mission.

That day, Samuel faced the scouting group who had just received their orders in the briefing room. "I don't have to remind you how crucial your mission is and how grateful we all are." The officers glanced at each other and smiled at the Admiral's words.

"Your primary task is to get the most detailed intel you can on the Moîrai expedition, discover the terms of their relationship with the Kritas, and collect hints of its possible development."

The officers nodded and took notes on their own mission logs floating in front of them, linked back to the Fleet AI.

"That's the easy part," Telle added, provoking chuckles among his companions. His faced turned serious. "We need that intel at all costs." Samuel nodded and let those last words sink in. "Dismissed... And good luck, gentlemen."

From the observation deck, Telle watched the small group of fighters and the pilots' unit leave the vessel to set course toward Protusa. They disappeared as soon as they activated stealth mode. He took a deep breath. *"Good luck."*

⁂

In Xrusé, troopers boarded the last transporters. Protusa watched with pride as the fleet left. From the Supreme Council tower, alone on the highest terrace, The One grinned.

The imposing Moîrai fleet assembled in space. Aboard the lead vessel, in deep thought, Ekahau supervised the operations.

It wasn't as he had planned, it wasn't what he worked hard for, and he only had the Kritas to thank. *"They will pay for this,"* he thought. *He* took them to Eridu, *he* made them experiment on the humans until they managed to control their primitive minds, and the Kritas inepts screwed up everything and failed him.

"The Keepers!" He couldn't hide his disdain for them and hissed a raucous whiff. He regretted he'd missed the opportunity to deal with those zealots who roamed freely and arrogant and disrupted everything in Xrusé. He longed for the day when he would make them all pay for their haughtiness. Many were still unaccounted for; they were a major concern and an unneeded distraction. *"The Wisest,"* he snorted, "*the fools!"* They hesitated and let the Keepers escape. *"I will deal with them on my return."* He laughed in rapid coughing sounds. "And they call themselves The Wisest."

"Sir?"

He realized he had voiced his thoughts out loud. "Nothing. Honoring the Wisest, as we all should. Focus on your tasks and set the course for the Alliance space sectors."

"Yes, sir." The Moîrai officer lowered his head.

The ships created the wormholes to prepare for the jump into hyperspace; in the cover of the stealth cloak, the human pilots felt the disturbance and planned for the same journey.

⁂

Despite Alaston's reluctance, Mênis and a small group of Keepers decided to stay and fight in Xrusé.

Night was safer. In the deepest guts of Protusa was safer. Everywhere but on the surface was safer for the remaining Keepers, and for Mênis.

He could have left with Alaston, but escaping had never been for him. Besides, he understood the need for the Brethren to rescue the largest possible number of the Keepers' fleet vessels and leave Xrusé, but not everyone made it in time to the base.

They regrouped wherever possible, reinvented their organization, and battled for months to keep fighting the Supreme Council. They nagged, harassed, and sabotaged—however they could—the coup d'état perpetrated by the Wisest. Maybe they were just an irritation—a nuisance, at best—but the Keepers devoted all efforts to exasperate the traitors.

The Supreme Council members gave the order to extract vital information from the Keepers held in custody using any means; they didn't hesitate to condone brutal force and torture, mental and physical.

The ones still free—roaming from hideout to hideout—watched and protected all their remaining vulnerable resources, the ones the Council hadn't managed to find yet, the ones that were left untouched in the short warning before everything changed, when the impossible happened, when the Wisest struck.

"In the worst case, you will make me wait for your return for too long, and I will get bored," he told Alaston.

He remembered the Brethren's sad expression when he heard him say those words.

"We will be back. This I promise you, Mênis. The Keepers will be back."

"You better be."

In the darkness, Mênis couldn't stop a smile surging to his lips, but skilometres were inappropriate in those moments, as Moîrai would die. *"Either them or us."* He turned around for a last check; the Keepers were ready.

The leaked news reported an imminent guards break-in at a valuable target, two compounds concealed under a warehouse in a larger industrial complex, a laboratory and a safe residence. Both were crucial assets for the Keepers active in the area.

The complex provided the perfect hiding place under the hunter's nose. The warehouse stored detection devices and probes in use by the Supreme Council Guards, or SCG, units. Administrative personnel occupied the upper level of the premises during the day. If the SCG had discovered the location, it only meant one thing: one more Keeper had been broken by torture.

Protusa was quiet that night. The mobilization of the recent weeks gave the Keepers a pause, but now the hunt ran wild again. Mênis rolled his neck. They waited.

In complete silence, and using passive remote sensors as guidance, the guards' vehicles approached.

The perimeter security announced the arrival. "Council's Guards access request." Hiding, Mênis and the others exchanged a brief look. The automated system acknowledged. "Granted."

The shields lowered and the main entrance to the complex dilated. Vehicles landed on the large esplanade and ground troops took position.

Nothing happened for a few moments while the guards performed a passive scan of the various buildings. The Keepers' scramblers recreated the probes' signals to send back evidence of an empty compound.

"We need someone alive," he whispered in the minds of all Keepers. He waited for a few moments before adding, *"at least for some time."* The mental agreement from the Keepers arrived at once.

Outside, the guards muffled sharp orders and initiated deployment. The Keepers followed the operation as it unfolded on the small rendering panels floating above their blasters. The best targets pulsated among the others, different for each Keeper.

It was a search–and–destroy operation, judging from the equipment the guards brought with them: anti-personnel seeker-mines with bio-detection and penetration cluster ordnance.

"This is going to be bloody." Mênis worried for the safety of his group. *"Forget what I said before. We can't add the risk to take prisoners."*

The guards searched each building in turn, and soon the warehouse would be the next one under scrutiny. For sure, they would find the secret entrance to the underground facilities. On a nearby building, the guards sent probes in and seeker-mines before breaking in for a more in-depth search. As they got out, they yelled. "Cleared!"

"What do we do?" He heard the question in his mind. *"What are our chances of fooling those mines?"* he asked.

"We can fool them, and any bio-detection probe, but we won't escape their manned search," a Keeper replied.

Mênis had learned a lot from them in the past months, and if a Keeper said so, he had all reasons to believe him. *"Okay, then,"* he said to all minds. *"We will let them analyze the building with the probes and grow their confidence that it's clear in here. Then, once they get in, we need to ensure no one gets out."*

Someone shifted his weight in the dark and changed position. *"What about the others, the ones outside?"*

"I guess we need to trick everyone in."

The silence that followed was charged with doubts. The Keepers spread out through the warehouse and got ready for the welcoming reception. A clicking noise announced the entry of the mines. Timid at first, the swarm rolled inside and paused as the AI decided where to send each individual device. Then, the mines dashed in all directions with a hissing noise as if they tore the air at their passage.

As they proceeded, they sent back to the guards outside a detailed representation of the warehouse interior. The Keepers waited for the sweep to conclude. After a few long minutes, the mines retreated back in order.

Through the dilated entrance, the first guards stepped in with blasters ready to shoot. Behind them, engineers' squads followed, equipped with neutron-spallation devices. The engineers probed every surface and corner of the warehouse with intense pulses of high-energy proton beams and measured the neutrons driven away from the nuclei.

They would obtain a detailed neutron spectroscopy of the complex, and no spoofing technology could have hid the underground Keepers' facilities.

"Here comes the problem. They will find the entrance."

Mênis smiled. *"This changes the balance, though. Those engineers are not a personal threat. We need to split and take care of those outside, too."*

The guards had to be dealt with the first, swiftly and without mercy. The ones outside the compound as well, but that would have required a different, tougher mission.

The Keepers knew of the implications and why Mênis refrained from giving orders that were more specific. *"I will go,"* one of them said. *"But I need at least five with me."* Volunteers risked their lives once in the open. Five stepped forward without hesitation.

"Okay. Warn us when you are in position. We will attack at the same time." The group of six headed deeper in the warehouse, toward a disguised exit. Meanwhile, the engineers kept advancing and probing, protected by a shield of heavily armed Moîrai guards.

Time was essential, as the surprise factor would have been lost if the engineers found the hidden cavity before the joint assault could start.

The six checked the surroundings on their security screens, then they left the hideout. The solid metal columns that provided the building with buttresses became fluid for a moment as six Moîrais in strange uniforms emerged in the esplanade.

"The SCG are two hundred units that way." The leader expressed in words what each of their floating screens revealed. "Activate the bio-scramblers."

Brushing the building perimeter with their shoulders, they reached a point where no more physical obstacles provided them with a screen against the only detection devices they could not fool—ears and eyes.

"They are too many."

"I know," the lead said. "It will be an all-out strife. We will not survive the fight."

The Keepers glanced at each other and nodded.

"Okay, then. Select your targets. I will warn Mênis we are ready."

Inside the warehouse, time passed, and each elapsed unit brought more tension.

The guards stood now in front of the concealed main entrance to the covert compounds. The Keepers behind the secret entry wall, and the others scattered in the warehouse, knew time was running out. *"Any communication from the others?"* the question resonated in all minds.

"I am afraid not." Mênis replied for everyone. Then he addressed the ones next to him, in the corridor. Only the wall separated them from the SCG personnel. "I hope they are not in trouble out there."

"Get ready. Engineers approach." They aimed their blasters at the wall.

The first engineer prepared his proton beam, the receptacle of the particle detector, and examined the wall.

"It is all clear so far. We process this last side then we can move on to the remaining buildings."

"There is no rush. Just do your job and we will do ours." The guard smiled and jerked up his blaster in his direction.

The engineer nodded. "Nothing anomalous here." He kept moving the beam along the wall and check the results. "Wait a moment..." The guards stiffened, the engineer grinned. "Umm, false alarm." He smiled and looked sideways at the guards, who shook their heads.

"Too many and too close," Mênis said, "and the wall dilates too slowly for an all-out attack."

"There's an alternative, but we can say good-bye to our compound." The Keeper next to him harbored unfounded hopes.

"It is lost anyway." Mênis twisted his neck to look at him. "So?"

The Keeper lowered his head. He sighed. "The wall can blow up outward."

"That will do it. What do we have to do?"

"Nothing, I will tell the wall."

Mênis rested his right hand on the Keeper's shoulder. "Do that." The Keeper nodded.

"They will all gather right in front once they discover it." Mênis stared at the entrance.

Outside, the six set their blasters to pulse-explosive jolts and maximum energy. They would have depleted their guns in a short time at that rate, but they didn't expect to remain alive to fight for a long time.

In the esplanade, crews watched the SCG vehicles and talked casually. In small groups, guards equipped with assault vests and pads created the backbone of the enemy threat.

The six needed to avoid immediate casualties and create an initial diversion. From their cover, they took aim at the group of vehicles, ready to fire. The soil trembled and an explosion lit up the warehouse.

The guards yelled and dashed toward the building. From inside the warehouse, screams and blaster screeches and flashes tore the night and sent long shadows on the tarmac.

The lead Keeper's eyes dilated and his jaw dropped, but he regained control. "Now!" he yelled. White pulses of energy reached six of the landed vehicles. The hulls trembled on impact, then huge fireballs erupted and the ships broke apart, sending burning debris in all directions and damaging the nearby vessels.

The explosions made the guards who were still running in the esplanade cower, and sent them flat-bellied when the blasts' shockwaves reached them.

The Keepers dashed into the open toward the burning wrecks and fired with their blasters against all that moved.

The flames and blaster hits fought against the night's darkness. The Supreme Council Guards in the esplanade recovered and opened fire around as they ran for cover toward a nearby building, searching for the assailants. The Keepers fought back with a simple first goal—staying alive.

In the reigning confusion, they reached the remaining vehicles and disposed of the stunned enemy crews.

The Keepers assessed the situation and glanced at each other. "We are cornered!"

The guards pounded their position with precision hits. "If one of these blows up..." The lead pointed at the ship but didn't need to finish the phrase. "We need to reach the building!"

Another explosion shook the warehouse. "Set the mines!" he ordered.

The Keepers tossed them inside the nearby vehicles. "Run, run, run!"

⁂

Inside the warehouse, the engineers confronted the anomalous reading on their neutron spectrometres. "There is no doubt. This wall hides a cavity, and it is not on the blueprin—" The main wall burst into a powerful directed explosion that maimed and slaughtered the nearby guards and engineers.

Mênis and the other Keepers dashed out, blasting away at everything that still moved and in the direction of the markers in the blasters' targeting screens. The red dots blipped out at each casualty. The guards still alive responded with their own fire.

The air filled with fumes from melting metals and flesh where blasters hit. Maimed Moîrai lay contorted on the ground and shredded parts of bodies adorned the walls and the containers nearest to the explosion.

The Keepers took cover as more blaster spurts fused the first pillars that supported the vaulted roof. The screeches of the energy bursts and the liquefying matter covered and muted the last laments of the wounded.

The roar of a multitude of blasts came rolling through the entrance and shook the entire structure. For a few moments, gushes of colored lights painted the warehouse interior with billowing red and yellow bursts.

The Keepers knew what they were from; the guards didn't and hesitated for a too-long moment; fright blocked their reactions and it was just what the Keepers needed. They felt the fear exuding from the Council Guards as a signal and assaulted their positions en masse. A container ruptured under the heavy blaster hits. "Take cover!" Mênis cried, but it was too late; he heard the bang and saw the flash, then everything happened as if he wasn't there and it wasn't his body flying across the room, crushing through a wooden panel and landing like a ragdoll on the floor.

He heard the screams of many Moîrai and felt Keepers die, while others survived; his head spun and he couldn't stop the powerful wails blaring in his ears.

"Mênis, Mênis!" He thought he knew the meaning of that sound. Someone was shaking him. He opened his eyes.

"We need to go. Now!" The face of a Keeper emerged from the dark cloud his senses had been lost into. The Keeper was covered in blood, and Mênis tried to understand why the Keeper seemed to be in such a hurry. Then he remembered.

"What happened?"

"A container exploded. Guards are all dead or in too bad shape to do anything. We lost many of the Brothers, too." He helped him to his feet. A few other pairs of eyes looked at him. The trembling lights of the flames hurt him.

"Don't leave any Keeper behind." He regained his senses. "Let's go!" He limped toward the exit and into an even worse scene. Like torches, the Council Guards' vehicles burned into the night and bodies littered the square.

"They are all dead," a voice said behind him. He turned and saw a Keeper activate the remote of their transporter hidden in stealth mode. The vehicle landed and the entry bay dilated.

They recovered the Brothers' bodies and planted the Keepers' entwined sign before leaving.

The transporter entered stealth mode and drifted away; a swarm of Supreme Council Guards and security unit symbols appeared on the tactical screen, converging on the scene of carnage.

"Do it now," Mênis said. The pilot entered a sequence of commands on the dashboard. Back at the industrial complex, the guts of the warehouse shivered as a set of deflagrations torn them apart. The structure collapsed with a rumbling growl and a hungry mushroom of dust rose high above the debris, but they couldn't hear it nor see the expanding cloud as they sped away to safety.

Chapter 20 – The Night Fall

Eridu's most formidable war effort materialized in space at a safe distance from Xrusé to avoid any Moîrai detection of the space-time ripples the human Fleet caused.

In the distance, a planetary nebula blossomed with its dwarf star safely tucked within, an improbable destination and an unforeseen and favorable twist for the humans in the intricacies of every possible multiple timelines. From the main deck, Samuel wondered what kind of mysteries hid in that part of the galaxy.

The vessels—as a precaution—sent out probes to set up a passive remote detection network, and the information filled the space-sphere in the FCC.

"Link with Hekate established, sir."

He nodded to the communications' officer and smiled when Chris Telle appeared on deck.

"Good to see you, Admiral." The colonel saluted first and lowered his head.

"Chris, I bring my father's greetings and his congratulations add to mine for a job well done."

He smiled. "Thank you, sir, but it's premature. There's a lot to do still."

"Don't shy away from your merits. How's the scouting?"

"We've recovered their first buoy; we're analyzing the data as we speak. We'll soon have details on the Moîrai fleet's composition. And the scouts confirmed their final destination; the Moîrai are reaching out to the Kritas."

"So the treason that started in Eridu continues today."

"We could say that, sir."

"Chris, you need to help the Keepers with the resistance on Xrusé. They need to know we're coming." He waited for a moment to let the colonel understand the full complexity of his new mission. "Ohtlinell will lead the expedition from their side, and we need to have our Space Marines on the ground too."

"Sir?"

"I know it's risky, but we can't win with the Fleet alone."

He frowned, unsure of what the Admiral meant.

"The Keepers are on their way; we'll stay in the nebula for the time being. Your brief is underway."

"Aye, aye, sir."

Samuel closed the link.

On the lead battleship's bridge, Telle saw the Admiral's eidolon freeze and fade. He sighed.

"Get me the Marine commanders to the briefing room in five time units." His serious gaze left no doubt to the petty officer that they were preparing for something big.

"Right away, sir."

The Keepers' flotilla announced its arrival to the Hekate task force. Their leaders sent the composition of the convoy and the waypoints to their route while in stealth mode. Telle surveyed their approach on the space sphere.

The Space Marines Commander in Chief, Amy Norton, looked at him. "Are they really on our side?" She graduated first from all her classes, and her mind was able to simplify complex strategic and tactical problems to those simple elements able to turn anything to her advantage on the battlefield. Her green eyes pierced Chris' and told him she didn't expect half-term replies.

"Yes, they are," he said as he watched the flotilla maneuvers.

"We'll trust no one on the ground, sir."

Telle turned and stared at her haircut of a combatant before capturing her gaze. The Marine's stern expression told him about the risks implicit in those words. "And yet you will have to if you want to survive in Protusa."

Amy snorted. "Who guarantees they'll not betray us again?"

"Eridu's Primum, for one. Besides, the Keepers have always kept their word."

"Keepers, Moîrai—they're the same race." She stressed the last syllable.

Telle looked straight at her, then enunciated his words. "You will make this mission a success, Norton."

She raised her right hand. "We will, sir, but if they attempt anything to hurt this mission, there will be more Moîrai corpses on the ground. Keepers or not Keepers."

From the bridge, a voice announced the convoy had joined the Hekate task force. On the space-sphere, the Keepers' ships closed in, still within the stealth cloud. "Keepers request permission to send a delegation, sir."

"Granted," Telle said, staring again at the Marine. "Let's have a good first meeting with them."

The shuttle docked, while in the Command and Control Room Chris Telle, Amy Norton, and the Marine squad leaders revised the mission details and its main objectives—Protusa and the Supreme Council.

The wall announced the visitors and Telle let it dilate. One Moîrai led the group and advanced without hesitation toward the centerpiece of the room, the interactive mission tactical simulator. Norton gestured and the various rendering and details shrank and vanished.

"I am Ohtlinell," the Keeper said.

"I'm Colonel Chris Telle, commander of the Hekate task force."

"I recognize you." The Keeper's black eyes locked on him.

"Excuse me?"

"Your image in Samuel's memory."

A loud groan made them both turn. Amy's eyes narrowed to a thin slit. "You've scanned the Admiral's mind?"

"With his consent, of course."

"Of course." She rolled her eyes. "Well, know this now." She stepped forward. "You won't have *my* consent. Ever."

The Keeper bent his head.

Chris gave her an oblique look. "Good. Now that the rules of the game are laid out, we won't allow anything to interfere with the success of this mission."

"Of course." Ohtlinell smiled at Amy.

She fixed her eyes on an imaginary point beyond the Keepers. "Yes, sir."

"Ohtlinell, I know you have information to share. Will you?" Telle showed the tactical simulator. With a sigh, Norton resumed the session and the panels blossomed up again.

"We do, indeed." The Moîrai showed a crystal in his hand. A receptacle opened in the simulator and the crystal fit into it. The biocomputers learned details about the planetarian defenses and around Protusa, and the complete mapping of the Supreme Council. Details only the Keepers knew.

⁂

The day after, Telle had everything ready for Samuel in time for the briefing with Eridu's Council. Together with Norton, they waited in the main briefing room for the links to establish.

A pedestal rose from the floor and its bulb blossomed. Half of the room turned into the image of a hemicycle portion of the Council. As expected, the entire Council honored the appointment. Samuel's connection went live and he appeared, standing on the bridge of the flagship. The briefing started.

After the operational main lines received the unanimous approval, Eridu's Primum rose from his seat. "This is the first step of the new humankind, and it is momentous that a hundred years after the Moîrai's descent into Eridu..." Dan hesitated. "...Earth, we are led to start a new era with our descent into Xrusé." He paused and his cold stare paused on everyone. "If need be, our descent will bring the same destiny to the race of that planet."

Amy grinned and turned to glance at Chris, who stared at the floor. She looked in turn at Samuel, but couldn't decipher anything from the Admiral's expression or from the Council members'.

"If need be," Dan continued, "every non-human in Xrusé will be considered an enemy and a threat."

Amy sighed. "Every single one, sir?"

Dan stared at Amy's determined green eyes and his mind went back to someone he had lost decades before—Laura. Now her diamond, too, rested on a memorial boulder in Civita. He chased the imaged before replying. "I'm sure the Marines will show no hesitation on the battlefield."

She smiled. "If need be, sir."

After the briefing, Telle waited in his quarters for a private communication with Samuel, but for some reason, it took longer than expected. He asked the Communications Department many times for an explanation, but the answer was always the same: "We're in standby, sir."

A whisper made him jolt from his desk. He never realized the stem took such a long time to rise from the floor before it started to render the visual.

"Admiral!"

Samuel sat at his dashboard station in the bridge. "Chris, I couldn't get to your call sooner."

"If I may, sir." He stood up. "What the heck is going on?"

He sighed. "We are in a need-to-know situation, Chris. You're not in the need."

"The hell I'm not in the need!"

"Colonel!" The word slashed in the air like a whip.

He mumbled, "Apologies, sir. But I respectfully disagree."

Samuel stood up and stepped closer to the rendering. The two men looked as if they stood right in front of each other; and to their own senses, they were.

"Hekate will not intervene in Protusa. But you know that. So what's the problem here?"

Chris shifted his weight from one foot to the other. "Amy Norton seemed to expect that declaration; I felt sidestepped."

"You're not, Chris. Hekate's role is to watch our back. If need be, your task force will consider any vessel approaching the star system as hostile. And that's the risk our scouts need to evaluate."

"Indeed, sir. But what about the Keepers?"

"We need to be prepared for all possible scenarios. I hope for their sakes they'll not decide to put themselves in the line of fire of the Space Marines."

⁂

The docking bays in the battleships showed the same spectacle; the engineers loaded up the Marine squads' gear and equipment in the deep landing devices, and small stealth transporter units swallowed and packed Space Marines beyond their regular limits.

The Keepers did the same, though with less equipment, as they counted on the support and assets of the underground resistance in Xrusé.

Chris observed the overall preparation details. By his side, Amy nodded from time to time as she verified the loading operation on the floating screens projected by her belt.

"Once on the ground," Chris said, "you'll be on your own, Commander."

Amy raised her eyes. "I'll be in the best ever company in the whole bloody universe, sir; my Space Marines." She smiled. "Those bastards in Protusa won't even know what hit them." Looking at her, Telle understood she meant every word she said.

He noticed the Marines were about to board the last ships and reached out with his right hand to their commander. "Good luck, Norton."

Amy looked at the open hand for a moment, then smiled. "I'll wait for you, sir, when it's over." She gripped his hand in an firm clasp.

Telle gave her an intense look. "You do that, Amy."

She nodded and turned to board her ship. A smile rose to her lips.

A few minutes later, on the main bridge, Telle verified everything was set. Ohtlinell confirmed the same from the Keepers. "We are awaited on the surface. We will communicate only to confirm a successful touchdown and rendezvous. The next time will be when in position."

"Agreed." He glanced at all vitals from the Marines and he envied them, but he had a crucial role too. Soon, everyone would know whether wisdom led their path or if madness was about to engulf the whole galaxy in a burning hell. He took a deep breath and announced. "Operation Prometheus is a go."

The docking bays opened silently to the outer space; the transporters rose one by one to drift away in order from their mother ships. A small swarm of ships assembled, protected by the Keepers' stealth cloak, and moved in toward the Moîrai's cradle planet, Xrusé.

At minimum impulse, after a few hours, the planet grew in their visuals, a golden gem with blue and green touches; like a precious stone, it captured the eyes of every Space Marine onboard.

"Get ready. We are in for a long jump, lads." Amy adjusted her suit while looking at the floating visual. She verified her blaster and the ordnance. She smiled, happy, and couldn't wait to set foot on Xrusé.

The vessels entered the atmosphere at high altitude. On the ground, hundreds of kilometres away from Protusa, the rebellious Keepers waited, secured a deserted area and set the passive beacons that would lead the Space Marines and the Keepers to destination.

On all vessels, the same voice announced the time to the troops eager to start their mission. "ETA to jump, two time units."

Amy got in front of the bulkhead, ready to hop in the air and dash down like a bullet toward the surface. Their gear and equipment would follow but with a different, more dramatic result on the ground.

"One time unit." She checked her timer.

The Marines pressed forward and lowered their visors; the bulkhead dilated over the main continent in Xrusé, still at rest in the night shadows. Large cities sparkled within the obscured lands and an oval of pulsating dots, invisible on the ground, appeared on their visors and marked the landing area.

"Target down below at forty kilometres. Have a nice jump and good luck, guys," the transporter pilot announced.

Amy Norton raised her fist. "For the Third Loss!" she said and jumped out of the vessel. For a moment, the Marines could not refrain from marveling at the spectacle nature offered them before they dove in head-down position to their rendezvous. The thin layers of Xrusé's atmosphere caressed the planet's curvature and were ignited at the fringe by the Moîrai star. The dark space above greeted them, and they felt the heaviness of unknown constellations and a myriad of stars.

During their descent, small jets from their suits kept them within the optimal trajectory. Their suits maintained the inside temperature constant and kept them alive. They countered the coldest temperature of the rarified layers of

Xrusé's atmosphere, then neutralized the burning friction when they crossed more dense layers. Amy silenced her transponder and gave a mighty battle cry as the planet's gravity pulled her down faster and faster. She enjoyed every moment of her descent.

Their gear and equipment passed them, accelerating inside threaded cones that spiraled their way through the air as they targeted specific impact points at their destination.

On the ground, Mênis and the other Keepers gazed high above and distinguished the brief blinks of tiny flashes when the invading Marines' rain commenced. "They made it!" A sense of liberation and expectation filled their minds.

A Keeper monitored the descent on his tracking device. "They have slowed down from supersonic speed to terminal velocity, now." Mênis nodded.

"What about the equipment?"

The Keeper raised his eyes off the screen. "They will impact the designated area in three time units. We will hear them." He smiled.

At the altitude of three kilometres, the cones opened their flaps to slow down while—at the same time—increased the spin rate to maximize their penetration into the ground. The Keepers felt their arrival as a multitude of thuds when they impacted and dug deep into Xrusé's soil. When their downward momentum stopped, they unscrewed onto the surface and the bases opened up and deployed around like the petals of a composite flower.

The free-diving Marines and Keepers' commandos sped through the last five thousand kilometres. Amy verified her altitude and smiled when the visor showed the equipment cones notifying their successful arrival and deployment. "Goodies are awaiting. All squads' commanders report on landing. See you on ground. Norton out."

She released the slow-opening black parachute. A gentle pull at first, then, as speed decreased, she changed her position to a foot-first descent and waited for the parachute to gradually open and lower her to the assigned landing area. She touched down a few moments later.

In the darkness, the infrared visor showed the rest of the Marines landing all around her. The parachute folded back into its case and she located the nearest cone. She recovered her blaster from its back-casing, checked it with a glance, and ran to what looked like a mound in the distance. As she ran, the other squad leaders reported their successful landing, too, and assembled their units.

Amy walked up to the cone's rim and smiled. Turning around, she contemplated for the first time the Xrusé deserted location—a raw, rocky plain with strange tree-like formations. They were large and narrow at the base with protruding thick branches with dark sprouts of some sort of leaves. Other tall—but sparse—vegetation patched the ground, and seemed like a contorted dream of a mad sculptor, ending with a reversed umbrella structure, bony and woody at the base with shoots of finger-like leaves at the top.

In different times, the scenery would have captured her interest, but she had other things in mind. After a last glance, she ran the status check of the cone contents, and notified her location to the rest of the commandoes. She raised her eyes again to check for the assembling Marines. In the meantime, the visor had acquired all cones' locations and the various squads verified each of their loads. She looked up toward the night sky and opened the encrypted channel. "Prometheus touched down." The visor confirmed the message had been received.

The tactical screen blinked and new unknown dots approached on the surface. *"Keepers..."* she thought.

"Commander Norton here," she voiced on the common channel to warn both the Marines and the Keepers squads. "Locals are nearing."

"Yes, Norton," Ohtlinell's voice replied at once; she snorted.

Two squads of Marines joined her. As the troop acquired and distributed the equipment and ordnance, both their captains approached and saluted. "Squads fully operational, sir. Nothing to report."

"Well done, gentlemen."

The tactical screens showed details of small transporters approaching and identified them as friendly units. Hovering only a few feet above the ground, the welcoming reception for the Prometheus operation reached the commandoes.

The ships came to a halt and rested on the ground. Ohtlinell, with a few other Keepers, moved forward as the sides of the vehicles dilated. A tall figure emerged from the closest one and seemed to search for someone. "Ohtlinell. Finally."

He lowered his head and opened his palm to the Moîrai emerging from the vehicle. "Mênis."

Amy strode forward and interrupted the scene. "So you're the leader of the resistance in Protusa." She nodded as if she were evaluating the Moîrai. "How many of you are still active?"

Mênis looked at Ohtlinell and bent his head.

"This is Amy Norton. She leads the humans, a group they call 'Marines.'"

Mênis lowered his head. "We have conducted undercover operations in all major nodes in Xrusé. The brain is in Protusa, and it is where we concentrate our efforts." Then he turned toward Ohtlinell. "I expected to welcome you in a greater number."

"The Fleet is ready, but we need to ensure that the Supreme Council does not flee to reorganize elsewhere."

"We are more than enough." Amy shook her head.

Mênis glanced at her. "They are well protected."

She grinned. "They won't be protected from us."

The two Moîrai exchanged a glance, but didn't comment further.

"You just take us inside. The rest is our business." She turned, raised her left arm, and signaled the Marines to hurry up and reach the rally point.

⁂

Protusa's buildings towered high above the plain. Luminous cusps and shimmering structures sent a diffused glow that lit the sky above the capital, creating the sensation of a vault protecting its buildings.

On the brim of a terrain elevation, not far from the ruins of Alaston's residence, the Keepers and the Marine leaders observed. The commandoes waited near what Mênis indicated was a *den.*

"How close to the Council can we get?" Amy examined the view through the tactical screen, raised to the level of her eyes. The added information provided her with details on the city plan and buildings.

"Right under it."

In the silvery light coming from the city, she turned to look at the Moîrai. Mênis felt her glance. "But from there it will be a fight to reach the top of the Council Tower."

She went back to study Protusa's skyline and, unseen, smiled.

They faced a rocky formation covered with the same desert vegetation they'd seen when they landed, but here it grew thicker and larger at the base. The Keepers said they were in front of the entrance to the den. The humans could see nothing but rocks around them, yet the Keepers insisted they'd penetrate Protusa from there.

While the Marines looked at each other, their eyes filled with muted questions, the Keepers' soldiers waited patiently. A few metres away from the two groups, Mênis and Ohtlinell stared at each other. *"I don't like the human female much."*

Ohtlinell glanced at him for a second, then thought, *"Dan of Eridu says she is able to face any situation, and when the moment comes, no obstacle will stop her from accomplishing her mission."*

"I have the impression she knows more than we do."

"She will be tested soon. The Supreme Council Guards are not that easy to face."

"I know. We lost many Brothers in the last months. We need to break this stalemate."

"What are we waiting for?" They both turned to face Amy, who approached them with large strides but quietly as a wild beast.

"It will not be a long wait." Mênis made a floating screen blossom up from his belt for a quick control. "They are almost here."

"They?"

"Our Brethren."

The rocks seemed to swell; they detached from each other along a contour that ran from top to bottom and revealed a massive swiveling door. The Marines grabbed and aimed their blasters, but relaxed when they saw no reaction on the part of the Keepers' soldiers.

A faint light showed through the fissures that grew larger, making no sound, until a steep descending gallery came into view. "Welcome to Kamerye." A Keeper with a long tunic came out of the gallery, lowered her head, and opened wide her palms to her Brethren and to the bedazzled Marines.

Once inside, for once, Amy expressed surprise—and in a positive way. "This looks like your base in the Antarctic, Eremia. I've been there a few times."

Ohtlinell turned to look around; his eyes caressed the walls, the vaults, and the large central hall where the commandoes gathered and checked once more their readiness for combat. "Eremia is much younger than Kamerye, but you are right, our bases are similar to each other."

His voice sounded... *"Sad,"* Amy thought. She hesitated. "How many? I mean, what kind of casualties have you suffered?"

The Moîrai turned and his black eyes saw beyond the human. "Keepers have been slaughtered, tortured, and murdered even within our sacred walls in the Supreme Council." He stared at her and Amy felt his dark, ancient eyes reflect the depths of time. "You still harbor doubts in your heart about our resolve."

"I..." For the first time, she didn't know what to say. She was too accustomed to feeling scorn for the Moîrai.

Ohtlinell lowered his head and then left to join the others; with her eyes, Amy followed the Moîrai as he walked away.

She took a deep breath, activated the tactical floating screen, and called her squad leaders for one more check, even though she could see the Marines were ready.

Guided by the Keepers, the commandos took their places on the elevator platforms. Amy was the last to join them, and she looked at them with pride: the bravest breed she'd ever had the privilege to command.

She nodded to herself when she found Ohtlinell among the others. Obeying a sudden impulse, she lowered her head. The Moîrai smiled, and the platforms initiated the descent to the bottom level and the millennia-old tunnel connecting the base to the Supreme Council.

The platforms accelerated until they reached a steady speed and the levels they crossed dashed upward with a hypnotic rhythm of light and darkness.

The base once resonated with the sounds of Moîrai presence, and her mind filled with their ghosts. A brief look at her men taught Amy more than decades she'd spent nurturing resentment, becoming stronger than the strongest; the Marines blended with the Keepers, in mixed groups, chatting. They shared the same equipment and, to her own surprise, Amy thought that maybe they could share more than just gear.

The platforms slowed down and fused into the bottom level. Looking way up, she couldn't distinguish the level they came from. The Keepers at once moved forward toward a massive archway that opened into a dark gallery. The Marine squads followed.

Mênis and Ohtlinell approached. "The gallery will take us under the Temple."

She noticed the last word. "The sacred walls you mentioned before, right?" Amy walked closer as she watched the troops moving.

Mênis fixed his eyes on hers. "The Temple was first, before the Supreme Council; before we knew of the galaxy. It is the oldest place in Protusa, and in Xrusé. It is where Dan of Eridu became part of us and us part of him, and of the people he represents."

She stared back and frowned. "I hope you'll nurture the same feeling after our mission's over." Without giving the Moîrai time to reply, she breathed hard. "It's time for me to join the troops." With a swift pace, she reached them under the arch.

"I wish Alaston were here," Mênis said.

Ohtlinell smiled. "He will be soon."

Amy Norton stood tall and addressed the Marines. "There's a time when what is required from you exceeds everything you're capable of. There's a time when you won't have the chance to mend your mistakes, and a time when others will accomplish deeds that won't be told if you fail them and just take care of yourself." She paused. "Beyond this arch, there is a place where it won't matter if you stand defeated, but it matters if the last one standing is a Marine. Then we all will have mattered." She stared at them. "For the future that was robbed, for the future that was given, we are one!" She raised her right hand clasped in a fist. "For the Third Loss!"

With one powerful single voice, the Marines replied: "For the Third Loss!"

The emotional waves rumbling from the humans hit the two Moîrai as if they emanated from one single entity; they understood in that moment that a new, different human race had risen in the galaxy.

The Marines crossed the arch and stepped into the tunnel. The force field reacted to their brainwaves and set them in motion; the troops drifted to their destination.

Chapter 21 – The Wisest Choice

The Moîrai fleet emerged from hyperspace at the fringe of the Alliance borders, the Kritas' realm; they sent a beacon deep into their main space sector and waited.

In the space-sphere rendering of the main bridge, Ekahau's eyes followed the device's symbol traveling deep into Kritas' sectors while the tactical officers prepared for an imminent encounter with the Alliance.

The resolution of the screen grew as the beacon traveled until the Kritas' star system came into sight at the boundary of the sphere. He didn't have a doubt that the Kritas had already detected their arrival, beacon or not, but he felt the need to be cautious; he had too much to lose.

The device reached its assigned location and activated; with a sigh, he saw its symbol pulsate. A ping confirmed the Kritas had received and acknowledged the beacon's signal; the Moîrai wouldn't have too long to wait.

"Set all units to maximum alert." His eyes widened in anticipation of the next events, attracted by the flickering in the sphere that indicated that a disturbance occurred already in the space-time continuum.

"Maximum alert level." The confirmation from the bridge didn't suffice to loosen the knot he had in the back of his head.

After losing the base in Eridu, the Kritas had distanced themselves again from the Moîrai and from him, raising the tension between the Confederation and the Alliance to dangerous levels. *"At least,"* Ekahau thought, *"I managed to sew a solid truce between our empires."* The truce he made possible raised him to the highest ranks in the government and he enjoyed the favors of The One until they discovered the drug contraband.

Only the Kritas had the expertise to reproduce the drug in the galaxy, and yet, as much as the Supreme Council tried, they'd been unable to point the finger and accuse the Alliance, or their members, for the cloned formula. He shivered at the thought of the strange, vicious illness that had hit the interstellar pilots. The causes eluded all their research efforts.

"Cit Ekahau Tum?" A voice distracted him. He turned and realized he had been lost in thought. The space-sphere had filled with blinks from Kritas vessels; a daunting and massive presence as if the Alliance expected them and was ready for a direct confrontation. "Not exactly the welcome from someone who has nothing to hide," he said.

He took a deep breath. Their numbers were enough to balance the technology disadvantage they had compared to the Moîrai's fleet. He frowned. "Any sign of hostility?"

"None that we can detect, but their shields are raised." The officers enlarged the panel detailing the information on the newly arrived vessels.

"As are ours," he grunted. "Message them that Cit Ekahau Tum, Supreme Commander of the Moîrai fleet, demands to meet with Xiucaman, Kritas' Martial Master."

Right after the communication officer carried out his orders, the visual of the front section of the Kritas flagship appeared. "Receiving an incoming communication," the officer muttered.

In the main bridge, the scene of the imposing vessel, flanked by some of the largest battleships of the Kritas fleet, was a menacing view. The officer glanced at Ekahau, who kept staring at the screen.

The image grew larger and showed the commanding dome of the ship, before it zoomed into its interior.

A group of high-ranking officers stood next to their military ruler, Xiucaman. On one side, and dressed in Fleet uniforms, three humans shared the stage. Ekahau's eyes widened, his neck extended in surprise before he recovered and controlled his reactions.

"So, not every rebel died in Eridu." He betrayed his surprise.

"Ekahau, I am pleased to meet with you again. Why the wonder? The events in Eridu required us to expend a considerable effort. It would have been a pity to lose all our investments." He grinned at the humans.

"Besides," he continued, "they have proved themselves valuable. They are a cunning species, the humans, and see things with a natural shrewdness." He gave a nod to the men in uniform. "You should try them. Ah," he laughed, "I forgot you're expert in humans."

Ekahau frowned; things had taken an unexpected turn. The Kritas' impudence struck a nerve. "Maybe, but history shows you have not selected the best ones." He stared at the three men. The humans lost their grins at once, one in particular. He clasped one hand into a fist; Ekahau noticed it missed part of one finger.

A low-ranking officer entered the visual, approached Xiucaman, and whispered in his ear. The Kritas bent his head to listen, tightened his lips, and nodded. He raised his eyes back to the Moîrai. "For the moment, your fleet is tolerated in our space. Do not initiate any wormhole creation. Do not leave the sector and keep your communication links open. We will be in contact with you again, Ekahau."

The image faded and the was link interrupted from the Kritas' side. Ekahau stiffened, incapable of any reaction. On the bridge, he felt the stares of the officers as a provocation. He clenched his teeth. "Resume your duties!"

⁂

Deep inside the planetary nebula, the neurotrophic Fusion drug factory operated now under human control and produced new formulas targeting more races and with a faster activation time. The dwarf star flickered, mute spectator of the humans' efforts to rule their destiny. Meanwhile, with the Fleet in formation, the time was set for the humans' invasion.

Aboard the flagship, Samuel and his staff officers contemplated the latest information retrieved from the scouts' buoys.

The Moîrai and Kritas reunion didn't appear to be that peaceful. The bulk of the Moîrai fleet faced an even larger Kritas deployment in a space standoff, but the scouts hadn't yet acquired further details.

The round hall was dimly lit, and the only illumination came from the tactical analysis centerpiece. The Fleet composition and the timeline of extrapolated events—in the case of a confrontation—ranged from the most to the least probable, and their details were exposed on floating diagrams and schemes. Information migrated from one panel to the other as relevant intel was acquired. Symbols and visuals floated and replicated with added information into the integrated dashboards. The officers picked the most urgent and distributed them to expert groups for in-depth analysis.

The humans knew every technical detail of all the Moîrai and Kritas' vessels. Why had they stalled in front of each other? The face-off constituted a factor capable of bringing unforeseen consequences for their mission in Protusa; a real nut to crack before launching the invasion with confidence.

Samuel's eyes met briefly with everyone's in the briefing room. "Gentlemen, please, your candid opinion. Time is of essence."

The most senior among them cleared his voice. "Sir, unfortunately, all communications between the two parties take place via direct, modulated phaser beam. The scouts are too far from it to have a chance to intercept, and getting closer for a resonance analysis is too risky."

"I know this." His eyes dug deep into the officer and urged him to develop his thoughts even further.

"Sir, any conjecture at the moment would be baseless, but we can infer that there isn't a formal pact between them, yet. Maybe, they are discussing terms..."

He nodded. "We need to know that for sure."

The officer glanced at the floor for a moment. "It risks to be a no-return mission for the scouts."

Samuel sighed. "What are the Huitzilin saying?"

"They report the Kritas are aware of the crisis in the Moîrai empire and that the Keepers are now considered hostile, representing a huge unknown." He paused.

"What do you think?"

He snorted. "I believe Kritas will be opportunistic, as usual."

"Right. Especially after what happened to them in Eridu." Samuel looked around. "Anybody else?"

A younger officer muttered. "We..." he said, but then he shut his mouth again.

"Don't stop. Go on."

The young captain's gaze went to his colleagues as asking for support, but no one accepted the invitation and many avoided eye contact with him.

"Well..." He started with a feeble voice. "We could leak the intel and make the unknown known..."

The senior officer grunted. "What?"

Samuel halted him with a gesture. "Go ahead."

The captain took a deep breath. "We know how Kritas behave—they do not truly ally with anyone; they always go with the winning party. If we provide them with enough information so they get convinced that the Moîrai's time is up..." He allowed himself to exhale. "They might decide to take our side."

Samuel eyes tightened. "And how would you do that?"

Encouraged, the officer's torso straightened. "The scouts, sir." Everyone's eyes turned toward him.

At that moment, an urgent classified communication from the FCC prompted the opening of the security floating screens from everyone's belt. The Marines had reached their position in Xrusé.

"Get a team and fill in the details." Samuel glanced at the officer highest in rank. "Gentlemen, we have an invasion to carry on." He turned and strode toward the FCC.

The order of the Fleet arrival in the Moîrai star system aimed at a swift destruction of their Bridge Stations first, then a sweep of the entire sector with the fastest and more agile vessels available, to end with opening the corridor for Xrusé. The second phase consisted in the annihilation of the planetary defensive systems, overruning the ground troops, and entering Protusa. At the same time, the Marines already on the planet would have had to seize the Supreme Council and capture its leadership.

On the observation deck, Samuel watched the various task forces line up and waited for the wormholes to open.

His flagship—and its own squad group—moved forward to reach the assigned location.

The interstellar pilots received the coordinates with the departure orders and the nebula filled with growing wormhole singularities whose fringes trembled as the fabric of space-time itself quivered with expectation.

Under the watch of the dying brown dwarf star, the nebula shimmered when the tunnels opened and the task force dashed through them.

The space around the Moîrai's Bridge Stations crowded with flashes when the vessels emerged from hyperspace. An instant later, the ships swerved into offensive formations and released a massive load of antimatter torpedoes. Even before any reaction could come from the Moîrai, the battleships' heavy particle generators screeched in an effort to sustain the colossal energy required by the blaster jolts that pounded the stations' defensive shields. The first torpedoes hit and deflagrations lightened up the space.

From the battleships, clouds of medium and heavy fighters emerged to counter the defensive units that scrambled after the Moîrai recovered from the stunning violence of the attack.

Inside the stations, chaos erupted in the various departments and deafening alarms stressed every hall. The bulkheads that separated each section sealed and isolated all internal divisions. The wounded personnel screamed, and those who could ran to the nearest safety pods. Inside the stations, an insidious breeze blew where the structures had collapsed. It meant death to those inside.

"Under attack! Under attack!" The message shouted in the Moîrai's guttural language, repeated without interruption, echoing within the isolated compartments for the ones still alive to hear it. The message went unheard and lost where the hull had given in and a mist of maimed corpses floated into outer space.

On the bridge, after the first astounding moments, the Moîrai officers reacted and provided tactical support to the resident defensive fighter units scrambling from a multitude of docking bays. The stations' structures vibrated and shook amid the explosions while the Moîrai fighters rushed out against a yet unknown enemy.

The breeze became a wind and acquired the strength of a tornado as the bridge ripped apart. The commanding officer's last vision fixed on the alarms and distress signals that appeared in tens of floating dashboards sent by every Bridge Station. His jaw dropped, but his lungs had no air to allow him to scream. The light in his eyes paled.

The scrambling fighters faced the impossible—a wall of spaceships greeted them and obliterated from existence many ships before they could even attempt to fire. Those pilots fastest to react reversed course. Their hearts sank when they encountered the same maddening scene; the enemy vessels had surrounded each station and closed off any escape route. The bravest opened fire—out of instinct, maybe—before they turned into dust in huge balls of fire or vanished in flashes of matter antimatter annihilation.

The distress signals reached Xrusé's near-space stationed military vessels. "This cannot be!" Their Moîrai leader slammed his hand on the dashboard. "Re-run all probe analyses!" The yell made the nearest technicians jolts as they operated their dashboards. Their hands dashed through rushing floating symbols and diagrams. The chief frowned and lowered his head. "Confirmed."

In shock, all units acknowledged the destruction of the Bridge Stations, an event that had lasted only a few seconds. With a shiver, the space-sphere rendered the multitude of enemy ships regrouping, and plotted the forecast of their route. Xrusé flashed as their destination. "Hostiles will reach Xrusé sector in one time unit."

The inexpressive voice from the biocomputer left no doubt. "Survival rate estimates... less than one percent."

All eyes turned on him. "Send a distress message to the fleet. Get Cit Ekahau Tum immediately!"

The response took only a second. "We cannot reach the fleet. All communication links with the Kritas' sectors have been severed."

The commander did not hesitate. "Set course to quadrant thirty." He rushed to the dashboards and highlighted a far-away destination deep into an allied star system.

"Sir?"

"We will not be of any use when destroyed and dead. For all we know, the bulk of the fleet is no more. Do it! Now!"

The navigation officers lowered their heads—relieved—and issued the orders.

On the FCC hall of Samuel's flagship, wormhole creation alarms resonated and the floating screens showed the warning and the singularities parametres. The tactical and intel officers jostled as they rushed to correlate the new flow of information, and the tactical biocomputers integrated the new data.

"The Moîrai are leaving!" the first officer announced.

Samuel smiled. "Difficult for them to consider their own death a necessity." He turned away from the space-sphere. "Set direct course for Xrusé. Space Marines ready."

He activated the omni-channel to reach every unit and every crewmember. Priority notifications on floating panels blossomed in front of every man and woman in the Fleet. The Admiral's crest camped for a moment before Samuel's smiling face appeared on the comm units.

"Today we'll write a new chapter in the history of our race. There will be no more Losses. Today, we'll walk on Xrusé."

⁂

The Marines and the Keepers waited underground. The chambers that gave them shelter had been cut in the planet's crust eons before, but to the Keepers' Founders, they were never intended to nurture a threat to those who walked on the surface. Yet, the Moîrai who sat at the Supreme Council had become a fatal curse for everything those chambers stood for.

The last hours brought a fundamental change in the relationship that bound the two groups together. Amy felt that the initial diffidence had vanished. The Marines checked their gear ad nauseam, but no longer kept their fingers on their triggers. The Keepers went through the same exercise with their arsenal; some glanced at her, some mingled with the humans, too.

Mênis observed Amy and the other Marines, though, with a growing sense of worry. The Keepers now considered the humans as peers rather than the uncomfortable presence of an inconvenient and cumbersome ally, difficult to handle and who grew too dangerous to manage.

He was there when the first discussions examined the possibility of a Selection process for the humans. Thousands of years before, much younger, he advocated the necessity to preserve the race of man in the galaxy.

Indeed, they'd been preserved, but what did the Moîrai preserve? He had contributed to saving mankind from oblivion, but he hadn't foreseen what they had become in the span of a few generations.

He stiffened when the humans jumped to their feet. The security screens became visible to each of them, Keepers included. The assault had started; the Moîrai bridge stations had been destroyed with a massive demonstration of power and the human Fleet was only one time unit away from entering the Xrusé atmosphere.

The Marines shouted and exulted; the Keepers digested the news with a bitter satisfaction. Their Brothers were coming, but the taste of victory wasn't entirely sweet.

Amy advanced and stopped in front of Mênis and Ohtlinell. "The invasion is under way. We need to coordinate and move in to seize the Supreme Council."

Her expression was tense, and Mênis wondered why. He nodded. "We will be flanking you in the assault."

"Negative." Amy took out a data-crystal from a case. The Moîrai exchanged a worried look. "It's all in here." She held the crystal between her fingers. "You'll provide access to the towers. We know what to do and where to go. We cannot ensure your safety once in. The Keepers will have to watch the outside perimetres and guarantee no aid from outside reaches the Council Guards trapped inside."

Mênis took the crystal and turned it in his hand as if it were an unfamiliar object.

Amy nodded at it. "It's better for you two to listen to the message in private."

Ohtlinell faced her. "What does this mean?"

She didn't flinch. "I have my orders. It comes from Alaston and Dan of Eridu. I suggest you hurry." Her green eyes pierced deep into the Moîrai's.

Ohtlinell pondered the situation for a moment, then turned to a wall and gestured with his hand. The wall dilated into a recess. Followed by Mênis, he entered and sealed the room.

Amy rejoined the Marine squads. "Move up!" The Marines moved onto the platforms ready to reach the ground level inside the temple.

The Keepers' squad leaders watched their security screens all blossom at one time; after a brief look, they issued orders in their guttural language, then rushed toward the wall where Mênis and Ohtlinell had disappeared a few minutes before. The wall opened and they formed a circle, in silence. Amy Norton watched the scene from afar and understood the Keepers communicated using their minds. She knew the content of the message and turned to signal her captains. The Marines armed and aimed their blasters. Her hands embraced her gun and got ready to fire.

⁂

The Kritas' battleships had the Moîrai vessels locked in their targets acquisition system. Unbeknownst to all, a small group of volunteer human fighters closed in to the sector where the precarious standoff risked turning into a danger for the humans if the aliens' fleets reached any kind of agreement.

"Approaching Kritas' deployment. ETA six time units." From within the stealth cloak, the fighters filled a data probe with the latest details of their mission.

They risked getting close enough to release the phaser intercept array net, sensible to the nanometer wavelengths of the communication beams. The array widened, thin, practically invisible to any detection. Each node created a field that would have been altered by the phaser link between the two fleets and the interference decoded. Only one little detail remained: its complete calibration and the decryption of the beams weren't ideal procedures to conduct in a stealth mission. The interference would be detected before they could reach full calibration and the array of detectors discovered.

"Array in place. Calibration procedure started," the scouts announced.

The confirmation triggered the pilots' wormhole programming for the rest of the ships: destination, Protusa.

⁂

Xiucaman waited for the image of Ekahau to disappear, then shouted, "Who dares?" His eyes dashed to the humans near him and stared cold at them. "This is madness." Then a thought traversed his mind and his eyes squinted. "Or pure genius."

He turned and shouted into the deck, "Find them!" The humans wondered what he had in mind. He smiled to himself. "Join me on the bridge."

On the bridge, the Kritas detected the interference created by the human array net and started to correlate the signals.

Xiucaman questioned his Chief Scientist. "They can't be Moîrai; they must be humans?"

The scientist looked back and raised his eyebrows. "Humans? They use a new stealth technology we've never seen before. We wouldn't have noticed anything if it wasn't for the attempt to decrypt our communication links." He frowned. "It's weird, though."

"What is?" Xiucaman had no time for conjectures.

"That they made such a mistake..."

"I'm not sure it's a mistake."

The scientist mulled. "They must have known we would detect them."

"Indeed. How long before we can pinpoint their location?"

He sighed. "If they insist calibrating...only a few more time units."

"Excellent. Communicate at once the coordinates to the battleships."

"Yes, sir." The Chief Scientist returned to his dashboards.

On the bridge, the tension grew strong among the Kritas. Only a few more minutes before they would discover who hid out there. Xiucaman stared at his human Councilor, intent to observe the analytics. He needed confirmation.

The correlation completed and the coordinates flashed on all dashboards. He grinned as the battleships converged at maximum impulse and armed their antimatter torpedoes. Whoever hid out there would have to counter Kritas' might.

The human scouts saw the enemy battleships surround their location. "The bait is laid."

A jet of blasters illuminated the sector and the bug devices in the phaser beam-intercepting array exploded one by one. On the Moîrai battleships' screens, the scene shone bright, but no one noticed a wormhole open and close in the blink of an eye.

The Kritas released the torpedoes, ready to be launched, and issued a warning in the common language.

All units in the sector had two time units to leave stealth mode and surrender.

Silence fell aboard the battleships as the countdown limit approached. Xiucaman and his Councilor humans stared at the surrounded space sector on the main screen.

The one with a mutilated hand grunted as the fighter ships appeared on the screens. As they left their stealth cloaking, the Eridu's Phoenix insignia shone with pride on their hulls. Xiucaman eyebrows rose and he nodded.

"Bring them in." He turned to the one with a mutilated hand. "Always full of surprises. It seems you'll be useful once more."

⁂

Xrusé filled all 3D renderings in the middle of the tactical screens and space-spheres in the FCC of every ship. Samuel squinted his eyes. "Send a dispatch to Eridu. We initiate the descent."

The planet grew, and its continents emerged into view from beneath the clouds. In the nightside hemisphere, the Moîrai cities rivaled the darkness with silver and golden glows. On the visible horizon, the star lurked, and it seemed to Samuel that it greeted him in its wisdom—that it had always expected this moment to come...one day.

The vessels violated the planet's atmosphere and filled it with uncountable traces of condensation. From the ground, the crystalline vault of Xrusé's sky looked like it cracked under an unbearable pressure, pixellating into an infinite number of shimmering dots. The surface defenses activated at once and lightning reached the sky, aimed at the invading spaceships.

On the FCC, the alarms resonated just before the first hit impacted. The vessels' shields fizzled as they absorbed the energy of the Moîrai fatal welcoming; in response, the Fleet gripped the planet with its most lethal embrace. Samuel ordered the attack. "Open fire! Hit them hard!"

Clouds gathered where the atmosphere burned and depleted, and Xrusé saw what the ancient race of men and its poets—in its multiple dawns—described as the wars between the titans and the gods.

On the tactical rendering, Samuel surveyed the targeting AI system choices and his officers, directing fire to the bigger threats first. The ground trembled and the entire planet resonated with a lugubrious vibration. Thousands of small fighters scrambled from bases around the planet and their symbols set alarms on all dashboards. "Enemy fighter scrambles," a tactical officer lashed out.

Samuel smiled. "Let's meet them." Small human fighters left the larger battleships that still delivered death from above. The two swarms met in mid-sky. With a technology matching that of the enemy, only the personal skills and the numbers of opposing fighters dictated the issue of the deadly ballet that played until one of the opponents succumbed and the blasters turned the ship and its pilot into a cloud of ionized molecules. With a keen eye, Samuel stared at the live data on the dashboard with the results of the battles and the balance of forces.

On the ground, the Moîrai troops gathered, determined to make the invaders pay a high price. Their eyes were glued to the fights in the higher layers of the breathing shell of Xrusé and hoped for their own to be victorious, but the clashes got closer, and closer...

⁂

In the depths of the Supreme Council, the Keepers watched the Marines raise their blasters. Ohtlinell fixed his eyes on those of Norton. Then he saw the human hands contract on the grip of the blaster, fully charged.

Amy watched the Keeper raise one hand, and those already on the platforms lowered their heads. The others stopped and turned around. They all lined up and gathered in a tight formation, then moved away from the Marines and marched toward a lateral gallery. A long, harmonic murmur came from their ranks in a language the humans didn't recognize.

"We will not interfere." Mênis and Ohtlinell approached. "May you see another day."

Amy relaxed and nodded. The two Moîrai lowered their heads and turned to rejoin the others. Then they disappeared in the distance.

"Let's go!" Amy ran toward the platforms as the first one started to lift upward.

The platforms rose without interruption and the ceilings dilated to let the platforms fuse into the floor of the temple. The vast hall was silent, but the echo of turmoil reached them the same, even if vague, as in a dream.

The Marines spread out. The blueprints shared by the Keepers detailed the entire complex. Amy examined the rendering on her tactical unit; the various squads acknowledged their readiness and confirmed their orders. She and the Marines in her squads didn't have much time. "Release the sniffers."

Tiny rods, floating only inches above the ground, sped out in search of molecules that would lead them to their targets—the Wisest.

The search-and-destroy mission started, the huge metal doors swiveled, and the Marines left the temple. On her tactical display, Amy signaled all units to engage.

Out of the Keepers' temple, the battle raged, but first they had to reach the higher levels where the Wisest could still hide. The rest of the men had to seal any escape route and deal with the Supreme Council Guards; Amy hoped the Keepers would fulfill their part, too.

The ground trembled and shook; an eerie sound reached them from the outside. "This way," she shouted, and ran to the vast central hall with the blaster shivering at each of the bolts she delivered with deadly precision. The blaster screeches marked the walk of death among the ancient colonnades.

⁂

The Supreme Council received in silence the bitter news that the rear guard of the fleet had fled when the invasion started. The military attaché stood in the middle of the Council. "The last communication stated that it was not necessary for the fleet to suffer further losses when faced with overwhelming enemy forces."

The One—who had not reacted thus far—moved his eyes to the officer and fixed him as his lungs filled. "Necessary? *Necessary? I* decide what *is* and what *is not* necessary for our military leaders. He will not live through his decision!" His dark eyes looked like obsidian cuts into an even darker soul. "Where is Ekahau?"

The military attaché trembled under that uncontrolled fury. "We cannot establish contact," he muttered, "and the envoys we sent... They have disappeared. Someone must have intercepted their path."

"Someone?" The One's shout echoed in the hall as the entire world shook and trembled; dazzling bolts dashed from the ground to counter the impossible vision of an invasion. A gesture from The One turned the walls and the ceiling transparent. The attention of everyone moved away from his waves of anger and incredulous eyes turned, blinking, toward the sky above Protusa.

"Seal the Council!" The One yelled, and his hands danced over the symbols that emerged from his dashboard.

The Wisest watched in awe, and some gripped the edge of their seats to prevent their minds from falling into a forgotten and neglected terror. Alarms jangled in all recesses of the Supreme Council complex; the walls flashed with the orders and procedures to be followed in the emergency. The shouts and the rhythmic pounding of feet from guards running from all posts resonated under the ancient vaults.

The walls dilated and a platoon of heavily geared soldiers rushed in. An officer stepped forward. "We are to escort you to the crypt. There is a security breach."

After a moment of bewilderment, the Wisest hurried to the exit. The One looked up again; lights slashed Protusa's sky and glowing red flowers bloomed by the thousands. The sight would have been beautiful if ancient words didn't haunt him and fill his mind with the weight of fate: *"They broke the seal of death... The end is the start."* He slammed his fists on the dashboard and sent ripples on all floating displays. His mind struggled to formulate the words. *"Be damned, Keepers and their mutant human!"*

"Honorable!" A voice charged with urgency broke the connection that had formed in his head; visions of humans and Keepers spun with rage in front of his eyes. He joined the officer who rushed him out.

⁂

Above the surface, the human Fleet continued to spread downward like a plague; as a fatal disease, it decimated the Moîrai in droves. In the FCC room, Samuel and the staff officers surveyed the evolution of the invasion. "Moîrai's resistance's deteriorating, sir."

Samuel nodded. "Message Eridu with the details and keep an eye on our casualties."

"Yes, sir."

They had prepared for decades for this moment; the end of it was nigh. He watched the battles on different areas of the planet, shifting the images from one location to the other. The Marines had landed at the focal points identified for them by the Keepers. These last participated in the conflict and their presence sapped Moîrai troops' morale, even more so when combined with the overwhelming deployment of forces the humans had brought to Xrusé. The Keepers fought alongside the humans!

They were a fabled organization, feared but revered in all layers of the society. The Supreme Council hadn't factored in—in any proper way—how much the cruel hunt and vile repression they unleashed against the Keepers undermined the credibility of the accusations they had fabricated. The One aimed at destroying them before any trial, denying any open confrontation.

Security by obscurity saved the Keepers, but now they were in the eyes of everyone, and the Moîrai troops' determination faltered when the Keepers manifested to them, and many units surrendered. They had been told humans had come to destroy, strong in their cruelty and disrespect for any form of life, and Keepers instead came forward in the front line. Who was serving the principles at the base of the credo of every Moîrai?

In the FCCs, officers exchanged skilometres of satisfaction at each completed objective. The expected opposition the Marines faced on the ground, when they landed, faded faster than any could have predicted.

Samuel nodded, glad the Keepers helped avert the genocide. He wouldn't have to share the guilt and the same shame as the Moîrai, but humans would make them pay the price. Father wanted a brutal message to be sent, nonetheless. He waited for the Marines engaged at the Supreme Council to confirm that the target had been found and treated, then he would give the order.

A communication officer stood nearby and cleared his voice. "Eridu quantum link established, sir."

Samuel realized the officer had had to repeat the announcement.

"Thank you." He nodded and left the command deck, walking through the dilated wall of the annexed briefing room.

Alaston, from the main bridge of a Keepers' battleship, agreed. "We will meet at the Supreme Council esplanade soon." He lowered his head and opened wide his palms.

From Eridu, Dan smiled. "Samuel. You will walk with me as we once did in Civita."

"Father..." A vivid memory rose in his mind; he remembered how he put his chest out while walking on the tarmac of the spaceport, next to his father, the day of the inauguration of Eridu's fleet. He smiled.

"You honor me again."

"No, Samuel. You did."

Alaston stepped forward. "Ohtlinell and the Keepers have secured the complex. Nothing can get out or sneak in."

Samuel's smile faded as he looked again at his father. "We'll proceed as soon as the Marines are ready."

Dan stared at his son. "It is necessary." The scene froze and the communication ended. Samuel left the room and went back to survey the Marines' advance inside the Supreme Council complex. The squads were about to reach their assigned locations. He gave a quick look at the casualties and sighed. The Marines were paying a high price for the mission, but they'd be soon out of danger.

Chapter 22 – Resolutions

The Kritas escorted the scouts into a small cell with bare walls and an empty floor. They rushed them inside and the entry coalesced.

"Well, at least there are no torture devices around," one of the scouts said. "That we can see..." another replied. "Wave to the wardens. You can bet they're watching." A middle finger rose.

The rendering of the cell and its occupants filled half of the space in the surveillance room. Called in as councilors, the three men in Kritas uniforms walked through the 3D image to examine the prisoners and their behavior. They listened to their chatting and exchanged brief looks among them, nodding. Meanwhile, the Kritas surveyed the details of their body signatures—blood pressure, the chemical analysis of their transpiration, their eye movements and pupil contractions.

"So, what can you tell me?" Xiucaman followed their gait among the prisoners' images.

"They're calm and resolute. They're trained soldiers and they know we're watching them, but they're not afraid." He turned. "Am I right?" He made a gesture with his mutilated hand toward the floating diagrams showing details of the prisoners' metabolisms.

The Kritas glanced at them. "No, they are not."

The man nodded. "They're here for a purpose. I'd like to examine them. Personally."

Xiucaman looked at *his* human, the one he created back in the early days in their base on Eridu. "They're all yours, but keep them alive." He grinned. The human smiled and left with the others.

The scouts' vitals showed how much pain his man inflicted, always stopping short of the danger zone. *"The human knows his job,"* Xiucaman thought.

A smile rose to his lips, but the screams annoyed him. "Shut them off."

A technician acted at once and he welcomed the silence.

The scouts had been laid on bare tables that rose from the floor. They didn't need to be restrained much, as the human with the mutilated hand controlled their minds. The scouts' vitals reached alarming levels when he focused too much during his mental probing.

The man kept his eyes closed as he extracted all information from the scout's tortured mind. He trembled and breathed deeply as if he enjoyed the moment.

After a while, Xiucaman saw him nod, then straighten up and open his eyes wide. The man grinned and seemed to stare at his Kritas master through the visual rendering. "Your most secret desire is about to come true." He looked back at the scouts with a pinch of admiration. "And it explains the loss of the flotilla you sent to Eridu."

⁂

Amy glanced at her tactical device's screen. The rods had acquired their intended target and were converging. After all, the Keepers were right—the coordinates matched.

"Status report," she asked of all squad leaders. Casualties were within the expected figures, and the Marines kept advancing through the last resisting nodes.

She turned to check on her own squad. The Marines lined up along both walls of a secluded gallery, far from the main battles in the lower levels. Tucked away at the top of the main tower, what the Keepers had mentioned as 'the crypt', their target appeared at the fringe of the tactical screen. The rods pointed all to the same coordinates and advanced quickly. She smiled. The Wisest of the Moîrai... *"Hiding like little girls,"* she thought.

She signaled the men to stay low and raised her arm for squad leaders to rally on. They knelt around her.

"We're not far from the crypt." She pointed at the screen. "We'll wait for the rods to hit their hosts, then we move in." She turned her eyes to the chief engineer. "The Keepers say their devices will disable the security in place. But let's check for ourselves."

The engineer nodded. "I'll activate the scramblers," he said, and issued the orders on his floating screen.

A high-pitched ping, inaudible to the old human race, confirmed the activation of scramblers' spheres. The devices flew at mid-height past them and disappeared from view as they turned at the first corner in search for signature signals revealing alert and security devices along their route.

The spheres deployed and stopped at regular intervals, blasting the Moîrai sensors that were invisible to the naked eye. Amy checked their progression until they reached the hall that served as the entrance to the crypt.

The chief engineer confirmed. "Full deployment, Ma'am. The path is clear."

The rods reached the hall and sent the 'target acquired' warning, then waited for further instructions.

Amy turned and nodded, hoping not to find any ancient trap not using a technology detectable by the spheres, but she kept her worries for herself. "Okay, quiet now, and keep your eyes and ears wide open."

With caution, Amy walking in front, the Marines advanced in the gallery. The scramblers hummed and glowed with a reassuring green light. They reached the main hall.

The ceiling resembled the vaults of gothic cathedrals back in Eridu, with stone ribs joining at the top into a ring. At the center, on the floor, camped the Keepers' symbol. Multicolored stones reproduced the four and eight pointed stars of the Palladium, and the hall recalled the main shape of the overall architecture of the Supreme Council complex itself. Around the walls, at vertices of the larger star, the statues of past Wisest surveyed the place with their gaze fixed down to the Keepers' symbol.

Amy looked around. The rods floated in mid-air, evenly spaced near the perimeter wall in front of the statues. "Let's see if the Keepers are true to their words."

She entered the code received by Alaston. The rods rose to the level of the face of the sculpted Wisest and modulated the emission of hyper-frequency tone sequences.

Nothing happened at first, and Amy glanced at the chief engineer, who frowned. The sequence activated a mechanism that ignited an ancient process inside a cavity in each of the stone torsos. "Look!" he said.

The opaque crystal of the statues' eyes became transparent; inside, invisible lenses adjusted their focal point. The statues emitted a whistle when the internal chemical reaction pressure increased, and the Marines retreated a few steps back. Then the eyes emitted faint infrared laser beams that hit the tips of the star shapes in the Keepers' insignia on the floor. Alarmed, the Marines stepped further back and raised their blasters, but Amy kept her calm and observed the process. Her green eyes sparkled.

The tips shimmered; the star shapes on the emblem swiveled and created slots that matched the rods' dimensions.

"Fascinating." Amy clenched her fist when green lights on the tactical screen confirmed the seal had been opened. She licked her lips with satisfaction and entered the code to activate the rods for the second phase.

The devices spread atop the newly opened cavities and descended. They fit perfectly and disappeared inside.

⁂

The One had his eyes glued to the floating screens and dashboards all around the oval room. For fear of an immediate retribution, the other Wisest didn't dare making any comment on the news that reached them in their impenetrable retreat. They were the most powerful Moîrai, and yet, when all seemed lost, they were the only ones now at the mercy of his ire. They looked at him in fear, and among them, the words of an ancient Keepers' litany resounded like a prophecy: *"...over the brink, the mad will fall."*

If it existed, Fate would have watched the events with a sardonic grin. The Wisest hunted the Keepers, tortured them and killed them, and here they were, trapped in a millennia-old Keepers' refuge. The guards made them feel secure, though. For the time being, they were safe, even if "safe" was a relative word in that enclave.

Nobody noticed or heard the feeble scratching of stones moving against stones. In the vault, tiny holes opened and the rods broke through to enter the crypt, the inviolable sanctuary. All at once, as though driven by a demonic will, they dashed, with a hiss, toward their prey. The Wisest yelled. The guards pointed their blasters, but couldn't fire against those tiny, fast flying targets for fear of hitting one of their masters who scrambled, waving their hands and arms to stop the rods from reaching them, as if a swarm of stinging animals attacked them.

The first one to scream in panic made the guards turn to watch in horror as the rod reached a nostril and penetrated. "Help me!" the Wisest cried with a broken voice and felt to his knees, sticking his fingers up his nose in the desperate attempt to stop the invader.

The guards hesitated as all other Wisest howled in pain and fell on the floor, their bodies contorting under the assault of powerful spasms.

Once inside, the rods released an aggressive genetic compound that spread to all tissues.

Amy checked the security device as green, bleeping dots appeared. A smile rose to her lips. "They're ready." She turned to a captain nearby. "Release the chemicals."

Through the whole Supreme Council complex, the Marine squads received the order on the tactical screen. They stopped returning fire, took cover, and activated the drones. Like bacteria spreading inside an unprotected host, the drones scurried through all galleries, halls, under all vaults and crossings—overcoming all obstacles to reach all locations in the Supreme Council.

The Moîrai tried to target the devices with their blasters, but for every drone destroyed, more came to take their place. From the wrecks, thick fumes exhaled and widened like oil spills; then they drifted toward each Moîrai.

The same vapors leaked from the flying drones as they spread, and the fumes crawled up in search of an opening—an exposed part of the Moîrai's bodies. When they found it, they stuck like glue. The halls filled with the guards' screams. The reaction, at the chemical bonds level, started in a few seconds after the first contact.

In the crypt, the guards looked in horror at the Wisest lying on the floor, now motionless. Bending over them, they tried to resuscitate their masters when internal spasms made those bodies contract. Their eyes widened and their mouths opened. A viscous fume came out, floated above the Wisest's faces for a long moment, growing, hesitant, then it searched for the guards as if it was a living thing. The first guard screamed as the fumes condensed into a thin layer of gooey foam when in contact with his skin and penetrated.

The muscles contracted and relaxed with increased frequency as the genetic compound broke the chemical bonds of the Moîrai molecules. The internal tissues melted and the organs collapsed. The guards vomited their organic fluids, brown as dirt; they died without even the decency to bleed.

The Supreme Council galleries, corridors, and the ancient and majestic domes seethed at the screams of terror and pain. They turned into a dreadful gurgling sound as the Moîrai soldiers' bodies ejected the liquefied tissues from all orifices.

The Marines left their cover. They frowned with disgust, but felt pity, too. They shot the few Moîrai still shaking on the floor with pinpoint accuracy. They aimed at their brain, but the brains had turned into mud and were seeping through their ears. Bodies lay reversed over puddles of sticky glue reeking of rotten flesh and putrescent matter; an acrid stench stung the eyes.

Amy checked the vitals of those in the crypt; the rods had worked as planned. The genetic antidote they had released preserved the Wisest and turned them into the carriers of death for their guards. "Get those stretchers. We're done here."

Silent fell all around. The Marines moved forward and the gallery resonated with their steps as others reached the hall. The engineer squad proceeded with the instructions received from the Keepers. Amy's eyes went in turn to each engineer after they took position in front of the old statues. They placed their hands and looked at her for the signal. At her command, they pressed on the stony eyes at the same time.

The floor trembled and the central symbol on the floor revolved and lowered. A large, circular staircase appeared. They climbed down, followed by the floating stretchers with their crystal canopy. At the bottom, a large door, made with a single slab of stone, constituted the last barrier that separated them from the crypt.

Amy climbed down the steps looked at by the Marines waiting at the bottom. She stopped at a bas-relief carving on the door, and touched—in the order specified by the Keepers—the stars' symbols that mapped the Moîrai's dominion in the galaxy. With a huff, the stone rose, and a vile odour made the Marines turn away from the entrance. Amy grunted but peeked inside. Inside, it looked like a giant pool of puke. The envelopes that once were Moîrai guards still trembled from internal fermentation. She stood at the entry and cheked the Wisest's vitals. They were stable and ready for the trip to Eridu. "Put them in the stretchers."

After the Marines secured the last Moîrai, she gave one more glance into the crypt. What remained of the bodies of the Moîrai guards kept rotting from the inside. They looked like flaccid dolls with empty eye sockets. It was good the Keepers didn't take part in the operation, she reasoned.

⁂

Aboard the lead vessel, in his private briefing room, Xiucaman pondered whether he could take the risk to act upon the latest revelations and change the course of history for all Kritas. The dashboards kept him abreast of all that went on in the space sector. He paced the floor under the impatient gaze of the human looking at him from the other side of the central table. "We can't let this chance pass," he told him. "As much as I loathe Dan of Eridu—"

"Don't!" He stopped in the middle of his stride; he didn't let the human end the phrase. "Don't ever doubt my resolve to have the Moîrai pay their dues." He pointed his finger at him.

"My apologies, it wasn't what I implied." The human raised his hands to his chest, and Xiucaman couldn't but look again at that mutilated hand. "What do you humans say in cases such as these?" He raised his eyes. "Too good to be true?" He grunted.

The man smiled. "And yet, Ekahau lamented he couldn't reach the Supreme Council. I think he lies, but maybe he doesn't."

The Kritas resumed his brisk walking. "He didn't lie." He stopped. "There's something you don't know. We can't reach our agents there, either." The human raised his eyebrows and the Kritas continued. "Communication from all sectors around Xrusé is dead."

At these last words, Xiucaman went to the main dashboards floating above his desk. The first officer on the main bridge appeared on a floating screen. "Prepare for an attack, and call in the destroyers." He didn't wait for an answer, but interrupted the communication and turned. "We'll know the truth soon. Get ready for a long journey."

The man squinted his eyes and filled his lungs.

⁂

Chris Telle stood in the FCC room. The hall hummed with muffled discussions among the officers and the noises from the all the intelligence-gathering activities. The space-sphere, in the middle, showed both the Kritas and Moîrai fleets facing each other. Telle had ordered the most complete report on all scenarios in case he had to face them both. He hoped the scouts had succeeded; the report of those who made it back to Hekate confirmed, though, the lack of a formal alliance between the two parties. He checked the Huitzilin units in the rear guard and hoped they'd be able to provide the support they promised.

"How long still?" his first officer thought aloud.

"The scouts were instructed not to resist. It won't take long. I hope the Kritas will not harm them. They'll use the scouts as leverage to deal with us; later on, that is." He sighed.

The FCC space-sphere showed an increased rate of activity. "Something's up." The first officer raised his gaze to the ship symbols shifting on the sphere.

Telle observed the rendering of the lead vessel of the Kritas fleet and its supporting group retreat into more protected coordinates while larger battleships took formation in their previous positions. The Kritas units moved and changed formation; the fleet spread out. "It sure is; they're preparing to attack." Telle's eyes widened.

The alarms howled as a multitude of wormholes opened in the space sector and additional units emerged from hyperspace. The Kritas opened fire and the Alliance showed its resolve against the old enemy.

Chapter 23 – The Finger

The Alliance paid a hefty price against more capable enemy vessels, but all the might of the Moîrai fleet couldn't face the additional forces brought into the battlefield. Their capitulation came after hours of intense fighting. When the odds became evident, beaten and baffled, Ekahau ordered the fleet to surrender to avoid further unnecessary slaughter. All vessels lowered their shields and floated inert, surrounded by the victorious Alliance battleships.

On the main screen, the stern face of Xiucaman addressed him. "You were right, Ekahau."

The Moîrai didn't reply, too shocked by the events, and the words of the Kritas only nagged his resigned spirit.

"You chose the better human, after all."

He raised his eyes to those mocking words. "What do you mean, Kritas?"

The lack of respect made Xiucaman laugh. "The same arrogance, in all situations. Your empire crumbles, but I bet you're not aware of anything yet." He laughed. "Don't oppose resistance; my troops are boarding your vessel and my human assures me you will be a valuable gift."

Ekahau blanched and turned to the sounds of a commotion getting nearer; orders shouted in the Kritas language and the occasional blaster's screech marked the demise of members of his crew as the sounds grew more menacing.

Xiucaman smiled when Kritas troops erupted on the main bridge and grabbed the Moîrai by his arms. "Don't break him, I need to have him wrapped nicely." His laughter resonated in the hall.

⁂

Xrusé waited for the arrival of Dan of Eridu. Muted, stunned, and in distress, the cities and the communities of all continents watched the humans—flanked by the Keepers—take control. Their battleships hovered, imposing, and cast a shadow that demolished the latest hopes of resistance. All Moîrai military personnel had been corralled and were closely watched by the Space Marines.

The empire collapsed, headless, and the Keepers maintained the order under the watch of the humans. They spread a reassuring message: the real traitor had been defeated and, after a transitional phase, the future would smile again for the fate of the Moîrai, with the Keepers' role restored—in the open this time—and the ancient values strengthened. The Keepers and the humans came as liberators.

The captured Supreme Council members were en route for Eridu when the Hekate task force reported the latest events from the Kritas space sectors. The Alliance offered to agree to new terms with the emerging leadership and was clever enough not to engulf all races in a galactic conflict. A special envoy would be sent to meet with the humans.

On the Supreme Council esplanade, Alaston watched the approach of the Eridu's Primum's battleship and its supporting squad. All around, ranks and ranks of Space Marines, Keepers, and other Moîrai crowded every flat surface of the huge symbol of the Confederation power. The battleship slowed down and came to a rest over the esplanade. A gigantic Phoenix was painted on the belly of the ship, and all eyes watched in awe when the painted fires and burning ashes in the hull opened to let the shuttle with the Dan of Eridu's crest leave the mother ship.

The tension rose as the shuttle descended without haste. It touched ground, the bulkhead dilated, and a forceful roar erupted from all throats—humans and aliens alike—when Dan of Eridu appeared on the threshold, followed by the Eridu's Twelve and Samuel.

"Welcome, Eridu's Primum." Alaston's thoughts resonated in his mind. *"The mad has fallen."*

"And others will follow," Dan replied. *"But today is a day of rejoicing. A break before the next stage, when other painful decisions will have to be made."*

Manfred's thoughts resonated clearly. *"Well found, Alaston. Good to see you're fine, Ohtlinell."* The Twelve, too, revealed themselves to the Keepers with mental greetings.

Waves of surprise rippled from the Moîrai, Alaston first. *"The humans will never cease to surprise me."*

The humans advanced to the middle of the esplanade to meet with Alaston, a wounded Mênis supported by a floating med-unit device, and Ohtlinell. A few steps back, Amy Norton and Chris Telle saluted. Dan saluted back and nodded to both. "Mênis, I've heard you had a rough time."

"But I am still here." He lowered his head.

Dan stepped forward and offered his right hand to Alaston, who looked at it, unsure of what to do.

"Just hold it and let me do the rest." Dan smiled.

The crowd roared when the human and the Moîrai shook hands.

⁂

Protusa saw intense and profound changes. The people of Xrusé's fears of a human occupation faded when the Keepers, instead, took control of all matters in the Moîrai society. Trust needed to be rebuilt and the Brotherhood carried an aura of fear that had to be dissolved soon in everybody's minds.

The Keepers led the initial negotiations with all members of the Confederation with the presence of human representatives. The Huitzilin pressed for a swift resolution and were the first to propose and swear their allegiance to a Confederation lead by Eridu's leadership. The news of the massacre in the Kritas sector also played a crucial role in those decisions, as not one race entertained the option of bending under an Alliance rule. Besides, the Keepers revealed the treason perpetrated by The One, and the Supreme Council took the blame for the oppression of other races. The confederates welcomed the change—any change, actually.

Eridu prepared to judge The One and the members of the Supreme Council. The accusations stemmed from the Moîrai's own laws in place for millennia. The main charges brought forward comprised of the treason perpetrated against the Keepers and the genocide against the humans. The flaws in the decision process that started the Selection and culling of the human race appeared to be coming from within the Supreme Council itself. The pivotal role of Ekahau in helping rogue Kritas establish a base in Eridu had been proved. The case left no doubts over the final verdict; their fate was just a matter of time.

The Kritas delegation pressed for a summit. Their ships would emerge from hyperspace at a location authorized by the humans. They issued a formal request for the accredited chief of the delegation to have a personal and private hearing with Dan of Eridu before the works of the entrusted representatives could start.

They had to wait for an answer. Alaston and Manfred worked out the security measures to adopt. The Keepers and the Eridu's Primum personal guards would carry them out. The request was granted only when the Kritas accepted that the delegation would travel to Protusa on a single transporter vessel, escorted by human battleships. They didn't question the request and that surprised Alaston; the Moîrai were used only to confrontational interactions with the Kritas.

The events had set in motion a sequence of changes beyond any initial assessment. It was remarkable to notice how much resentment emerged against the Moîrai when the pressure of the ancient regime was no more, and the Keepers, too, learned something about how their race had been perceived in the last century. The sentiment created a rich peat for the human ascension to power and establish solid roots for their authority.

⁂.

From the ex-quarters of The One, in the main tower of the Supreme Council, the view on Protusa eclipsed the one I had enjoyed the first time I visited the Moîrai capital and their planet.

Marina's soft voice broke the silence. "You're always in deep thought when you look out of the walls." For a moment, I had forgotten that Marina was *there*. "You dismantled the Supreme Council, exposed the treason. Wasn't this your goal?" The voice came from everywhere in the room, but I turned to stare at the memnosphere.

"It was. The billions who died on our planet, and the spared ones—everyone now has received an answer to their cries. Yes, and it still is my goal."

"But there's more, isn't it?"

"I've lost everything and everyone, Marina. Only Samuel remains, and he, too, will be gone before me. Don't you think I've reasons to be in deep thought?"

"You have me." The sphere showed a series of bright tremors dancing and twisting in its interior.

"Do I?" The sphere subdued. "I'm glad I have *you*, but it's not exactly what I had in mind." I walked toward the pedestal where the sphere rested and spun. "The Moîrai have just started to pay the price."

"Just started?"

"Just started. This is a beginning, Marina. And now..." I glanced at the transponder's floating screen that blossomed above the desk. "I need to go. The Kritas delegation is landing."

"Glad to see you again, Selected."

I froze. I hadn't heard that *voice* in years. *"You!"*

I sealed the room. "Marina! The Kritas' puppet is here."

"What?"

"The leader of the spared ones' insurgence in Eridu provoked by the Kritas. He's their special envoy." I laughed. *"I see the Kritas have spared you, after all. They must be a more magnanimous race than I believed."*

"I'm sure you'll change your mind about the Kritas. I'm not coming to fuel long-gone hatred. You did in a hundred years what the Kritas tried to do for eons."

I snorted. *"My judgment is not easy to be influenced by words. What should I call you? Kritas salvaged specimen?"*

The mental sound of laughter filled the aural sphere around me. *"My shuttle has just landed. I'll see you in person soon."*

I breathed hard at the flood of memories that assailed me and let the wall dilate. "Marina, record all discussions, will you? Warn Manfred and Alaston for me."

"No need to ask..."

I left and headed to the encounter with my alter ego.

The guards saluted as they saw me approach the room we prepared for the private session. The wall dilated and I entered. Manfred insisted on providing a special room, a cube with two active seats. The integrated brain wave scanners reacted to violent mental patterns, and they were under my control as well. We would face each other, and the seat would constrain my guest if so I wished. My personal guards, armed, were ready to intervene right beyond each of the four walls.

I considered the precautions excessive, but Manfred took his role as Security Chief to the letter; he was the chief, thus, the last words were his, and I didn't interfere.

"The delegation has entered the Supreme Council, Dan." Marina made a security screen activate on the wall and showed me the Kritas delegation. I nodded. Among the Kritas, like taller and thinner humans, three men led the parade, dressed with high-ranking military uniforms.

At the end of the main hall, between the colonnade and under the watch of the huge statues of the Wisest of the past, the delegation reached a mixed squad of Keepers and Marines. They took one of the men aside and let the delegation proceed, escorted, to the Council Hall.

I gestured the screen to be reabsorbed into the wall. I sensed the Kritas envoy's arrival. The Keepers had him scanned one more time outside the room, and we mutually acknowledged our presence with a mental nod. He was bemused. The wall dilated and he stepped in.

"A Kritas general. What a meager result." I snorted.

"But with extended powers." He advanced and offered his right hand to shake. "Michael," he said. The past caught up to me with the impact power of a freight train. His left hand missed the last phalange of the little finger.

Chapter 24 – Through the Flames

Retribution, payback, retaliation, vengeance, punishment—all these sentiments animated the people in Eridu. Some thought of settling the score when the Council decided the prisoners would receive their trial in the same dome where my daughter Hope left her life.

The Kritas extradited Ekahau and all captured Moîrai military personnel as a sign of goodwill. Michael told me of his first encounter with the Kritas, how it all began for him. He came from New York, he said.

Ludicrous coincidence. I kept the secret with Michael; I knew already his story and his past. I didn't reveal that he actually had met with me via emails, when we both were once humans, when we were just wary survivors. Those times were uncertain; Earth had seen the sudden death of almost its entire population, and who knows what I would have done if Kritas had found me first, instead of the Moîrai. Which camp would I have embraced?

Besides, Kritas looked more human than the Moîrai, and I understood how their story could have carried a greater appeal to a bunch of scared people. But the Moîrai had gifted each of us with a Palladium, and through those we lived the lives of many, and knew of the many ages of the race of man. The Palladium had our destiny sealed.

For the time being, Protusa became my home. I hadn't returned to Eridu, yet, and I didn't know how long it would be before I could go back. Besides, I had no one to return to.

The Keepers—and Alaston, more than the others—felt the betrayal of the Wisest as their own watershed moment in history, defining anew their role among the Moîrai; they abandoned secrecy and covertness.

"We are very old, Dan." Alaston came forward one day when the investigations I always wanted had finally given the results I looked for. The conspiracy touched the highest levels and personalities among the Moîrai.

As once before, we admired Protusa from above, from the top terrace of the Supreme Council in those that I chose as my own quarters.

"The original decision foresaw that the Brotherhood had to operate unseen and unrevealed, but it allowed for other forces to sneak through unseen and unrevealed." He sighed, his eyes fixed to the horizon. I let my friend get rid of a burden and I sensed how much it haunted him. "I was blind, Dan, and I am sorry."

I stared at the horizon. "The Keepers took too many things for granted. You based your decision on what you knew then. A limited knowledge, but one you believed was whole and full."

"And this is the worst of sins, for which I am shameful." He looked at me, a grave expression marked his face. "I have resigned as Brethren of the Keepers."

I grabbed his arm. "You did what? Why?" I frowned.

He lowered his head. He seemed very human to me in that moment. "The events tested me and I proved inadequate. The Keepers have already accepted it."

I sighed. "What's next, now?"

"We are living through changes every day, and we are not certain where things will lead us and what more the investigations will reveal."

I took a deep breath. "The Keepers should have supported me when I asked for your help. My efforts and my requests had to be honored when it was easy."

"Do you regret anything?" Alaston bent his head.

"No. But many will."

Alaston stared at me but didn't reply.

"I'm to meet someone, Alaston, if you don't mind..."

"Of course not."

We left the terrace, not without a last glance to Protusa, and I accompanied him to the dilating wall. In the corridor, Amy Norton was waiting. I welcomed her in.

The memnosphere blinked and twisted when the Marine walked in with a measured pace and stopped in front of my desk. I reached the other side and sat.

"I wanted to thank you personally for what you did, Commander. Please have a seat."

"If you don't mind, sir, I'm already at ease."

I smiled. I noticed she had a few scratches left from the battle. She followed my gaze and anticipated my question. "They will heal naturally. I don't waste my time on a med-unit for minor things."

"Do you know why I called for you?"

"No, sir. Admiral Amenta already honored the members of our operation, and I was planning to return to Eridu."

I took a dossier from a drawer and placed it at the center of the desk. On the cover, it had 'Prometheus' in block letters. Amy glanced at it.

"I've read your report." I looked at her. "You did an impressive job, you and the Marines, but I read more than just the military assessment."

"Sir?"

"You added personal considerations—about the Keepers, about your perceptions and judgment." I probed her mind. "The operation changed you."

"I learn from every operation, sir." Her eyes met mine for a brief moment.

I smiled. "I want you to stay."

She shifted her weight. "I beg your pardon? ... Sir?"

"The Keepers respect you; you changed them, as well. Protusa will be the most difficult star system to control—at first, at least. I cannot stay here forever, but whenever I leave, I want to do it with confidence that things will not derail."

The memnosphere pulsated as if Marina tried to show me her approval, or was it jeaulousy?

She bent her head when my words started to sink in and formed a meaning in her mind. I sensed pride, although she kept her serious expression.

"And in Protusa there will be the largest contingent of Marines stationed abroad."

She nodded. "I understand, sir."

She didn't looked like any of the women that had shared their life with me, Mary, Laura, Marina. All gone, all alive within me, but Amy had qualities I recognized from all of them. "I want you to be the Protusa Proconsul, Amy."

⁂

Eridu continued the war effort as if nothing had happened, and the Fleet grew even beyond what the Moîrai had been capable of in the past. The Huitzilin—Samuel worked hard to make that happen—became our strongest ally in the Confederation. Our vessels, and theirs, visited together every star system once under Moîrai domination. At each visit, our Fleet established bases and we stationed our units, setting a foothold that provided us with a more convincing argument than any of our delegations and previous negotiations.

We established an Alien Administration Affairs lead by a Proconsul in each star system. Communication and trade resumed through the interstellar traffic regulated via star-gates. Each race built on for their system from our instructions. We controlled wormhole creations and established hyperspace routes for any ship to travel, with or without an onboard star-pilot. Each race received just enough amount of Fusion, the neurotrophic drug we produced, for the number of star-pilots allowed to them.

We held the monopoly of the drug, and Kritas received it free in exchange of their neutrality and for their role in the Moîrai demise. But it was our formula, tuned for each race in the galaxy, and via the drug, we held a trigger to a gun no one knew about.

It took a few months of negotiations to reach the point where we could call for a summit in Eridu, and we waited to make it coincide with declassifying the extent of the Moîrai conspiracy.

The delegates knew why they had been summoned, and our Fleet stationed in their star systems reminded them of our determination. I returned to Eridu for the occasion; the humans were ready to send a message to the entire galaxy.

The dome in Nova Roma hosted the leadership of all races in the Confederation accompanied by all our Proconsuls. It was the final page in the chapter of the Moîrai's dominance. Also, the Kritas Alliance had sent their representatives. Whatever their motives, or their aspirations, the delegates didn't hide their immense satisfaction, and all accepted the invitation at once.

The most advanced race in the galaxy had raised their successor, and it was time for the humans to grab the scepter.

The list of the prisoners' names ran in the thousands, and they knew their fate. Eridu's Council of the Twelve allowed the Keepers to be part of final judgment, to fulfill my promise to reinstate them, though in the Moîrai society only.

The delegates followed the verdict on giant screens all around the dome. They saw the prisoners held in the vessel that had been their prison since their apprehension. It was stationed between Eridu and the Moon; other screens showed the reddish glow of a wormhole creation in front of it.

The appointed members of the Tribunal gathered on the central podium, and a silence fell when it rose, lifting to the focal point of the dome hemisphere.

The Judge Principal, a Keeper, stood up. "The Moîrai Supreme Council, their military leadership, and those who participated in the conspiracy have been found guilty of the highest crime against the human race, against the Moîrai race, and against the Keepers' Brotherhood." The Tribunal went on to announce measures to compensate many races. The Moîrai leadership was found guilty of dampening growth and progress in the galaxy to ensure their supremacy.

The Judge Principal ratified the capital punishment, then asked Eridu's Primum to administer justice on behalf of the Confederation. The podium lowered.

The loge where the Council of the Twelve and I sat detached from its location in the dome and drifted to occupy the place vacated by the Tribunal podium.

"The corruption in the Confederation vilified justice." I stood up and waited for complete silence. "Humans paid the highest price, but have risen again from their ashes. Wrongs were committed against many, and justice today punishes the perpetrators. We disband the Confederation. Long life to the Union." Murmurs rose at those words. "It is now the time for integration, for a new order, and for a new guidance." I raised my arm, and the Twelve stood up as well. "I called for each of you, and some have responded, too." The loge occupied by the Huitzilin High Councilor detached and drifted to join and fuse with ours.

"It is time for you to share the burden and reap the benefits in the Union." The loges of those who had sworn allegiance followed. Manfred came forward to my side and declamed, "Eridu's Council of the Twelve has voted for free access to the neurotrophic genetic compounds to all races." The dome resonated by deafening roar from all delegates.

I raised my arms until silence was reached again. "The humans are reborn from their ashes, but there is another step before we can close the chapter to the injustice and the grief. We owe it to our ancestors, we owe it to those soul who will find peace at last." I paused. "From today, the end of the Confederation marks the end of Eridu, too. All interstellar maps, all reference to the planet of the race of man, will bear one name and one name only. Earth!" The delegates rose from their seat, and the clapping, timid at first, became a deafening thunder under the dome.

I turned to my right to the second row in the loge. Amy smiled and her eyes were wet. I felt a knot growing in my throat. I saw the skilometres of all the women I loved—Mary, Laura, and my daughters—and I thought of Joshua, too. But it was only a moment.

Now it was time to administer justice and send a message that needed no words. I put my hand on the dashboard and the sound of a grave horn resounded under the dome. The screens zoomed to all detainees held in the prisonship. Individually restrained, they watched their own downfall.

Separate displays showed the members of the once-powerful Supreme Council, they lulled themselves like mindless dolls. The scene silenced the dome.

The mental extraction process we authorized in case of treason had destroyed their minds little by little. The process was initiated with The One, and we let the other members witness the progressive mental degradation before they suffered the same fate. At the view, a murmur rose from the delegates. Those in the dome, the population of Earth, and all races connected in the galaxy through the quantum links received the same images and heard the same words.

"The verdict is unanimous. The traitors will bear a subjective detention of nine hundred years before the capital punishment by annihilation."

The screens showed a battleship approaching the space-prison. Its tug beams grabbed the vessel as the wormhole grew to show its singularity tunnel into hyperspace. The fringes of the wormholes diffracted the light from the stars, and the battleship maneuvered behind the prison and flung it into the tunnel that closed right after engulfing the ship.

What we showed kept the dome in silence, and Earth, and the whole galaxy. For the first time ever, we captured the events in the horizon of the wormhole tunnel. The nine hundred years of the sentence passed on the screens in a matter of minutes. Time is a quantum dimension, and the human pilots bent it as the vessel traveled toward its final destination. The silence of doom accompanied what everyone witnessed. The prisoners' lives, their body corruptions, the decay and—in some cases—their death flew by in front of billions and billions of eyes.

We showed them death; we showed them a power that flirted with the divine. Maybe not everyone grasped it at first, but some understood immediately the message, and the power we held each time anyone jumped into hyperspace.

The images shifted to focus on the end of the Supreme Council members, the mindless parody of the once-feared and revered tyrants—as many perceived them. Their flesh wrinkled and their absent eyes, deprived of intelligence, turned opaque and dark like coal; their mouths drooled. Their limbs turned into flaccid appendices and they lost control of their body functions. In a matter of minutes, we vilified them, humiliated them, and showed the galaxy *we* held the keys of time.

With the Twelve, we stared at the delegations in the dome. Without blinking, we transitioned the galaxy into the era of Earth's Pax. The Huitzilin High Councilor fell on his seat, glad of the choices he made in the recent past.

A larger, giant floating rendering showed the solar corona in its entire splendor and might. The light hurt, as if the Sun itself made its appearance inside the dome. Gasps and choking sounds echoed all around.

A wormhole blossomed in the corona, defying the laws of nature, and pushed aside the solar plasma. My jaws tightened and I clenched my fists. I was too young to forget, too young not to remember, and too young to feel compassion. I shouted, "Let the Third Loss be avenged!"

With a flash, the vessel emerged from the hyperspace tunnel into the corona itself, and from that point on, the time bent matched ours. The Sun grabbed the ship with ferocity and pulled it deep into its fury. Those prisoners still alive had no time to scream as all organic matter ignited; only their flesh screeched and echoed in the dome. Then, even the atomic bonds fractured, and all vanished in bursts of energy and light.

The last images showed the battleships of our Fleet—with the new Earth emblem—emerge around our planet from hyperspace, and their number eclipsed the stars.

Chapter 25 - A New Beginning

It was a warm day in May and Samuel brought his vehicle down, following the banks of the river Brenta. The navigation panel showed where he would land in a matter of a few minutes. In the distance, he spotted the ancient villa. The building stood on a high pedestal, raised on a podium like an ancient temple. Guards watched the perimeter and they acknowledged his arrival. "Good morning, Admiral." He looked at the officer who addressed him from the floating communication screen. "Please, engage the autopilot and authorize the remote guidance link." He nodded and complied with a gesture. The vessel jerked as the link established and guided the vessel to enter the landing corridor. The villa came into view.

The main front wall and the portico faced the water and—during the approach—he had time to admire the majestic twin access ramps. The vessel touched ground with a gentle touch. He stepped out. The landing platform imposed a kind of a ceremonial route to the visiting guests. Austere, the façade of the building watched the visitor ascending along a path ornated with the green and blue spots of luxuriant plants of sage in flower. He smiled.

The guest of the villa waited for him at the center of the portico, grave as a high priest in the pronao of his own greek temple.

Samuel raised his eyes and met with the man's, then he bent toward the left stairs.

"Admiral. You flatter me with your visit," the man greeted him.

"How are you, Anton?" He stopped when centimetres apart from his host. They resisted only for a second, then they fell into each other's arms.

Once inside, in the library, Anton Sage watched out the window, toward the river; sentinels guarded the embarcadero. "I'm not complaining, mind you, your father is magnanimous."

"There's no need to measure your words with me." Samuel fixed his back and probed his mind, as his father had taught him. He didn't find resentment. Resignation, rather.

Anton turned. He was smiling. "I didn't know of the extent of your father's humour..."

"Pardon?" He bent his head.

"This villa has a history." He raised his eyes to the ceiling and pointed at the frescos and the bas-reliefs. "It was known as the 'Malcontenta,' the 'Disgruntled.'" He paused. "Do you know who was its architect?" Samuel shook his head.

"An Italian. He was known as the 'Palladio'. Do you see the irony?"

Samuel laughed.

Anton snorted before changing the subject. "I watched the ceremony. It was beautiful."

"Seems only yesterday when Hope left us, and it's already twenty-five years."

Anton went to the bar and filled himself a glass. "Want some?"

Samuel declined. "I'm okay."

He took a sip of the liquor and savoured it as it flowed down his throat. He sighed. "The Memorial to the Third Loss is touching..." He stared at Samuel. "Is it true any of us can trace back his genes to the original mother and the first Selected?" He raised his eyebrow.

"Yes, a perfect match, no errors possible."

He nodded. "I'd like to try, one day."

"You will. Soon." Samuel stared back at him.

He stopped drinking. "What do you mean?"

"Father thinks you can be reintegrated into society, and that you have character traits that might be useful."

"Do I?"

"You will be trained, instructed, and I will make sure you'll be able to visit the Memorial before your departure."

"My departure?"

"To the Kritas' Alliance."

Anton Sage frowned. "Kritas? What are you up to, Samuel?"

"My father cited words from when the past generations rediscovered the atomic energy." Samuel stood up and approached the window. "He mentioned a scientist of his past, a certain Robert Oppenheimer. He led a team of scientists to create and test the first rudimentary atomic bomb. After the first successful test, Oppenheimer said 'Now, I am become Death, the destroyer of worlds.'"

Samuel and Anton exchanged an intent look.

"You're going to war!"

"The time for another plague has come, Anton."

⁂

Earth's Primum's flagship emerged from hyperspace, accompanied by its escort of battleships of new generation. Earth never looked so beautiful to Dan's eyes as in that moment. The flawed jewel had been polished, regenerated, hardened, and its might reached the farthest stars in the galaxy.

"Your shuttle is ready, sir," the ship's commander announced on the communication link. In his quarters, Dan looked at the planet and glanced at the traffic of ships entering and leaving the high orbit levels.

"Thank you, Commander."

The shuttle entered the atmosphere veil and approached the Mediterranean Sea region. Marina's voice sounded sad in his ear's implant. "Dan, there's no need. You have to turn the page."

He had learned to trust her more than anyone else. The memnosphere with Marina's thought process was connected now to all intelligence links and had access to any data or piece of information recorded in the vast network of quantum computational devices; an artificial neural cluster that enhanced his capabilities to know everything of everyone at any moment.

He grinned. The shuttle descended toward the Tiber Valley and the energy dome surrounding Civita blinked in the distance.

"You're right in that, Marina. I have to turn the pages. What else could I do? But the book of my life is not finished, yet."

"You'll cause more grievance... After all this time..."

He sighed. "Time? Time is just a dimension; it's not a cure. And I'm made so I cannot forget, remember?" He sneered.

The shuttle slowed down as it approached the dome. The pilot announced, "Landing now, sir." Dan nodded. The dome enveloped the hull as it traversed the threshold and coalesced again as the shuttle landed on the esplanade. The bulkhead dilated and Dan stepped out. "Wait here."

"Yes, sir."

He smelled the air and looked around. Everything was as he left it the last time he visited Civita, to place Joshua's stone in its slot in the memorial. Saint Mary's gate was polished and clean, as time didn't matter anymore. The bas-relief with the two lions still protected the citadel.

"This is the first time for you, right?" he asked Marina. She didn't answer, but he expected that from her. He walked on the cobblestones of the esplanade and crossed the gate. The vivid memory of his daughter, Annah, walking hand in hand with Federico, her soon-to-be husband, filled his vision for a moment. They were both teenagers, Annah and Federico, at that time, only hundred and twenty-six years before. Memories, though, didn't bring their load of pain and regrets anymore, and his heart continued its mechanical duty undisturbed.

Reaching the square, the boulder came into view. The embedded diamonds, one for each member of his family, sparkled in the daylight and contrasted with the dark reflections of the black onyx stone remembering Joshua, his grandson. Samuel had questioned him why he chose that particular stone, but he didn't share the true reasons. The black onyx also stood as a symbol of the changes he went through and the sense of duty that became his only drive.

Dan walked up to the boulder and caressed each diamond, one by one. His face had no expression. No one lived in Civita or was allowed to visit without his explicit permission. In those days, though, no one had any reason to, either—but Samuel, maybe.

Then he touched the onyx and it felt warm under his hand.

"May I ask you something?" Marina's voice filled the aural vision around him. "I wonder why I'm not there, too."

Dan sighed. "You can still ask me questions. They can't."

"But where's my body?"

"You searched for it and found nothing, right?" But Marina didn't reply and Dan smiled. "It means my orders have been executed." Dan took his Palladium and donned it. "Now, I have to turn one more page, Marina."

Manfred's eidolon formed in front of him. "Well found, Dan. The Council is unanimous."

Dan nodded. "Put the Kritas' puppet under arrest and authorize the memory extraction. He will resist. Break all resistance, follow brute force protocol, and ignore any safety concerns."

Manfred nodded. "For the Third Loss."

"For the Third Loss," Dan replied.

All started in Daimones, *and the new race of men understood its role in the galaxy in* Once Humans.

Note to the Reader:

There's one more thing I'd like to add after this journey together in the "Daimones Trilogy."

Sales are great, press releases, interviews, live radio guest appearances are exciting, climbing the ranks and entering the Top 100 Authors for my genre is exhilarating, but nothing beats the support of all readers and friends and fellow writers who share the thrill with me. You're the best readers any writer could ever have. Without you giving my stories a chance, nothing would ever be possible.

"'Tis the good reader that makes the good book; in every book he finds passages which seem to be confidences or sides hidden from all else and unmistakably meant for his ear; the profit of books is according to the sensibility of the reader; the profound thought or passion sleeps as in a mine, until it is discovered by an equal mind and heart."

~Ralph Waldo Emerson

Humbly yours.

http://massimomarinoauthor.com

Acknowledgements

1) By Alden Brooks, US Army Topographical Engineer—December 27, 1864—Chattanooga, TN

From a historical manuscript written and compiled by Gloria Brooks Forsyth. Used by permission of David P. Forsyth.

37070394R00180

Made in the USA
Charleston, SC
26 December 2014